# The Guiding Lights

*By Mathew Keller*

# Reel One: Into the Light

# Prologue.

Special Agent Simpson felt her shoulder bone splinter as she was slammed against the wall, caught off guard by the immense force of the blast from the incendiary device that had landed a few metres behind her. Dammit… she already had to deal with the fact that she had less than a minute to find the light and get away from here, and now this! There were sharp pains down her back and legs caused by shrapnel wounds from the blast… but she had no time to deal with pain right now.

The light... she had to get to the light…

The room ahead was filled with brick dust and smoke, circling in the air around her in great clouds, like the dense London smog her commanding officer had always called a "pea souper". She'd always found that curious turn of phrase amusing to her American ear. Her head began to swim as the room began to shift in and out of focus, the after effects of the blast. Suddenly she caught a flicker of light in her peripheral vision and turned her head too quickly towards it, the abrupt movement causing multiple images of the room to overlap across her vision. She closed her eyes to stop from passing out, focusing her mind on the task ahead of her. If the light went out permanently she'd be trapped here, buried alive by the next bomb that she knew was about to drop right where she was standing. Opening her eyes again she caught sight of the flicker once more and was careful to move her head slowly toward it this time. Her perception of time seemed to slow down, like a film running at half speed, as she gingerly felt her way forward through the smoke and dust, towards where she perceived the flicker of light to be.

Something touched her right ankle and made her jump out of her skin. She looked down to see a bloodied hand protruding from the tattered sleeve of a British uniform. The hand was grabbing at her, desperately trying to grasp hold of her leg like it was the last firm handhold on the edge of a cliff. She looked down and noticed her own hand for the first time since before the blast had hit her, the service revolver gripped tightly in it, mirroring the hand now clasped firmly around her leg. Without a thought she raised the gun and pointed it to the area along the length of the uniformed arm where the rest of the soldier should be, hidden deep in the clouds still circling wildly in the air, and fired a single shot into the gloom. The hand loosened its grip on her leg and fell limp.

There... The light appeared brighter now, more focused. She stumbled towards it, unable to keep a straight path due to the constant ringing in her ears affecting her balance. In an instant a second bomb landed behind her, at the point where she'd been standing only moments ago, and the explosion threw her forwards towards the brick wall the light was being projected onto.

With a sharp "yelp", she vanished.

# I.

Gertie Granger was standing in front of a wall made up of tall wooden boards wiping the sleep from her eyes. It was still pretty early in the morning for her and she was wishing she was somewhere else. Normally at this time on a Saturday she'd be in her pyjamas in front of the telly getting ready to watch Thundercats on Going Live!, clutching her action figure of Cheetara. But no, today her annoying dad had dragged her and her equally annoying younger brother Walter to the quiet back streets of Brighton on a mysterious outing to some derelict old building. Actually, she didn't mind really, secretly she was a little excited, but it was still too early in the morning for her liking.

It seemed to Gertie that every street these days was filled with empty buildings, their doors padlocked shut and their windows boarded up to stop their windows getting smashed. Back when she was younger she was sure every street corner had a local baker's shop, or a butcher, or a greengrocer's on it. When she'd queried it with her dad he'd explained that the "blummin' Tories and their blinking recession" had meant they'd all gone out of business. She missed those friendly little shops where everyone seemed to know each other and talked about "Mrs so-and-so from number 43" and "Mr whats-is-name from number 11". The shopkeepers always used to give her sweets, which she liked, and ruffle her hair, which she definitely didn't. Then one day they had quietly shut their doors for the last time and moved away, now the shops stood abandoned and empty. Everyone did their shopping in one of the huge supermarkets in the centre of the town and no one talked to each other anymore it seemed.

She shuffled her feet, kicking at the chewing gum stuck to the pavement and looked at the bright colours of the spray painted graffiti on the once whitewashed wooden hoarding. She was bored and getting colder by the second. She glanced over at her brother, hunched down in his green parka with its hood up, the cold spring air condensing his breath as it appeared out of the fur rimmed opening like steam from a dragon's nostrils. The weather man on the telly had said it had been the coldest January on record and the sky still seemed pregnant with the promise of more snow. She had very much enjoyed the snow, but it had quickly turned to ice and she'd fallen over more times than she cared to admit and got bruises on her bum.

"Come on dad! I'm freezin'" moaned Walter. He looked over at Gertie and stuck his tongue out. Her brother was alright most of the time, but he could sulk for England and still sometimes cried and threw tantrums when he didn't get his own way. Pretty childish behaviour for an 8 year old in her opinion, thought Gertie. He did have a point though; her dad had been fumbling with the padlock on the door section of the wooden hoarding, trying to find the key that fit it out of a big bunch of others, for the last five minutes. He was on his sixth or seventh try, she'd lost count.

"Ah ha! Got it!" he finally exclaimed.

After more seconds than she felt it should have taken him, her dad finally worked out that the door swung outwards and not inwards. He pulled it open after a couple of forceful tugs and stepped through. Her dad was like that, a bit clumsy and forgetful, but kind hearted in his own way.

Walter just stood, hands in his pockets, belligerent that he wasn't going to move until he was forced to. With a "tut!" she pushed past him and peered through the opening into the gloom beyond. Her dad, of course, had completely disappeared.

What she saw through the door of the hoarding took her breath away. Rising upwards out of the gloom was the expansive and ornate facade of the most incredible old building she had ever seen.

She took a step forward to take it all in but was rewarded with temporary blindness from the morning sun glinting off tall windows that rose majestically upwards and seemed to disappear into the sky. It took a moment for her eyes to adjust, which was good because she quickly realised she'd forgotten to keep breathing. She took a few quick gasps of air and collected herself.

Below the tall windows she could now make out an elaborate curved metal framework covered in coloured glass with the letters P I C T U R E  H O U S E picked out in leadwork. Below this stood a huge brass revolving doorway, just like the one she'd seen at a department store in London. It was, without a doubt, one of the most beautiful things she had ever seen in her life.

Above this cathedral-like stained glass signage sat baroque balconies bordered with carved stone frescos of the harvest, with barley, grapes and vegetables spilling forth from horns-of-plenty and a hog's head surrounded by mountains of fruits. As her eyes travelled upward toward the sky she saw that the windows that had blinded her upon her entrance were fronted with ionic-topped Grecian columns and guarded on either side by vast statues of the most elegantly dressed ladies. The left-hand statue held an arm-full of wheat sheaves and the right an ornate longbow with a quiver of arrows just poking up behind their shoulder. At the very top of the building, she could just make out the outline of two octagonal spike-topped turrets, the small windows of which she imagined command impressive views of Brighton's rooftops and the sea beyond.

She slowly became aware of her dad's voice calling to her. "Earth to Gertie!" he joked, "Beautiful isn't it? Come on, let's go have a look inside". She could now see him standing off to the side of the entrance, gesturing towards a courtyard to the right of the building.

"Oi, Walt! Shift your bum and get 'ere." Gertie's dad exclaimed. She glanced back to see that her brother was still sulking the other side of the entrance through the hoarding, puffing out huge steamy breaths like a chimney. With an overly dramatic shrug he reluctantly shuffled forward towards them. Gertie turned back to watch as her dad spun on his heel and walked purposefully into the courtyard, keys jingling in time with the clip clop of his shoes on the hard ground echoing in the silence beyond.

# II.

Special Agent Simpson was struggling to find the precise location of the cache of supplies she'd been scrambling around this basement looking for for the last ten minutes. She was damn sure she'd got the right place. She'd followed the set of instructions, given to her on arrival by her fellow operative, to the letter, but nothing seemed to match with the last part telling her where the cache was actually to be found.

"Where is that blasted trunk! Come on Kitty old girl, think…"

Shocked by the sound of her mid-Atlantic accent ringing loudly off the walls she clasped her hand swiftly to her mouth, trying to stifle the echo. Feeling defeated, she sank to the ground, folding her long slim legs under her to land firmly on her bottom. This was always her favourite position to sit and think in. She was dressed in her trademark light coloured trousers and loose fitted blouse, rather conspicuous for Edwardian France, especially considering the war that was currently raging in the countryside mere miles from where she was sitting. So, after acquiring her instructions at her original entry-point, she'd helped herself to a large black astrakhan overcoat from the cloakroom, left behind by some previous theatre goer who had never returned for it. Thankfully, she'd only needed to blend in whilst travelling quickly on foot through the streets of Amiens to the abandoned tenement whose basement she was currently sitting in. She'd normally be better prepared and travel in the correct clothing ahead of time, but this had been an emergency jump and she had had to improvise. Exactly why there was a system in place for precisely these kinds of emergencies, she thought… if only she could locate the damn thing!

She couldn't understand it. She'd managed to follow the instructions successfully thus far, but was falling at the last hurdle.

"This has to be the place?! Why can't I find the damn thing?"

She stretched her legs out in front of her and fell gently backwards, enveloped in the folds of the huge overcoat. Lying on the floor of the dust covered basement she realised something, staring over her own head at the upside down room behind her... she'd been looking at this all wrong!

"Oh Kitty you absolute rube! The instructions are the other way round! You need to be looking from the window to the door, not the door to the window."

With cat-like agility she sat swiftly upright, and by sweeping her legs under her was up on her feet in two seconds flat. She walked forward with sudden purpose and pulled deftly at a dust sheet covering a large mound of items, jerking it aside and sidestepping the spray of brick dust and crumpled bits of masonry like a matador avoiding a bull. The dust sheet had been covering a stack of steamer trunks of varying sizes. Grabbing the handle on the lowermost trunk she dragged it around in a wide arc, revealing, tucked behind, an upright wardrobe trunk with large brass catches and what looked to be combination locks.

Stepping round the other luggage, she once more adopted her favourite thinking position, sitting perched on the projected portion of the bottom trunk, and attacked the locks, slowly rolling the rockers until they showed the numbers 1, 8, 9, and 6. She smiled as her patience was rewarded with a gentle "click" as the catches popped and she pulled the trunk open to reveal its contents.

Inside the right-hand side of the trunk she found drawers full of documents, medical supplies, undergarments, and in the bottom drawer, a service revolver and several boxes of ammunition. The left-hand part of the trunk contained hangers on which hung the various parts of a Red Cross nurses uniform: a light blue sack dress with leather belt, detachable white collar and cuffs, a long white apron, white Red Cross armband, a white head veil and at the bottom of the wardrobe, black laced boots. Pinned to the uniform she found a note which explained where to find various additional objects dotted around the basement which would allow her to make up a comfortable bed for the night. Kitty left the uniform where it was and set about following these new instructions. Best to tackle the mission after a good night's sleep, she had always maintained.

# III.

Gertie's dad had tried to explain it to them in the car on the way over to Brighton, but it was still all pretty confused in her head.

It had all started about six months ago, when her dad had received a phone call from a firm of solicitors dealing with the estate of Ms. Abigail Brown, who Gertie was surprised to discover having never heard of her until now, was her great Aunt on her mother's side. They had been trying to reach her mother in relation to part of Abigail Brown's Last Will and Testament, which the company, Betteridge, Boxell & Knight had been charged with executing.

So far so good, but this was where everything started to get a bit *complicated*.

You see Gertie's mum, Elizabeth, had been killed in a hit-and-run accident three years previously leaving her husband, Gertie's dad Edward, in charge of her and her younger brother. To Gertie her mother had been the most amazing person in the world and she was completely devastated by the loss. It was like half her heart had been removed from her body, leaving a vast empty hole. All the excitement and beauty she'd once seen in the world seemed to have fallen down that hole, never to be seen again. On Sundays Gertie and her mum had used to watch one of their VHS tapes of black and white films from Hollywood's

14

Golden Age on the television, huddled together on the sofa drinking hot chocolate. Gertie loved the glamour and the suspense of these films, much better than the non-stop action movies her dad took her and Walter to see at the cinema in town. To Gertie her mum was every bit as beautiful as the glamorous stars in their favourite films, Ingrid Bergman in Casablanca, Gene Tierney in Laura or Rosalind Russell in His Girl Friday. Gertie herself had inherited what she thought of as her mother's best traits: her thick wavy coffee coloured hair, her hazel eyes, her pleasing smile, and her taller than average figure, although she would never admit this to herself. Especially since now her mum was gone, Gertie always tied her hair back tight, wore jumpers that were too big for her and rarely smiled at anything.

Her dad was equally as devastated by Elizabeth's absence. He was prone to long spells of hiding away in the garage tinkering with bits of electronic equipment Gertie couldn't even begin to understand. About a year after her mother's death they'd moved house to one of the new builds that were being put up at the top of the small rural town of Lewes, miles from where they used to live. Her dad had explained they needed to "Get away from everything", secretly Gertie knew it was because everything in their old house reminded him of her mother, as it certainly did for Gertie. Now all that seemed to be left of her mother were a few photos on the mantelpiece over the fireplace and a shoe box full of keepsakes under Gertie's bed.

The house move had been the thing that had thrown a spanner in the works for Ms. Brown's solicitors as they needed to jump through hoops to discover the whereabouts of the Granger family. Apparently the old house was still the last known address of Elizabeth Granger, the new one being registered in her father's name instead.

Their trail eventually led them to the Granger's new home and to the phone call to her dad which would, in turn, change Gertie's life forever.

Her dad had explained that her mother had been named as a recipient of part of her Aunt Abigail's estate. In normal circumstances, Elizabeth's death would have meant that the portion of the will naming her would lapse and be shared between any other recipients. However, Ms. Brown had clearly had some precognition on the subject and had included the phrase: "Or any surviving female descendent" in the clause. So Abigail Brown's gift to Gertie's mother in fact passed down to Gertie.

The exact nature of this gift, coupled with the fact that Gertie had only just recently turned 12 years old, meant that, like the care of her and her brother, Gertie's gift was to be looked after by her dad until she reached adulthood. Especially as the gift in question happened to be a large plot of land in the centre of the coastal town of Brighton currently containing an abandoned building that once housed the Grand Picture House cinema.

Now, there are not that many 12 year olds in the world who know that in six years time they will become property owners. But to Gertie's relief, like so much of her and her younger brother's life, this particular worry was still firmly on her father's plate to deal with. Lucky then that he was such a kind-hearted, unflappable man, taking all the beatings life had decided to dish out like a punch bag and never letting the bruises show.

She discovered later that the Grand Picture House had been one of a dozen Victorian built theatres which had switched over to showing films in the early 1900s, and had continued operating as a cinema until it closed its doors for the final time in August 1974.

Thirteen years later, on a cold Saturday morning in February, the doors to the Grand Picture House were opened again by Gertie's slightly inept dad, the aging hinges sending out an eerie creek that echoed around the empty courtyard and reverberated off the wooden hoarding.

"Well, Gertie old thing, you ready to travel back in time?" joked her dad.

# IV.

Kitty Simpson felt her stomach start to tighten as she approached the outskirts of the once fortified town of Bray-sur-Somme, just north of the river Somme in northern France. Dressed smartly in her crisp Red Cross uniform, she was sitting, along with a group of fellow Voluntary Aid Detachment nurses and staff, in the back of a noisy and bumpy canvas covered supply truck, pressed in amongst the crates, sacks and barrels. From her vantage point near the rear opening she could see the once idyllic landscape scarred and damaged beyond recognition from the ravages of battles never meant to take place here. Where there was once majestic farmland now stood bomb crater dented fields of churned up mud, trails of barbed wire and the splintered remains of tree trunks. Cutting through the fields at all angles were deep riverlike trenches with walls and battlements made of wooden planks and sandbags, dotted with occasional flashes of mud splattered canvas.

She knew the bloodied history of this area well, and of the greater conflict that lay beyond, still years away from ending. Seeing it with her own eyes however was something else. If the once solid ground of this country could be completely destroyed by the fighting ahead, then she struggled to imagine the horror she knew awaited her at the field hospital she was heading towards. She pushed such thoughts from her mind, quashed the anguish in her stomach and before she realised it drifted into unconsciousness, the constant movement of the truck rocking her to sleep like a baby.

She woke with a jolt as the truck juddered to a halt, and almost leapt out of her seat at the immense "CRACK" of artillery guns going off in the distance, sending their shells of explosive metal destruction into the air and towards the German army entrenched to the north-east. They had stopped alongside a high barbed wire fence, a smattering of sandbags ineffectually protecting its flimsy iron gates, to offload passengers before the truck proceeded onwards toward the rear-supply station serving the frontlines. Beyond the fence she could see the L'Hôpital d'Évacuation, a vast collection of long prefabricated wooden huts for the care and treatment of the wounded flooding in from clearing stations closer to the front. It was here that her mission was to start, and she couldn't imagine it was going to be an easy one.

Stepping down from the truck she turned to grab the small travel case she'd brought with her from the basement in Amiens. When she turned back, the gates were being opened by two old men in khaki uniforms. She recognized them as Les pépères, literally translated as "the grandads"; men too old for military service who had volunteered as territorial reserves to act as orderlies in the hospital. Behind them, standing tall and proud like a stiff peacock in the crisp white nurse's uniform of the Croix-Rouge française, was the Directrice of the hospital. The woman she was here to save.

Along with her fellow passengers, some in uniform like her, some still in their civilian clothing, Kitty made her way through the gates to stand in line in front of the Directrice. This formidable woman in white, her dark brown hair rolling in waves from beneath her broad and neatly folded white muslin cap, then proceeded to walk slowly down the line sizing the group of women up, checking and tugging at bits of the uniforms of those who had, like Kitty, come from the VAD headquarters in Amiens. When she reached Kitty, she stopped and looked down her long straight nose at her, the woman's piercing brown eyes hard, but with a hint of warmth.

"Est-ce que tu parles français?" - *Do you speak French?*

"Oui, je le parle couramment Madam Directrice" - *Yes, I speak it fluently Madam Director*

"Good. You will need it. Most of the wounded that come through here are local men."

The Directrice moved on to the next person in line, but hesitated, and turned back to Kitty.

"Paris?"

"Yes, Madam Directrice, I spent quite some time there with my family before the war."

With that fixed, the woman made her way to the end of the line and, seemingly satisfied, turned and walked purposefully towards the entrance to the hut closest to them, firing off a curt "Follow me" to them, the constant crack of artillery counterpointing her every 10th step.

# V.

As Gertie stepped through the side entrance into the Grand Picture House's foyer for the first time, she was hit by the frankly rather unpleasant musty smell of stale air. It was clear no one had set foot in the place for quite some time. She coughed once then stopped suddenly, stilled by the scene that lay before her.

The foyer was just like something out of a lavish Hollywood film set. Warm light floated in from all directions and bounced off the still reflective surfaces of the room's brass fittings, down onto the autumnal colours of the carpet and up into its impossibly high ceiling. The space felt inviting, like a thick woollen blanket next to an open fireplace waiting to be crawled under.

At the lower end of the foyer she could just make out the revolving brass doors she had seen from the outside. Visitors to the cinema would have come through those doors and been welcomed with a luxuriously carpeted floor still complete with circular Art Deco patterns in warm red, black and plum on a cream base. The circle then extended out to mark lines around the lower steps of the twin staircases with their brass handrails, curving left and right around a deep, carved out space presumably reserved for the latest films promotional material. The staircases led up to the main foyer with its twin ticket booths at either side and matching confectionary kiosks at the rear, framing the brass and frosted glass double doors marked "auditorium". The walls of the space were covered in fan shaped swirls of combed plaster and in the very centre of the upper foyer stood a large sculpted column with a plush deep-red velvet sofa running all around the bottom. Right now it was covered in a carpet of dust, and parts of the sofa looked frayed around the edges, but she didn't care, it was simply stunning.

As Walter shuffled in behind her, she turned to take in his reaction, and it was totally worth it. The normally indifferent look on his face was slowly replaced by a grin, a grin which got bigger and bigger as he distractedly pushed back the hood of his parka and looked around the room. It was like seeing a little kid taste chocolate for the first time.

"Wow! Wicked!" he exclaimed in his laconic manner. It was the most she'd heard him say all morning.

Edward appeared behind them, and putting one hand on each of the children's shoulders said: "Great isn't it? But I reckon the auditorium might be even *more* impressive. Come on…" With that, he turned and walked off toward the double doors at the top end of the foyer. Edward was a tall man, a good head taller than most of the other parents, with scruffy dark brown hair which had started to get grey streaks above his ears. Gertie had seen her dad visibly sag since her mother's accident, almost as if he was afraid of standing to his full height. It was like the world was sitting on his shoulders and it was so heavy it made it hard to stand up straight. Now though, he seemed light and statuesque as he made his way through the foyer. Clearly this old building was having an effect on everyone in their own way.

During the remainder of the day, she and her brother would explore every nook and cranny of the Grand Picture House, but nothing could compare to what was waiting for them in the auditorium.

Through the double doors she found herself in a gloomy, wood panelled hallway. To the right she could just make out a curved wooden staircase, the wood matching and blending in with the walls, sweeping off and through a cut-out in the ceiling. Like the foyer, this was covered in fan shaped swirls and patterns in the carpet once again directed you either down the hall or up the stairs. Edward had gone on ahead and was waiting, silhouetted in the light coming from the rear end of the hall. As she reached him she could see he was holding open a curtain covered door through which he gestured for her to pass. As usual Walter was three paces behind them, but for once not because he was sulking, but because he was looking around at everything, taking it all in.

As Gertie passed her dad she entered a vast cavern-like room, framed on either side with ornate curved theatre boxes high up on the walls. The floor was carpeted with rows of plum coloured seating leading down to a velvet curtained stage dominating the far end of the room. In the centre of the impossibly high ceiling was a rounded crystal chandelier, with globes hung at points like planets, surrounded by a gilded sunburst. As if mirroring it, the morning sun shot long bright beams into the room from a half-dozen round windows high up above the theatre boxes.

"No idea if the power's on, but let me see if I can find a light switch or something" said Edward brightly. She turned to watch him fumbling around near the door they'd come in from for a switch, and discovered the doorway was surrounded by ornate carvings of clouds and curved sunrays, picked out in rich burgundy, cream, blue and gold. "Ah ha! Got it… let's see what this does".

As Edward flicked the brass switch, the room was flooded with light, both from the chandelier and from long strips of concealed lights in the plaster grilles above the door and all around the room under the boxes and above the stage.

Gertie stood silently, her mouth open wide. She had never even seen a picture of anything so spectacular in her life, let alone to be actually standing looking at it with her own eyes…

"I can't believe all this belongs to me." she thought quietly to herself, her eyes welling up as the sight of the room filled her with an overwhelming sense of pride and elation.

# VI.

Kitty had settled quickly into the daily routine at L'Hôpital d'Évacuation. Like all new volunteers she'd had to initially serve her time in the reception hut. This was where the wounded were first brought into the hospital, and was the first area the Directrice had shown them upon their arrival. The pépères would unload the wounded from the ambulances coming in from the frontline aid stations and place them in whatever space was available in one of the four long rows of stretchers. These were arranged into two rows each on either side of a central alleyway and with very little space between each stretcher. The men received triage upon arrival and were either prepped to be moved swiftly onwards to the operating theatres for the serious cases, their wounds treated and dressed awaiting transfer to the wards for the less serious, or given basic palliative care and transferred to the 'moribund' ward for those unlikely to last the day. It was distressing and laborious work, but it served as a perfect introduction to the rigours of day-to-day life for the new recruits coming into the hospital, "testing their stomachs" as the Directrice put it.

After only a week, Kitty had been moved by the Directrice to one of the main treatment wards of the hospital. It was to this ward that the most serious cases were brought for treatment, and during the last few days Kitty had come to witness firsthand the horrible effects of so-called "modern" warfare. It was gruesome and unrelenting. She had to attend more deaths in her first few hours on the ward than she had had to deal with in the entire course of her life to this point. The wounded arrived like tattered husks of what were once men, twisted and disfigured beyond recognition, missing legs, arms, noses, jaws. Others had been blinded or burned by chemicals or shrapnel, and more still suffering from the intensities of the conflict, mumbling incoherently or screaming relentlessly. They referred to this as being "shell shocked" and many of these men would cower under their beds every time the artillery battery to the south boomed and cracked, firing off their payloads of death and mutilation towards the enemy lines.

It was hard at times to remember the reason she was here… it wasn't to save the lives of these men under her care, as much as she poured her efforts into it, it was to observe and try to prevent anything happening to her charge, the Directrice, one Mary 'May' Borden-Turner. Despite her duties she was on constant alert. Any one of the orderlies, student doctors, surgeons or even fellow nursing staff, if they'd been corrupted, could be an operative sent to prevent the flow of events in Madame Turner's life and change the course of history.

In Kitty's eyes, Mary Borden-Turner was an inspiration. Born in Chicago in 1886 Mary had become a millionaire heiress at the early age of twenty. Rather than lavishly squander her money, she had graduated from college and decided to see the world. In the next few years she travelled extensively, married, settled in London, had two children, was arrested as a suffragette and published her first book. At the onset of Britain's declaration of war with Germany in 1914, she'd volunteered to work with the London committee for the French Red Cross. Her name caught the eye of the committee's président La Vicomtesse de la Panouse, who perhaps saw a strong kindred spirit in Mary. Taking advantage of Mary's finances the président asked if Mary, at her own expense, would travel to Dunkirk alongside two hospital nurses and start to treat the hundreds of soldiers suffering from typhoid there. She'd also believed that Mary's social standing would help persuade the French authorities to allow more English nurses to travel to France and staff their hospitals. After many weeks of distress, treating the wounded and sick soldiers pouring in from the frontlines, Mary wrote directly to the commander-in-chief of the French army General Joffree and offered to use her considerable money to set up, staff and run a dedicated field hospital. It was a bold gamble that ultimately proved successful. Not only did it lead to a second hospital, the very one Kitty was now working at, being set up much closer to the conflict, it also showed that nursing this close to the frontlines was a worthwhile risk and paved the way for over ten thousand more nurses to play their part in the war.

Although she came across as businesslike, stern and forthright at first, the Directrice had slowly warmed to her new staff and she and Kitty had quickly formed a closer bond. It was one of the reasons Kitty had been selected for this mission - her likeable personality - well that along with her command of French, her American background and the time she'd spent in London and in Paris, a beloved city for Mary as a young girl. Although she had needed to be very careful when talking with Mary about Paris, careful to never mention anything that might be different in her time from Mary's, anything that might make her question Kitty's cover story, anything that might jeopardise the mission.

To the staff at the hospital, Kitty was Béatrice O'Keefe, a debutante and socialite from Hartford, Connecticut, whose family had relocated to London in the spring of 1911 because of her father's work as a prominent engineer. After the outbreak of war, Beatrice had been appalled by the flood of wounded men returning home from the front, and felt compelled to sign up as a Voluntary Aid Detachment nurse to help in any way she could. After 6 months at the 1st London General she passed the criteria to travel to France to serve in frontline hospitals. This wasn't a million miles away from Kitty's actual background as it happens, which helped keep it plausible. "Beatrice" was also the name Madame Turner had herself used as a pseudonym to publish her first book under, a clever twist Kitty had added to aid in getting quickly closer to the Directrice.

The timing of her mission was critical. It was believed that the enemy would seek to prevent a chance encounter between Madame Turner and a British army Captain named Edward Louis Spiers. Captain Spiers was set to later become a prominent member of parliament, a personal confidant of Prime Minister Sir Winston Churchill and vitally important to the course of what was to be the Second World War. Their love for each other would become the fuel for

28

Madame Turner to write up and publish her experiences of nursing and the horrors of war for the world to read... and then to sign up and do it all again during the next war.

This encounter was due to take place on the 25th October, 1916... five days from now.

# VII.

Gertie spent nearly every weekend she could at the Grand Picture House, exploring its many secret rooms and hidden workings with Walter and her dad. Her favourite thing to do was to sit on her own on the big balcony at the rear of the auditorium surrounded by her drawing things, etching out elaborate sketches of mythical creatures on large bits of paper her dad got from work. That or sitting hidden away by herself in one of the high-up theatre boxes reading a book, she couldn't decide.

After trying and failing on their first few visits, Edward had finally worked out how to raise the projection screen at the front of the main stage. Gertie would roam around the empty space when everyone was distracted elsewhere, pretending to act or dance or sing to an imaginary audience, just as there would have been back when the Grand Picture House was still a Victorian theatre and opera house.

At school, she had a small circle of close friends, and wanted so badly to invite them over to play inside the Grand Picture House, but her dad had said that he wanted to "make sure the old girl was structurally sound" before anyone but them stepped foot inside. To be fair the place had been sitting untouched for 13 years and she was surprised that it wasn't a lot worse off than it was, to be honest. But it had survived intact for nearly a hundred years before that so perhaps that was testament to how well it was built in the first place. Secretly, however, she suspected that her dad just wanted to keep the place to themselves for a bit, and she didn't blame him… it was currently their "little secret", a hideaway from the world, and she still felt a bit magical every time they came here.

On this particular Sunday morning, Gertie and Walter were playing hide and seek, a popular choice for when Edward wanted to concentrate on playing around with the workings of the place. Today he was fiddling around in the projection room, a dust filled box of a room at the back of the auditorium, which housed the two main projectors used for showing films. Most of the "main features" came on multiple reels of film, which the projectionist would mount onto the projectors and fire across the room at the screen at the front of the stage. Their particular skill was to load the next reel in sequence onto the second projector and watch for cue marks at the top right of the screen which told the projectionist to start the projector rolling with its shutter closed. A second mark would then appear to tell the projectionist that they needed to open the second projectors shutter whilst simultaneously closing the first projectors. Once the second projector was showing on the screen, they were free to turn the first off, load it up with another reel of film and wait to do the whole thing again in reverse when prompted. It all sounded very complicated to Gertie, but her dad was fascinated by the whole process, as most men of his age seemed to be about complicated things.

He'd been trying to get one of the projectors to run, and had loaded a reel of film onto it from the huge stacks of them ranging around the walls of the projection room. He'd got the projector to start but now couldn't get the shutter to open. So that he could see when it had done so, the lights in the auditorium were currently off, with only the "exit" signs above the doors giving any light to the room. This made it a great place to hide, and Gertie suspected that's exactly where her brother Walter was, so she stalked back and forth down the rows of seating trying to peer into the gloom and spot him. They had a rule that no one was allowed to hide in any of the theatre boxes, this would be a form of cheating as it took ages to search them all.

Suddenly there was a blinding light and Gertie heard her dad shout "Got it!" After a few seconds images began to appear on the screen, as the film reel finally got through the first few feet of blank frames and onto the beginning sequence of whatever film dad had picked to load into the projector. He'd been particularly excited to find reels marked American Graffiti and Silent Running, but went a bit sheepish when Walter had asked him what Last Tango in Paris was. He hadn't yet worked out how to turn the sound on, so the auditorium was silent apart from the rhythmic "clack" made by the projector.

She turned from the screen to look back across the room to the opening where the projector was and spotted her brother standing up behind the rear row of seats staring at the projected images. "Found you!" she shouted.

"Ah, man!" Walter exclaimed, stamping his foot and punching the air in frustration, "thanks a lot, dad!"

"Kids!" replied Edward, ignoring Walter's comment, "Come up 'ere and have a look at this"

Gertie collected her brother en route and together they made their way out of the auditorium, into the hallway and up the stairs to the balcony, at the back of which was a secret door which led to the projection room. She'd always loved secret doors, how clever it was, she thought, that someone could make a door that looked like it was part of the wall, until it was opened to reveal its secrets beyond.

When they entered the room she saw their dad quizzically rubbing his chin whilst looking down at the table in front of him on which sat a large square metal box. "Now, what do we imagine this could be?" he asked.

# VIII.

Kitty's last five days had passed in a blur. She'd been kept busy by casualties coming in from the Anglo-French frontline at Flers and Lesboefs to the north, so heavy had the influx of wounded been that she'd been drafted in to work the reception hut again. The job of identifying and treating the men's injuries was made even harder by the layers of mud, agitated by the constant back-and-forth of the fighting and the persistent autumn rain that clung to the soldiers' bodies and uniforms. The floor of the hut was awash with a mix of clay, chalk, mud and blood, which the elderly orderlies tried to keep at bay with bucket and mop, fighting against the tide of rain water flooding through the doors every time they opened to let in more wounded from the ambulances.

Fortunately Madame Turner kept a small screened off area to one end of the hut and spent a lot of time there during the cold and damp days. It meant that Kitty could stay close by her and so didn't mind being away from her normal duties.

The constant rain on the wooden roofs made the long hut into an echo chamber and exaggerated every sound. She was on full alert now, her senses heightened, watching for any signs of the enemy… waiting for the arrival of Captain Spiers. Every time the doors to the hut opened she looked up to see, scanning the room quickly to make sure nothing was out of place, but it was always more wounded. More work to be done.

The temperature started to drop as the day drew towards twilight, and the pépères stoked the brick ovens down the centre of the hut in a futile attempt to fight off the cold. Kitty stood next to one of the ovens, trying to get the warmth back in her bones. She felt exhaustion flood towards her and for a moment her head swam. A cold blast of air shook her back to life and she turned towards the door at the end of the hut, to see a young man in a mud covered British army uniform standing next to an Alsatian dog.

"I…. I say! Can anyone help?" He called out, his English accent reverberating around the hut, alien in this mainly French speaking environment.

Kitty turned her head back towards the other end of the room, in time to see the Directrice come out from behind her screen and look to see who was making the commotion. Madame Turner and Captain Spiers stood, locked in time, the surprise of the moment rendering each momentarily speechless.

A movement in one of the rows of wounded caught Kitty's eye, a glint of metal. It was a gun being lifted, pointed in the direction of Captain Spiers. She leaped towards it, her feet flying out from under her as she stumbled blindly towards the would-be assailant. She landed awkwardly, her knee cracking down on the arm of the man, pinning his gun to the ground. He looked up at her, his eyes wild, his teeth gritted in determination. He went to cry out savagely at her, but her right hand, fingers pressed together like a blade,

35

stabbed him in the throat, knocking the sound out of him before it could reach his mouth. He started thrashing and bucking to try and throw her off, but she was trained to take down men twice his size and held her ground. She pressed herself down on top of him, covering his mouth with one hand, stifling the guttural wheezing from his damaged windpipe, whilst reaching out with the other to try and prize the gun from his hand. Lifting his arm and cracking it down hard on the wooden pole of a neighbouring stretcher, she sent the gun spinning away towards the next row of bodies. The assassin, still bucking and thrashing under her, threatened to send her sprawling to the floor at any moment and she held on for dear life.

Suddenly she was aware of Gaston, one of the old orderlies kneeling next to her holding a metal syringe in his hand. He must have assumed the man was having a fit. She grabbed the syringe by the barrel and stabbed it into the assassin's neck just below the ear, her thumb reaching for the plunger. The man's eyes suddenly filled with fear as the Potassium Bromide sedative entered his bloodstream. Slowly he stopped his violent movements and Kitty was able to relax her grip. Once he was completely still she slowly stood up, staggered back into the aisle between stretchers and collapsed backwards, her legs folding under her, the exhaustion overtaking her.

Within seconds her vision went dark and she fainted.

# IX.

The metal box was roughly 30 centimetres square and made up of what looked like a single sheet bent into a cube shape, with its edges folded over to form sides. It had a brass handle on the top, and was split across the front and diagonally down the sides in what seemed to be a lid, which was secured at the front with a brass clasp and some form of combination lock. On the front of the lid was an embossed shape, like a crest or shield, Gertie couldn't quite work out which.

She watched as Edward slowly rolled the tumblers of the lock one number at a time to see if he could work out the combination. Gertie knew you didn't need to be a genius to work out that that could take forever.

"Have you tried 1,2,3,4 dad?" Walter put forward.

"First one I tried, son. No such luck."

There was something familiar about the shield on the lid that Gertie couldn't quite place. Suddenly she remembered where she'd seen it and in a flash she turned on her heel and was out the door of the projection room running for the foyer.

A minute later she was back, a little out of breath.

"Try...", huff, "1, 8", huff, "9, 6", she panted slowly.

Edward looked at Walter, shrugged and turned his attention back to the lock, slowly rolling the numbers until

37

they read "1,8,9,6". There was a soft "click" and the lock popped open.

"How did you work that out, love?" inquired Edward.

She had finally got her breath back after running up and down the stairs, so smiled and said in a sing-song voice.

"Well… I remembered where I'd seen the crest on the lid before. It's on the end of the push bars on the revolving door downstairs."

"AND?!" chorused Walter and their dad together.

"And… underneath are the words 'Et Erit Lux' and the number 1896!"

"So clever! Clearly you are the light of my world, dear Gert, eh? Gettit? 'Cause 'Et Erit Lux' means 'Let there be light'? No?" Gertie and Walter exchanged glances then groaned at Edwards' bad joke at the same time. Undeterred he continued "Now, let's see what's inside."

She watched her dad turn back to the box, slip the lock off, flop open the catch and lift the lid. Inside was a single reel of film with the number 22041896 written on the label. As he lifted the film out of the box Edward spotted an old piece of paper underneath, but when he tried to pick it up it started to crumble to pieces between his fingers.

"Well, that's odd. Why would you want to lock up a roll of film?"

Edward turned the film over and over in his hands, looking closely at it, then pulled a small section of the film out and held it up. To Gertie it seemed like the film started to glow slightly in the light.

"Hmmm, no sound strip… must be an early silent one. Shall we spool it up and have a watch? It looks very short, only a hundred feet or so. You two head out to the balcony and I'll shout when it's ready"

Edward wandered over to the projector and started taking off the reel he'd been playing around with earlier. Meanwhile Gertie and Walter made their way out onto the balcony, to "the best seats in the house", the front row of premium seating: four seats on their own with lots of legroom in front. After a minute or so they heard their dad shout "Ready?"

"Ready!" replied Gertie and Walter in unison.

Edward shouted "Rolling!" and started the projector. All of a sudden the auditorium was filled with a strange purple-tinged light as the film projected onto the screen. There was an extra luminescence about the light, something almost ethereal, which sent a shiver up Gertie's spine.

She didn't have much time to think about this though as almost immediately there was an ear-splitting "BANG!" from the stage behind the screen, then a loud thud and the sound of masonry falling. In an instant the film shut off and all the lights in the building went out.

# X.

Kitty came to, with Gaston gently shaking her by the shoulder, to find only moments had passed since her blackout.

"Mademoiselle Béatrice, tu n'as rien?" - *Miss Beatrice, are you okay?*

"Oui, Gaston, tout va bien maintenant." - *Yes, Gaston, everything is fine*

She got slowly to her feet and looked around. To her relief the assassin was still lying on the stretcher in front of her, out cold. She quickly walked around the row of bodies to where the revolver had landed, snatched it up and discreetly tucked it into the leather belt beneath her apron.

She could hear the Directrice and Captain Spiers talking behind the screened off area at the rear of the hut. He was telling her that he'd been at the frontline trying to discover the whereabouts of a British unit which was currently "misplaced" and was told of this hospital and the woman who ran it, and thought he would stop in to see if any of the unit had ended up here as casualties.

She turned back to where the assassin's stretcher was and was shocked to discover that her assailant had completely disappeared. She looked around frantically but saw no sign of him. She questioned Gaston and the other orderlies but they hadn't noticed his disappearance either and refused to believe that a wounded man had just got up and walked out.

*     *     *     *

Satisfied that her mission was complete, Kitty resolved to set her mind to the task of making her way back to her exit point in Amiens. And so, a few days later, Kitty managed to hitch a lift back to Amiens with some of the wounded on the next ambulance out. She had arranged with the Directrice to travel to pick up some much needed supplies from the main station there, the fighting to the north had ground to a halt due to the adverse weather conditions, so there were less duties on the ward, and Madame Turner thought she could get some well deserved rest after she'd heard of her incident with the wounded man having a fit in the reception hut.

As soon as she stepped out of the back of the ambulance at the Hôtel du ville in Amiens, Kitty knew something was about to go wrong. Her plan had been to spend the night at the safe house again before heading to the exit point later the next day, but as she started to make her way towards the city centre she began to notice people looking up at the sky ahead of her to the east. Then she heard the tell-tale drone of engines. Three German AEG G.IV bombers heading for the city.

She had two choices, try and make it to the safe house, wait it out until the bombing was over and hope that the theatre survived the raid, or go straight to the exit point and initiate the jump herself. What if the theatre was hit and her exit point lost? She'd be stuck here with little hope of escape until the next available exit window in another location and at another time. Best play it safe and try to get away before it was too late.

As the first bombs began to fall on the train depot east of the city the people around her started to panic and run, heading for whatever shelter they could find. For her, the sight of bomber planes was a common one, but for the people of Amiens this was a terrifying new experience. It had only been thirteen years since the Wright brothers first manned flight, and few of them had even heard of aeroplanes let alone seen one. Certainly not one about to drop metal parcels of noise and destruction on them.

The theatre lay between her and the bombers so she would have to head directly towards them in order to get there. In minutes they would be above her and things would start to get decidedly hairy. She broke into a run, heading as hard as she could for the theatre, hoping she could get there in time.

The road was clear ahead of her and in less than a minute she'd covered the distance from the Hôtel du ville along the Rue Delambre towards the always busy La Place Gambetta. She could just make out the elaborate sunflower face of the l'Horlage Dewailly clock tower, with its bronze nude Marie sans Chemise ahead of her, marking the intersection of seven roads and five tram lines. The ground shook with the blast of an incendiary device hitting in the distant Rue Jules Barni, and she stumbled. The bombers were getting much closer. Regaining her balance she charged into the Gambetta, swerving to avoid a group of people anxiously waiting for the tram in order to escape, stood like statues dumbstruck by the approaching bombers. As she rounded the group she almost ran in front of the No. 25 tram as it slowed to allow another carriage to pass ahead at the intersection.

Her goal was now in sight. She just had to make it across the Gambetta and onto La Rue des Trois-Cailloux where the theatre was located. She dodged another fleeing tram car and reached the mouth of the road, the theatre visible ahead as the road curved right.

A woman ran past her shouting "Courez! Courez! Les diables arrivent!" - *Run! Run! The Devils are coming!*

She was swiftly followed by a crowd of people running and shouting, trying to get away from the approaching bombers. They jostled into her, almost knocking her off her feet.

"Où allez-vous? Ils sont presque sur nous!", shouted a young boy - *Where are you going? They are almost upon us!*

Almost as soon as she'd cleared one group of retreating pedestrians another was upon her. She dodged left and sprinted along the tram rail mercifully free of people. Just a hundred metres to go.

She reached the entrance with moments to spare, bombs were dropping only a few streets away in the Boulevard de Belfort and she didn't have much time. Thankfully she'd made sure to scope the place out on her arrival and knew where to find the entrance to the projection box in the theatre's small auditorium.

Inside the theatre a handful of off-duty soldiers, early for the matinee performance or just visiting the bar, were trying to calm the other patrons who were cowering under the tables. Another bomb hit close by and Kitty was knocked off her feet, dust falling around her like rain.

Deftly getting back up she sprinted up the hallway and through the door to the projection room, thankfully empty. She reached under the projectionist's cutting table and pulled out a large metal cube with a combination lock on the front. Quickly rolling the combination she was rewarded with the lock popping open. She slipped the lid back, grabbing the film reel from inside. The ground shook again and she half tripped, half stumbled over to the projector, tearing the reel from it and replacing it with the one in her hand, swiftly spooling the film through the machine, flipping the solenoid which started the projector.

With a loud "pop" the machine came to life. She now had to race to get to the exit point before the bombs were on top of her.

Running back the way she came, she flew into the hallway, turning on her heel to head down towards the auditorium. Several people were travelling in the same direction, trying to seek shelter, she couldn't worry about them, not enough time… soon it wouldn't make a difference anyway.

As she burst through the door into the auditorium, the bombers overhead scored a direct hit on the building. An incendiary device plunged through the roof, landed behind her and exploded. She was knocked forward by the blast and hit the wall violently, shrapnel raked her side and legs. The people seeking shelter in the auditorium were caught by the explosion, dying instantly or sent flying like ragdolls. The air was filled with smoke, brick dust, falling masonry and confusion.

Something grabbed at her ankle. A British soldier caught badly by the blast and severely wounded. She reached beneath her apron for the assassin's revolver and without a thought put the poor man out of his misery.

Stumbling forward she reached the end of the auditorium, its projection screen shredded and hanging in tatters, the images from the projector hitting the wall behind, throwing its ethereal light onto the brickwork, making it glow.

The second bomber scored another direct hit to the auditorium behind her and Kitty was thrown forward by the blast. Instead of striking the hard brick wall in front of her she promptly disappeared through it, just as the projector spluttered to a halt and the light died out.

# XI.

"What the hell was that?!" shouted Edward from the projection room.

"No idea dad!" replied Gertie, "I can't see a thing!"

The explosion had made Gertie's ears ring, a high-pitched whine filling her head and causing her to shout. Her eyes began to adjust to the light and she noticed a soft luminescence coming from the stage behind the projector screen.

Slowly she felt her way backward along the rows of seats to the rear of the balcony, down the stairs and along the hallway to the lower part of the auditorium. From there she inched her way along the wall to the lower end of the room, and through the lower exit doors. Reaching to her right she found the stage door and twisted its brass handle, pushing. The door opened slightly and then stopped, caught on something blocking it from the inside. She leaned her weight against it and it slowly stuttered open, with the tell-tale scrape of masonry on wood.

The faint glow was stronger here and she realised, as she felt her way along the wall and up the backstage stairs, it was coming from the backdrop at the rear of the stage.

To Gertie's amazement, lying face down on the stage, surrounded by pieces of broken brick and dust that didn't belong there, was the body of a woman.

46

The woman was dressed in what looked like a nurse's uniform, at least Gertie assumed that's what it was from the big Red Cross on the woman's armband. Edging closer she realised the uniform was exactly like the one she'd seen on display on her school trip last year to Preston Manor, which she seemed to recall was an Edwardian house? She couldn't quite remember...anyway, it looked old-fashioned, and nothing like the outfits she'd seen the nurses wearing when Walter had had to go to hospital with a broken arm.

The woman in the nurse's uniform let out a laboured groan and started to shift, turning her head towards Gertie. Gertie was routed to the spot, all she could do was stare at the woman in front of her whose face seemed to Gertie to be as beautiful as her mother's had been, even under the layer of dust and patches of blood that now covered it.

Just then Gertie became aware of another growing light coming from behind her, and up onto the stage came her dad and Walter. Edward thrust the battery powered lantern he was carrying at Gertie and headed toward the mysterious woman on the stage, who was now trying to sit up.

End of Reel One

# Intermission

"Brrrrrrring! Brrrrrrring! Click"

"Hello? Can anyone hear me? My name is Gertrude Granger, calling any Light agents listening. I've done a very bad thing. An idiotic, selfish thing and now I'm in deep trouble. Help me, ple…"

# Reel Two: Pathfinder

# XII.

Kitty awoke with her head swimming from the blast. She groaned and blinked, slowly turning her head towards the only source of light she could make out. Silhouetted in that faint light was a figure, but she couldn't focus enough to see who it was. She tried to move, but her whole body seemed to be on fire with pain. She summoned all her strength and pushed off the ground. Just then a light appeared behind the figure and grew quickly brighter. The sudden intensity of the light was too much and Kitty had to shield her eyes, but as this new light source settled and stopped moving she could now make out more clearly the figure she'd first seen. It was a girl of about 12, her hair tied back in a ponytail and looking lost in a jumper three sizes too big for her.

Before she had time to process this however she became aware of another figure approaching her rapidly and she tried to sit up just in case she needed to defend herself.

"Easy love, don't try and move, you look like you've had quite the accident" said the figure. She looked up to see a tall man with a kind face, sinking gently to his knee in front of her with arms outstretched, ready to help her up.

"Wha…where am I?" she managed to say, her voice raspy and dry, the sound of it seemingly coming from somewhere far away from her body.

"The cinema" said the girl behind her would-be rescuer. When she remained blank faced the girl quickly went on to say "In Brighton. The Grand Picture House".

Kitty wasn't entirely sure what the girl meant and turned her confused expression on the man currently helping her to her feet. This clearly wasn't the arrival room in the Æther, so where had the gateway taken her!? These people spoke English with a British accent, so she wasn't in France anymore. Obviously the gate had taken her somewhere, but not where it was supposed to. So where was this, and why had she exited here? She needed to be cautious, she was sure this would all make sense in time. Ironic isn't it, she thought, time was the one thing she believed she had a grip on, but here she was, God knows where and God knows when.

"Think you can stand?" asked the man.

"I...I'll try", she replied. Her voice seemed to be coming from her own mouth at last, so that was a start. With the man's help she pushed herself to her feet, but just as she thought she'd made it, the pain washed over her again and she couldn't help but cry out. Thankfully the man still had hold of her, so she didn't drop to the ground again. He gently slipped his arm around her waist and, with baby steps and winces of pain, together they made their way to some stairs and, from there, out through a door.

Beyond the door Kitty found herself in the cavernous hall of a film theatre, the sunlight streaming down from high up windows catching the rows of seating that filled the room. It was to the first row of these seats that the man helped her over to, entreating her to sit down.

"You rest here a minute, whilst I go and see if I can get the power back on", with this he disappeared into the darkness of the room.

So she was in the auditorium of a cinema, was she? she thought to herself. A picture started to form in her head of what might have happened. As the pain in her body had started to subside, Kitty suddenly became aware that her hands were shaking. She pulled them to her and crossed them against her chest, closing her eyes tight as she tried to push the sudden sensation of panic into the pit of her stomach. Slowly she became aware of a shuffling to her left, and opened her eyes to be greeted with the sight of the young girl cautiously edging towards her. Standing sheepishly behind her was a boy who, from his resemblance to the girl Kitty surmised, was most likely her younger brother.

"Erm…a…are you okay?" asked the girl.

"I hope so", she replied. The girl said nothing more and an awkward silence hung in the air between them for a painfully long time. Suddenly the lights came on and Kitty could see the girl clearly for the first time since her arrival. She was a pretty little thing, despite her stern expression.

"My...my name's Gertie, and this is my little brother Walter... What's your name?"

Slipping her white headscarf off her head and placing it on the seat next to her she paused for a second, unsure if she would need to maintain her cover. From the way these two were dressed this clearly wasn't 1916 anymore, so she decided to stick to honesty and replied, "I'm Kitty, pleased to meet you both".

# XIII.

Gertie thought the woman sitting in the front row of the auditorium looked pale and imagined she could make out a hint of confusion in her bloodied and dust covered face. She was still confused herself to be honest. Where was that explosion from, and how did the woman get onto the stage behind the screen? Perhaps she'd walked in through one of the emergency exits by accident and had followed the bright light of the projector onto the stage?

"Are you something to do with the festival?" Gertie asked the woman who'd said her name was Kitty.

"Festival?" replied Kitty, her brow furrowing ever so slightly.

"Yes. The Brighton Festival. I thought you might be an actress or re-enactor or something. To do with the Royal Pavilion? Dad says it used to be a hospital during the First World War."

The woman didn't reply but sat in thought for a moment before asking "Was that your dad who came to my rescue?"

Gertie thought Kitty sounded exactly like Katharine Hepburn or one of those other film stars she and her mum used to love watching. That strange old-fashioned posh sounding type of voice that wasn't quite American. That meant she had to be some kind of actress, right?

"Yes, that was dad, his name's Edward"

As if on cue, her dad came back down the aisle to stand with them.

"This is Kitty, dad. I was just asking her if she was from the festival... from the Pavilion?... and that's why she was dressed up as a nurse."

"Good point, old thing. Nice thinking. Didn't know they had anything going on over there, but anyway, how did you end up here?" her dad replied, turning to Kitty.

"I'm not quite sure. I think I must have had a dizzy spell and hit my head. I remember colliding with a door and then nothing until I saw the bright light, and then you coming towards me. Where am I please? Some sort of theatre?"

"You're in the Grand Picture House." said Gertie excitedly, "It's ours. It used to be a cinema before it closed, but now it's been given to us. Dad managed to get the projector working and we were just about to watch an old film we'd found and then there was an enormous bang and the lights went out"

Gertie thought she saw Kitty start to smile slightly, but only for a moment, and then Kitty winched in pain and put her hand to the back of her head. Her dad stepped forward and knelt down in front of Kitty, a look of concern on his face.

"I think we should probably try and clean you up a bit, find out if we need to take you to A&E or not. Walt, go and see if there's any cloths or tea towels in one of the kiosks. I'll go and grab a bowl of warm water."

After her brother and dad had gone, Gertie stood looking at the woman for a time. She seemed very composed considering her injuries and the fact that she had no memory of getting here. Definitely some sort of actress, she thought, to be able to take all this in her stride. Gertie was certain she wouldn't be so calm and collected in the same circumstances. Eventually the woman broke Gertie's scrutiny of her by asking "What film did you watch? Any good?"

"Don't know. It was just something we found in a locked metal box in the projection room. It had only just started when the explosion happened and the lights went out."

Kitty smiled at her then and said, "Oh that is a shame. I'm sure you will get a chance to watch it again soon though, as long as everything is still working properly that is."

Her dad arrived back with the water, Walter scurrying along behind him, and set to work cleaning the blood somewhat inexpertly off of Kitty's face. After Kitty's third or fourth sharp intake of breath, Edward stopped and she gently put her hands over the top of his, saying "Please. Let me do it. I am a nurse after all." Edward laughed nervously and let Kitty take the damp cloth from his hands. After a few minutes of dabbing and rinsing Kitty was looking much cleaner and less bloodied.

During all this her dad had been mumbling to himself, clearly trying to work out what had happened to cause the blowout. "Must have been a faulty fuse box or relay somewhere at the back of the stage... maybe turning on the projector overloaded it and it blew... can't remember seeing anything like that back there though… ah well, I'll take a look later…" Gertie put her hand on his forearm, and said "Don't worry about it too much dad, let's get Kitty home first yeah?"

"Yes, of course. How are you doing there, Miss?"

"Much better I believe." Kitty replied, "I think I might like to try standing up if I may?"

Gertie reached forward and took the bowl of blood coloured water from her and stepped back to give Kitty some room. She watched as Kitty cautiously placed her hands on the armrests and pushed herself up out of the chair. Once on her feet she wobbled slightly but seemed okay, so tried a step forward. This seemed to work fine for the first step, but when it came to the second Kitty's leg couldn't quite take the weight and she started to buckle. Edward rushed forward and caught her, helping her back up again.

"Well, that went well wouldn't you say?" Kitty joked with a small laugh. "I think I might like to go home now, properly get my feet up for a while. Do you think I might trouble you to help me find my way back?"

"To the Pavilion? Sure it's only a few roads away. Are you sure you're okay though? Don't need to go to the hospital or anything?" Edward replied.

"I'm feeling much better, thank you. I'm sure my colleagues will patch me up if I need it once I can get changed out of these clothes and properly assess the damage."

"Alright, if you insist you're okay. Let's go slowly though, eh?" With that Gertie's dad lifted his arm up and Kitty slipped hers through it. Together they slowly started to make their way out of the auditorium and towards the foyer with Gertie and Walter following behind. Gertie could see with each step Kitty was finding her feet again and was able to walk with more confidence.

# XIV.

As Kitty walked towards the back of the auditorium, consciously trying to support some of her weight on the arm of the man, she scoped out where the projectionist's box might be. She'd need to find some excuse to get away from these people and activate the gate. The film must still be attached to the projector as it was the last thing they'd watched, so all she'd need to do was rethread it, turn the machine on and get back to the stage at the front of the auditorium before being discovered. Simple, she thought, it wasn't as if she could barely walk or anything. She was still in shock and badly injured from her escape from Amiens, but she was sure if she could just get home she'd be able to get the proper medical treatment she needed... after her debriefing of course. She wasn't looking forward to that.

As she and her escort party reached the back of the auditorium they went out through a doorway and into a wood panelled hallway. To her left she spotted a staircase presumably leading up to the balcony she had seen on the way out. That must be where the entrance to the projectionist's box was, she thought. They were often kept hidden by secret doors, so she hoped it wouldn't be too hard to find if this was indeed the case. She'd need to demonstrate that she could walk on her own if she was to make her excuses and get away from this group, so she slackened her grip on the man's arm and tried to walk with more confidence. These people *seemed* very nice, but she couldn't be discovered, she wasn't supposed to be here, wherever or more importantly whenever this was. She'd have to do it soon, she couldn't let these people take her to their intended destination or her story would be blown.

By the time they'd all made it to the end of the hallway and the brass double doors into the foyer Kitty was walking on her own without any support from Edward and she slipped her arm from his as he stepped forward to gallantly open the door for her to go through. The others followed her and together they walked towards the revolving doors at the opposite end of the foyer. Reaching the top of the twin staircases down to the exit, she realised it was now or never.

"Oh damn, I've gone and forgotten my headscarf. Must have left it on the seat next to me. I'll just pop back and get it."

"I'll go", said the girl brightly

"No, please… let me. I feel steadier on my feet now and it will be good practice before we step outside. Don't worry. I'll be fine. I'll be back in two shakes of a lamb's tail, you'll see."

Without waiting for any more argument she set off at a steady pace, back to the brass doors leading to the auditorium. Once she was out of sight of the group she broke into a sprint, it hurt like hell but this had to be done quickly. She made the stairs, two at a time, and quickly spotted the secret door to the projectionist's box, which someone had thankfully forgotten to close. She found the projector which still had the reel of film attached, deftly swapping it to the other spool and rethreading it through the machine, just as she had in Amiens. With a flick of a switch the machine was running and so was she, back out the door, down the stairs and along the hallway to the auditorium.

The room was filled with the purple-tinged light of the gate reel, its black and white images of a man and woman standing in a garden of cabbages stuttering on the screen up on the stage ahead.

Kitty walked swiftly down the aisle of seats. Pausing to grab her headscarf from the chair where she'd deliberately left it, she turned back to the rear of the room to make sure she hadn't been followed. Satisfied she was in the clear she stepped up onto the stage and through the gate, disappearing through the screen like it was a curtain of water.

# XV.

Gertie was standing with Walter and Edward at the top of the twin staircases waiting for Kitty to return with her headscarf.

"She seems to be taking her time. Hope she's not taken another turn and fallen over or anything." remarked her dad "Perhaps I'll go check."

"Let's all go dad. I'm bored of standing here waiting" she replied.

By the time they had made their way back to the auditorium, the film had hit its final scene. The screen was bathed in light for a few moments, that strange ethereal light just as she'd seen earlier, before the projector shut off and the room became dark again.

"Kitty?!" Gertie called out. Edward went back to the doorway and switched the lights on. As soon as she could see again, Gertie ran to the front of the seating. Kitty's headscarf had gone!

"She must have slipped out the back door again" Edward suggested, "I'll go and look."

Before long he was back and shaking his head. "Door's still shut tight", he told her. Gertie couldn't believe it. What was going on? Who was this mysterious woman? She had appeared out of nowhere and vanished again in less than an hour. Where had she come from, why was she dressed the way she was, and why turn the projector on again before leaving? How had she gotten out anyway if the doors were still shut? She just couldn't wrap her head around it all. She was filled with confusion and disappointment, but underneath all that there were tremors of butterflies in her stomach, a tinge of excitement she'd only felt a few times in her life before.

*     *     *     *

Gertie, Walter and their dad spent the rest of the day pondering the mystery of Kitty's disappearance. Edward pulled up the screen on the stage to inspect the damage, but could find none evident. The stage was covered in dust and bits of brick and mortar, but he could find no place it had come from. They all pitched in to sweep up and pile the brick pieces out in the courtyard around the back. Once everything was squared away, they locked up the Picture House and took a visit to the Royal Pavilion to see if they could find Kitty there. No one had heard of her, and no one knew of any re-enactments or plays going on that had anything to do with the First World War or Edwardian nurses. Gertie felt a little sick. It was like some weird dream, like she'd fallen asleep and imagined the whole thing. Except her brother and her dad had experienced it all as well.

A lingering thought stuck in her head. What did the film they had found have to do with all this? Kitty had been there when they had run the film for the first time, caught and injured by the explosion her dad could find no trace of, and Kitty herself had played the film again to cover her disappearance. There was something very odd about that film. Why had it been hidden and locked away? Why did the light from the projector have a strange, almost purple tinge, when the film was only in black and white? They'd tried other films and none seemed to produce the same effect, so it wasn't the projector.

She decided she would make it her mission to find out more.

# XVI.

Kitty stepped out of the front door of her lodgings on the morning of the 27th June 1944, completely oblivious to the fact that today was the day her life would change forever. Today was the day she was going to die.

She'd come to England in 1938 as a girl of sixteen when her dad, whose work as an aviation engineer, had brought him to the attention of the Vickers-Armstrong company. Her, her dad and her mother had swiftly moved 'across the pond' from America to work in the company's new headquarters at Brooklands in Surrey. Being a bright and likeable young woman Kitty soon found employment as a secretarial assistant in the records department. The people were nice enough, but she wasn't particularly challenged and longed to take more of an active role in aviation. She wanted to fly aeroplanes like her hero Amelia Earhart. When Britain declared war on Germany in October 1939 she thought her chance might come. In March 1940, on the day of her 18th birthday, she hopped on a bus into Weybridge and volunteered for the Women's Auxiliary Air Force hoping this might give her an opportunity to pursue her dream.

A few weeks later she was shipped to RAF West Drayton for basic training. She aced every test and every physical challenge and was soon assigned to Fighter Command stationed at RAF Biggin Hill and moving swiftly up through the ranks. In a few short months she had earned the rank of Section Officer and started training on the maintenance and armament of fighter aircraft. It was about at this point that she learned her first piece of bad news; she would never be allowed to actually fly aircraft. All military pilots were men, the only female pilots were those who had previous commercial experience of flying and were attached to the non-military Air Transport Auxiliary. Even then they were only permitted to fly transport runs or ferry aircraft from base to base, strictly non-combat. This was a massive shock to Kitty, but a worse shock was to come a few months later, on September the 4th at 13:00 hours, when a group of German bombers dropped their payload on the factory at Brooklands. Both her mother and father were at work that day and were killed instantly in the bombing run. Kitty was now an orphan, one of so many during the war.

The death of her parents was a devastating blow and Kitty grieved for quite some time. When she returned to her work at the W.A.A.F she was more serious, more determined, more driven. She quickly came to the attention of a recruiter for the Special Operations Executive, a secret government initiative whose purpose was to set up and conduct espionage, sabotage and intelligence gathering reconnaissance missions into German occupied Europe. This transfer prompted her move from RAF Biggin Hill to Baker Street in central London and onward to various training camps at secret locations in Hampshire, Cheshire and the wilds of Scotland. After eighteen months of intense training she was "passed out" as a field agent. During this time the war in Europe had become more desperate and she was immediately cleared for active duty. Her command of the French language and knowledge of the French capital of Paris led to her being parachuted into the city on 14th February 1943 under the codename "Valentine".

What she did in France for the next year is a story for another time, although she did happen to return to England on a few occasions to recuperate from missions. One such occasion was in June 1944, which brings us back once again to the morning of the 27th.

Kitty had decided to walk down the Holloway road into Islington that morning and grab a late breakfast and some coffee before heading to H.Q. for her afternoon briefing. She'd been out dancing the night before with some fellow Baker Street Irregulars - the nickname SEO agents gave themselves - and had slept in a little later than usual as a treat. By 12:30 hours she was making her way back towards Highbury & Islington station through the Compton Terrace Garden when she heard the tell-tale sounds of aircraft overhead. Looking up she spotted a group of Spitfires out on patrol. As she neared Highbury Corner she heard another engine, but this one was different, a new sound she hadn't heard before, a much deeper throaty rattling, unlike that of a propeller engine. She became aware of other people in the street stopping to look up at the sky to see where this noise was coming from. High up she could just make out the wingspan of something small, but couldn't recognise the shape. Just when she couldn't imagine the sound becoming any loader it stopped. There was a moment of pure silence. Then the shape started to get rapidly bigger and she recognised it as one of the new German V1 'doodlebug' bombs. An air raid siren started howling, too late to make a difference. People around her were shouting and screaming. She broke into a sprint, hoping to find some shelter, some protection from the blast she knew was about to happen. She'd barely made it 10 feet before the bomb impacted in the street behind her and everything went black and silent.

*　　*　　*　　*

When Kitty woke again her head was swimming and her body felt like it was being buffeted by waves. She tried to move but seemed to have no control over her limbs. She tried opening her eyes but the shock of the sudden light was like someone had stuck a sword through her head. Slowly she became aware of a voice gently saying her name over and over, but the voice sounded like it too was underwater. Suddenly she felt like she was about to be sick, but then a wave of pain swept over her and she blacked out again.

When she came to once more she no longer felt like she was underwater. The soft cocoon of the ocean was no longer there to protect her and she missed it. Now it was as if someone had turned up the intensity of the world to be almost overwhelming. She could very definitely feel her body now and it was in pain, pain such as she'd never experienced. She breathed deeply, trying to push the pain away from her like shrugging off a blanket. When she felt up to it she gently tried opening her eyes again. The light wasn't as intense this time and slowly shapes began to form as her eyes started to focus.

"Ah, Valentine, welcome back to the land of the living" said a shape close to her. She blinked, trying to wash the blurriness away from her vision. Slowly the shape sharpened and took on the form of her SEO handler Flight Officer Adelaide Foster.

"Gently now... No sudden movements. You did just die you know", the figure said in her well-educated middle-class English accent.

Kitty tried to speak, but all that would come out was a rattle.

"Here. Drink this."

A glass was pressed to her bottom lip and tipped, the sudden flood of water into her mouth making her splutter and choke. "You never could handle your drink, Valentine." joked Flight Officer Foster, making Kitty smile despite the pain.

"Let's try that again."

This time she managed to swallow the water without incident. It was the most wonderful thing she'd ever tasted.

"Wha...what happened?" she managed to say, her voice still raw. She tried to push herself up, winching in pain as she did so. She felt Foster's arm push round her back and help her sit up as something was stuck behind her to help her stay upright.

"You were caught in the blast of one of Jerry's new V1 flying bombs. Dreadful things. Blew up the whole blasted street and buried you under a ton of bricks. It took the fire chaps two hours to dig you out, they presumed you'd popped your clogs and were about to cart you off to the dead house. Luckily I'd been keeping tabs on you and got to you first. Brought you here."

Kitty took the glass and drained it before handing it back to Flight Officer Foster. She looked around the room, trying to make out a little more of where she was. It was a dimly lit room with no windows, and filled with what looked like crates and storage boxes, could have been anywhere really.

"And where is 'here', ma'am?" she decided to ask.

"We are currently camped out in the glamorous surroundings of a store room in the Gaumont cinema, Holloway Road, Islington. It's the nearest exit point to the location of your little 'accident'. So it seemed like the best place to bring you", replied Foster.

"Exit point? Cinema? I...I don't think I understand. Why didn't I go to a hospital? Or to one of the medics at H.Q.?"

It was at this point Kitty noticed that Foster wasn't wearing her W.A.A.F. uniform, but instead was dressed in casual civilian clothing. This struck her as odd. As her superior officer Foster was due to have been at the same afternoon briefing as her and would have been required to dress for the occasion. It didn't take a spy to notice that something else was going on here.

"Valentine...I know you are already well versed in the art of making tough choices, but today may see you make the toughest choice you've ever made. To the world outside this building Section Officer Katherine Simpson is dead. Killed in an enemy bomb strike." Foster paused for a moment to let Kitty process the information she'd just given her.

"This leaves you two choices. You can return to the outside world. Go back to the war and resume your previous life as a spy, as if nothing has happened. People go missing all the time during bomb strikes. Things get misreported. Won't be a problem", again she paused, this time for dramatic effect.

"Or, you can leave this life behind and join a bigger fight. Be a part of something much greater. You'll need to use all the skills we've already taught you, and learn a hell of a lot more to boot. You'll visit places you never thought you would or could go to. Have adventures beyond your greatest dreams. Truly make a difference in this world. Right, its wrongs for the benefit of future generations."

Kitty sat stunned, completely lost for words.

"A bit grandiose, I know. Probably puffing it up a bit, but you get the picture. You don't have to decide now, think about it for a few minutes. In the meantime let's see if we can't get you up on your feet, eh?"

# XVII.

Gertie was sitting in the auditorium watching the strange, purple-tinged film for what felt like the hundredth time. Weeks had passed since the beguiling visitor had stumbled into her life and, within less than an hour, vanished again without trace. It felt like in less than six months her world had become bigger and more exciting. First she had learned about her inheritance of the cinema, then there was this strange incident with the woman in the nurse's uniform. When she thought about the woman and the mystery surrounding her, her heart beat so fast it felt like it would burst out of her chest. She'd not felt like this since she'd first read The Lion, The Witch and the Wardrobe. But she just couldn't seem to put it all together in her head. How had Kitty got into the auditorium? What was the explosion, and where had all the bricks come from? Why was she dressed like an old-fashioned nurse and why did she appear to have so many injuries? How had she recovered so quickly? Where did she disappear to and what did the film have to do with any of this? The whole thing made her feel confused, excited and bereft all at the same time.

Gertie was sure the film must be important. They had played the film just before the explosion had happened, and Kitty had taken the time to run the film again before she left the cinema… Why? Her head swam with more questions. Why was the film locked up? What was the significance of the inscription 'Et Erit Lux', Let there be light… Did this have something to do with the way the film gave off that strange purple-tinged glow? She kept looping back to why Kitty had played the film before she left. It was such a strange thing to do. The film was only about a minute long, it's not as if it would be enough of a distraction that it would have covered her exit. It had almost finished by the time they had realised Kitty hadn't come back and gone to find her. She thought about The Lion, The Witch and the Wardrobe and about Narnia and suddenly had an idea. It was crazy and pure fantasy, but she just had to see if it was true.

"Dad? Are you upstairs?"

"Yes, love." Her dad's voice replied from the balcony "I'm just up here looking through some old magazines"

"Can you go and run the film for me again?"

"Again? Well I can't see why not. Aren't you sick of watching it yet?"

"Daaaad?!" She moaned sarcastically.

"Alright… hold on"

Gertie stood up from her seat and walked towards the screen at the end of the room. She reached the front row of seats just as the film flicked into life. The white on black title card flashed up and disappeared again as she walked slowly closer to the screen, watching as a young couple entered a garden full of cabbages in purple-tinged monochrome. As she came near to the light her body felt electric, the fine hairs on her arm standing up as her flesh started to get goose bumps. As the elegantly dressed fairy reached into one of the cabbages to pull out a baby, she touched her now trembling

75

fingers to the silk canvas. She was surprised that she felt no resistance, no feeling of texture from the cloth, just air and a faint static charge which crackled up her fingers and into her hand. She pushed into the canvas and her fingers began to disappear, a purple glow around the area they once were. She continued to push and, first her wrist, then her hand disappeared through the screen. Taking a deep breath, she carefully lifted her foot up onto the stage, stepped up and pushed her whole body through the screen, just as the film hit its final foot of length and ended.

# XVIII.

Kitty stood in the auditorium of the Gaumont cinema, Islington facing the screen at the end of the room with Officer Foster supporting her weight. They had made their way slowly from the store room she'd woken in, into the main auditorium of the theatre, after a few failed attempts and a lot of reassurance. She was still a little unsteady on her feet and equally unsure of what was about to happen now they had reached this point.

"Now then Valentine. It's time for you to make your choice, I hope you've had enough time to think about it. In a moment I'm going to ask you to take a leap of faith. Either step up and enter into a new life, a new world... or stay still and return to your old one. Entirely up to you. Are you ready?"

Kitty took a deep breath, then another. Finally she said "I'm ready ma'am"

"Good, and do stop calling me ma'am... there's no rank where we are headed" Foster smiled at her and turned towards the back of the room. "Open the gate please, operator!" she called out to whomever, Kitty presumed, was in the projectionist's box.

The lights in the auditorium dimmed and she heard the distinctive clacking of the projector as it kicked into life. Suddenly the room was filled with an ethereal purple-tinged light and Kitty felt a strange sense of elation. Foster gently walked her forward towards the projection screen as images began to appear on it in black and white. The screen seemed to emit a tingle of static electricity which began to engulf Kitty's body as she approached. She felt her heart start to quicken with excitement and an uneasy feeling begin in her stomach as her fingers touched the screen for the first time. She watched as they disappeared leaving only a purple glow, but had no time to panic as Foster propelled her forward through the gate and toward her new life.

# XIX.

Gertie emerged on the other side of the gate but had no time to take in her surroundings before the light suddenly shut off. She was left alone in the dark with no idea of where she was. Fear gripped her without warning and she started to panic. Her breathing quickened, and the sound of it filled her hearing. She started to feel sick, her stomach tightening in spasm. She collapsed in a heap and brought her head into her arms and her knees up tight, curling into a ball with her eyes tightly shut. She stayed like this for what seemed like a lifetime. Slowly she managed to wrestle some control over herself and slow her breathing. When her stomach had settled and she was calmed and ready she tried opening her eyes. It was pitch black and she couldn't even see her own body. She listened for any other sounds over that of her own breathing but could hear nothing.

"He...hello?" She gently called, but all that returned was the echo of her own voice. Okay, she thought, if there was an echo she must be in a room, or something that had surfaces the sound of her voice could be reflected off of. She'd obviously managed to learn *something* during her Physics lessons. As her eyes started to adjust to the dark she could begin to make out shapes. She could finally see her own arms still wrapped around her and was pleased to discover that beyond them the stone floor she was currently lying on. Once she knew she was on solid ground she sat up but continued to keep her legs hugged tightly into her chest. Turning her head slowly from left to right she started to map out the features of the room as her eyes continued to adjust and it emerged from the darkness.

It was a large tall room, like that of a warehouse, with metal pillars from ceiling to floor at equal distances. The walls were whitewashed brick and there were no windows that she could make out. Behind her was a large white screen, like the projection screen in the Grand Picture House but smaller and fixed directly to the wall at floor height. As her sight became clearer she could finally make out a large door at the opposite end of the room. She was clearly alone here, so it seemed safe enough to get up and head slowly in the direction of the door, moving carefully from pillar to pillar. As she approached the doorway she could make out more detail thanks to the light filling in from the edges of the heavy black metal door. It looked like the door slid to one side on wheels and via a rail above it, but it looked pretty heavy. She grabbed the handle and tried it but it wouldn't budge. She summoned her strength and, channelling her hero Cheetara, she chanted quietly to herself "I am Cheetara. I am the strongest of my kind and I will not be DEFEATED!" A crack appeared, spilling light into the room. She continued to pull and the crack opened a little more, and a little more and slowly, as it overcame inertia, the door slid gently open.

She stopped and looked back at the room she was standing in. Something was odd about it and she couldn't quite place it. It was a strange room, just black and white and grey, nothing of colour in it at all. Even the rust on the metal door seemed to be grey rather than a deep orangey brown. Perhaps it was her eyes still adjusting. She decided there was no point in staying here and stepped through the door into another larger room. This one seemed to be filled with tables and chairs which had been stacked up against one wall. The only furniture left in the centre of the room was a black and grey bed shaped chair and a white sofa both with those fancy thin legs like the ones grandparents always seemed to have in the living rooms you were never allowed to sit on. The doors of this room were already open so she headed straight for them. The third room was an even larger room and had a glass roof through which sunlight shone, thankfully defused by a series of hanging blinds. This one was filled with racks and racks of clothing of all colours and styles, nearly all of it old-fashioned, but there were a few items she recognised from high street shops at home. Against the walls stood dozens of identical white painted chests of drawers. The room reminded her a lot of the shop in her favourite cartoon, Mr Benn, as there were piles of hats, and shoes, and lots of other accessories on every available surface. All the bright colours against the stark black and white of the room started to hurt her eyes so she decided to move on and keep exploring.

The next room she entered was even stranger, it had an incredibly high ceiling for a start, but the weirdest part was the massive warship, with huge white painted guns capped with black stars, rows of shiny metal rimmed portholes, and a spiral staircase coming out of the top of it, half built out of a wall of twinkling stars. On the other side of the room were rows and rows of banked seating, like you'd get in a sports stadium. Again, all of this was in Black and White, with no colour. She started to feel a bit dizzy and confused. Where was this? It was like nothing she'd ever seen before. She walked on and found herself at the very top of a massive staircase leading downwards into a huge room with lots of platforms, each with squared off stairs and immense white columns towering over her. She didn't like this at all, it gave her a very strange feeling deep in the pit of her stomach and she started to feel very disoriented. She ran down the staircase and onto one platform, then another, then another, on and on until she finally reached the bottom. She ran through a huge arched doorway and into a room filled with rows and rows of chairs. She looked around at the walls and they too were covered in boxes with rows of seats in them. The room curved on all sides, even the ceiling curved down like a huge bowl. She felt panicked and anxious. The rows of seats were all pointing the same way towards a huge spot lit platform draped in banners with a lectern standing proudly at the front. Behind it rose a giant banner emerging from behind striped curtains, showing a drawing of a man in a wide brimmed hat, the word KANE emblazoned above it in black square lettering. To either side of the platform she saw tunnels leading out of the room so without hesitation headed towards them as quickly as her feet could carry her.

The tunnel seemed to go on and on, for a very long time, but she could feel the anxiousness abate with each step so ploughed on. Eventually she could see daylight ahead, but it was so bright it hurt her eyes. Emerging from the end of the tunnel she had to shield her eyes from the sudden bright light of the sun.

Laid out in front of her was the most breathtaking thing she had ever seen. A limitless landscape made up of roads, and pathways, and lawns, and green parks, and city blocks, jumbled up together and stretching into the distance as far as the eye could see. And nearly all of it in glorious Technicolor. To one side she saw a vast marina filled with ships and boats of all shapes and sizes. Warships, aircraft carriers, ocean liners, boats, Viking long ships, sailing ships. Wait... wasn't that One-eyed Willy's pirate ship from the Goonies?!

She started down the steps in front of her and headed for the nearest patch of grass. The light was really hurting her eyes and she was starting to feel lightheaded. Perhaps she could rest a while on the grass, she thought. The building across from her looked very familiar too... it was just like the clock tower that gets struck by lightning in Back to the Future... and wait, wasn't that the Ghostbusters firehouse over there? Wasn't that in New York? Is that where she was? This was all so confusing. How did she get to New York? And where were all the people? Why was everything so bright and colourful? The sunlight was starting to make her feel really sick. Her vision began to go double and she stumbled forward to try and reach the grass lawn. As soon as her feet touched the green turf she fell forward, and by the time her body hit the ground she was out cold.

# XX.

*1st May, 1937*

Kitty stood once more in the now familiar auditorium of the Gaumont, preparing herself before signalling the operator to open the gate. Five years had passed since she'd been brought here by Special Agent Foster and had first stepped through into the Æther, even though at this point in time it was actually seven years earlier. The whole moving backward and forward through time thing had made her head go fuzzy at first, but she'd gotten used to it. Thank heaven it was just confined to the 20th Century… at least most of the time.

She'd just successfully completed a mission to persuade the English journalist Lady Grace Drummond-Hay against boarding a liner to New York to cover the first transatlantic passenger flight that year by the airship Hindenburg. Had Lady Drummond been present when it attempted to dock at the Lakehurst airfield in New Jersey in five days time, she would have been killed as the airship caught fire and crashed. With her mission completed Kitty was very much looking forward to some downtime before her next briefing in a few days. You know, she really would appreciate it if one day she could just vacation in the real world once in a while, she thought, but apparently there was too much risk of being caught or inadvertently causing a disastrous timeline distortion. That said, as she had on this trip, she didn't always return as soon as her mission was over, occasionally she'd take a couple of days in the world to herself. Just for appearances sake was always how she justified it. One didn't want to suddenly disappear, that would cause undue suspicion. "Leave a Clean Camp and a Dead Fire" as her father had always taught her.

She turned to the projectionist's box and signalled for the gate to be opened. Once it was established, she stepped through the screen and into the gate room on the other side. Even after years of gate travel it still left her with a feeling of uneasiness in the pit of her stomach.

She was met on the other side by one of the gate supervisors, Roberta Davis, or "Bobbie" for short.

"Hey Bob! What's cookin' good lookin'?" Kitty quickly fired off. Like Kitty, Bobbie was American, but had been recruited slightly later during the 1964 Harlem riots. She was one of Kitty's best friends in the Æther and they had great fun "talkin' jive" with each other.

"Nice of you to make the scene, Ms clean" Bobbie retorted. "I'm afraid you've got a bit of a mess you need to clear up."

"Well lay it on me sister"

"Seriously Kitty girl. Seems there's been a bit of a problem turn up after that little side trip you took, back when you was nursing in the Great War?" Bobbie explained. "Why don't you make with the feet over to the 'War room' and get the skinny. You might want to change first though, that look's a mite fancy."

"Thanks Bob, you're a peach" Kitty replied, switching back to her usual mid-Atlantic vernacular.

"Scoot, you crazy old lady." Although technically a few years older than Kitty, Bobbie liked to joke about the fact that she was born 18 years after her in the real world.

*　　*　　*　　*

After changing back into her usual casual attire - her favoured loose trousers and blouse - Kitty made her way through the topsy turvy jumble of rooms and sound stages to the area they had dubbed "The War Room". This was a strange rectangular room which had large video screens running the length of three of its four walls. Filling the rest of the room was a vast, horseshoe shaped, desk with blue cushioned office chairs placed around the outside. One of the techs recruited much later in the 20th century had once told her this was a set from the science fiction film 2001: A Space Odyssey. At the end of the room one of the senior directors in charge of "real world operations", as it was known, was talking with a junior administrator named George. The director was a glamorous, older looking lady with short grey curly hair who, like Kitty, favoured the fashions of her day, and was dressed smartly in a shirt and tie, pinstripe suit trousers and t-bar shoes. She was studiously studying the screen of a tablet shaped device. As Kitty approached, George nodded to her and left the room promptly.

"Ah Ms Simpson, how was your trip to London?" asked the director without looking up from what she was doing. Her southern-tinged American accent, slight and unassuming, a faint whistle on her S's caused by the gap between her front teeth.

"Successful I hope director, we won't know properly until the boffins have analysed the time stream data."

"Marvellous. Now, have you been filled in on our little problem yet?" The director finally looked up from her tablet device and directly at Kitty.

"Davis mentioned something on my arrival, director, but that's all I know. She instructed me to come straight here and speak to you."

"Right. Yes. Well we've had an incursion event I'm afraid. It seems to be as a result of your unexpected trip to that out-of-service gate on your way back from mission T slash 10 dot 16."

"An incursion event director? I thought we had safeguards in place to prevent those?"

"Yes, but it seems that particular gate isn't in our system for some reason. Didn't even know it existed until you dropped through it."

Kitty looked down at her feet for a moment, slightly embarrassed, then back up at the director.

"Apologies, director, I believed I'd followed protocol to the letter and covered my tracks. May I ask the nature of the incursion?"

"Why don't you come and see for yourself, Agent Simpson" The director motioned with her hand towards the door, inviting Kitty to leave the room with her.

Together, Kitty and the director walked swiftly down a brightly lit white hallway, the walls and floor split into rectangular panels edged in black. They stopped at a doorway and the director motioned Kitty into the room beyond. Unlike the hallway this room looked more like a museum, or a stately home, with ornate walls decorated with sculpted edged panels, brass candle holders dotted between each, and alcoves painted mustard yellow with white plaster figurines or paintings in the centre. They made their way across the room to a set of double-doors. The director knocked quietly on the door and then, without waiting for a reply, opened it and stepped through. Kitty had never been in this room before, and was surprised to find that the whole of the floor was lit by under floor light panels, split into wide squares. The room was furnished with the same style Victorian chairs and sofas as the gate room waiting area, but upholstered in mustard yellow like the alcoves, and at the rear of the room opposite the door stood a huge king size bed. If the room wasn't strange enough she was astonished to find that the bed was currently occupied by Gertie, the little girl who had discovered her after she'd unexpectedly dropped through the gate following her somewhat explosive exit from Amiens in 1916. The girl looked up from the book she was reading and her mouth dropped open in surprise.

"Kitty?! How are *you* here?" Gertie asked her in shock, "And where is 'here' by the way?"

Kitty looked from Gertie to the director, who tilted her head and raised one eyebrow. "Covered your tracks eh, Agent Simpson?"

"I'm so sorry Director Earhart, I honestly don't know how this has happened. I promise I will find out and try and make it right."

"Hm. Yes. You best see that you do just that, Simpson." The director replied sternly but kindly and turning on her heel left the room in long, purposeful strides.

# XXI.

Gertie sat in astonishment. Standing in front of her was the woman she had first seen weeks before and had travelled to this strange place in search of. She watched as the white haired older woman walked away and out of the room and was pleased to see Kitty make her way over and sit on the edge of the bed.

"Well", said Kitty, "You are a clever little thing aren't you?"

Gertie was pleased to see that Kitty looked much better than the last time she had seen her, no sign of any cuts or bruises. She looked a lot nicer when she wasn't covered in blood and brick dust.

"So, I'm guessing you figured out that it was the film that was the key to both my arrival and my exit?" Kitty asked her kindly. "Then you ran the film, stepped through the gate and ended up here?"

This was all too amazing. She felt like Lucy Pevensie meeting Mr Tumnus for the first time in Narnia. She had so many questions. Where was she? How did she get here? Where even *was* here? She remembered feeling dizzy and fainting by that weird clock tower that looked like the one from Back to the Future, and then she had woken up in this room, in this bed. She wanted to throw her arms around this woman who she had only known for less than an hour of her life, ask her all the questions that were running around her head, but in the end she just nodded. When it came down to it, she still felt a bit scared and a bit shy. She had no idea how long she'd actually been here. The other people she'd seen so far - a woman with black hair, and a bald man with glasses - had just asked how she was feeling and what she wanted to eat. They had checked her pulse and shone a light into her eyes. Most frustratingly they had refused to answer her questions about where she was. They had just come in and gone again with only a minimum of talking. She'd been brave enough to ask for the bathroom and they had shown her a bookshelf with something to read on it, but aside from that she'd just stayed in this bed too frightened to leave the room.

"What happened when you came through the gate? Anyone waiting for you in the gate room?"

Gertie shook her head.

"Was there no one around at all?!" Kitty probed further.

Again Gertie just shook her head, letting a sad look spread across her face without realising it. Kitty shuffled up the bed and gently put Gertie's hand into hers.

"Did you get a bit lost?"

Gertie nodded again.

"You...you didn't end up outside did you?" Kitty's voice had a twinge of sympathy in it and Gertie couldn't help herself, she really wanted to cry. Her lower lip started to tremble and she felt a tear run down her cheek.

"Oh you poor dear. Was it all a bit overwhelming? I'm going to take a wild guess and imagine that you started to feel dizzy and sick?"

Gertie really had to put all her efforts into stopping herself from crying now, but she thought about her favourite cartoon characters and people in books who were brave and fearless, and managed to let out a quiet "Yes". She took a deep breath in and out, then told Kitty "I...I fainted, I think. Then I woke up here."

It was Kitty's turn to nod. "It's the light outside." she explained "It affects everyone the first time. Those of us who aren't here all the time still have to wear eye protection if we want to go outside."

Gertie plucked up the courage and finally managed to ask Kitty, "Sorry… where is 'here' exactly?"

"Well" said Kitty with a sigh, "That's a bit of a tricky one. Hmm. How about I go rustle us up some Tea and I'll try my damndest to explain it to you as best I can. Will that be okay? Will you be alright here on your own for a little while?"

"Yes, I'm sure I will be," said Gertie in what she imagined was her bravest voice.

"Good, be back in a flash, you'll see." When Gertie looked doubtful she added "I promise this time. I really will be back."

With this Kitty got up and walked out, leaving Gertie absolutely none the wiser than when she'd walked into the room in the first place.

\*  \*  \*  \*

Kitty returned after about five minutes with a tray containing a big silver teapot with wooden handles, two cups and saucers and a plate with what looked like chocolate biscuits on it. After querying whether Gertie wanted milk and sugar, she brought over a hot cup of tea and the plate of biscuits. Placing the tea on the bed stand and plate of biscuits on the bed next to Gertie, Kitty went back to fetch her own cup and then resumed her previous position on the bed.

"So" she began "I'll tell you the story of 'how' in a little while but first, let me tell you 'where' we are."

Kitty took a cautious sip of her tea, but it was too hot so she returning the cup to the saucer carefully perched on her lap. "Do help yourself to a biscuit, I'm pretty sure you're going to need one or two to get through this" With this she winked at Gertie.

"This place we are in right now is what we call the Æther. Now you may have heard that word before but it might have a different meaning to the one we use for this place we are in. There's the Ether that's used in medicine to knock people out for surgery, then there's the Ether that's to do with outer space. But the Ether we use actually has a funny looking A and E joined together at the beginning of it. That one means 'light'... and we mean it in terms of the specific light that's produced when you use a piece of movie film, called celluloid or cellulose acetate. Are you keeping up with me so far?"

"I think so", Gertie replied, although she really wasn't.

"Excellent. So this version of the word Æther is actually named after a primordial Greek god, brother of

Darkness and Chaos and son of Chronos, also known as 'Father Time'. Not really important but I like the symmetry of the thing. Light, and time, brother of darkness and chaos… anyway, more about that later."

Kitty took another sip of her tea and went on.

"Now this is the really tricky part, so pay attention. As far as we know it, this place, the Æther, is in something called a dimensional singularity. It's a world that exists completely apart from our own. As such it doesn't conform to any of the known laws that define our world, the important one here being time. Are you with me so far?"

Gertie reached for a biscuit. She definitely needed one now. This was all hurting her brain, and she felt it still didn't explain anything at all.

"Not really, but I'm sure I'll catch up" she joked over a mouthful of biscuit.

"Good girl," noted Kitty after another sip of her tea "So now we come to the 'how'. Back in the year 1882 a man called George Eastman created the first roll of film. Little did he know however, that when that film was exposed to light and then combined with certain chemicals that something magical would happen. I'm not just talking about movies here, although they can be very magical in my opinion. What I mean is this: From that moment on, everything captured on film would be recreated here in the Æther. A perfect copy. Nothing living however, not the actors or the animals or the plants and trees, but everything else. Now… what do you think of that?"

"I...I don't know what to say." stammered Gertie, it all seemed too incredible to believe. "So, everything that has ever been filmed is here somewhere?"

"That's what we think" replied Kitty "Although, as I said, we've not actually managed to explore everything and everywhere yet, that would take a very long time. But what we've seen so far makes us think that is what has happened."

Gertie sat in silence for a minute. Then turned and took a big gulp of her tea, which was now getting a bit cold.

"More tea?" Kitty asked.

"Erm… yes please."

Whilst Kitty went and put some more tea in Gertie's cup she tried to put it all together in her head. Could this really be some kind of magical dimension made up of stuff from films? She must be dreaming... this couldn't be real, could it?

Kitty returned with her tea. "So, what do you think? It's all a bit fanciful isn't it? I didn't believe it myself at first, but then again, I had a lot of time to put it all together. And I didn't arrive here by accident like you did. Anyway, take your time and help yourself to another biscuit."

Gertie reached out distractedly and took another biscuit off the plate without even thinking about it, her head reeling with information.

Finally she said, quite matter-of-factly "That would explain all the crazy places I saw when I first got here… and this room?! So that WAS the clock tower from Back to the Future? And the Goonies pirate ship? And the Ghostbusters fire station?"

"Probably, but I have no idea what those things are. You see, if those are movies, then they were probably made a long time after I was born. I'm a lot older than I look, don't you know." Kitty paused and smiled "Now this is really going to mess with your noodle… What year were you born?"

"1974" replied Gertie. "In August"

"So, in the year you were born I would be 52 years old. Do I look 52 to you?"

Before Gertie could say anything Kitty replied "Don't worry, you don't need to answer that, I'm actually 27. I was born in the year 1922 and I first came here in the year 1944. This room we are in was apparently filmed in 1968, but it has always been here…although, to be honest, I've never been in here until today."

Gertie just stared, a look of utter confusion on her face. This made Kitty laugh out loud.

"Sorry. I don't mean to laugh. It's just you look absolutely at sea! Don't worry about all that stuff, it's a lot to take in all at once. You'll get your head 'round it eventually." Kitty said kindly.

It was true, Gertie did feel utterly lost trying to process all of this. She picked up her cup and took a drink, then stared into the rippling liquid. Finally she looked back at Kitty, a resolute question in her mind.

"What about the film?" She asked.

"What film dear?" replied Kitty.

"The film we used to get here. The film with the cabbages. The one that made everything go a bit purple. We played it the day you came to the picture house, and you played it to leave again. I finally worked that out, then I got dad to put it on, and my fingers went through the screen, then I stepped through and ended up here. Is it like the wardrobe in Narnia?" blurted Gertie. It was the most she'd said to Kitty since being here.

"Once more dear, I'm not sure what that is, but I would hazard a guess it has something to do with travelling between two places?"

Gertie nodded, slightly embarrassed at her sudden outpouring.

"In which case, yes. It's a bit like that. The films are very special indeed. They are the reason we found this place, and they are how we can travel back and forth between here and our own world. Originally they were used to bring everything needed to survive here, until it was discovered they could be used for something far more important. They can be used for time travel."

Gertie's expression changed then, as the realisation dawned on her of why Kitty had arrived wearing an old-fashioned nurse's uniform. She couldn't believe it. Kitty was telling her that she was a time traveller.

"Do… Do YOU travel through time?" she asked. Kitty nodded. "Is that what you were doing when I first found you?" again Kitty nodded.

Without realising she was doing it Gertie exclaimed "Bloody hell!"

"Language young lady", Kitty scolded. It was Gertie's turn to apologise.

"Sorry. Didn't mean to say that. This is all a bit too much." She thought for a moment, then asked "Why do you do it? Travel in time I mean...just to see what it's like in the future or something?"

"No" said Kitty rather seriously "We have a much bigger purpose than just sightseeing."

Just at that point a 'Bing bong' sound like a doorbell came into the room, presumably from a hidden speaker or something, and made Gertie jump.

"Ah" said Kitty "That noise means it's almost time for lights out. Let's turn on your bedside lamb here before that happens shall we?"

She got up and clicked the switch on the lamp that was sitting on top of the bed stand and sat back down on the bed.

"One of the things you have to get used to here is that there is no day or night. Only areas that exist in either perpetual day or in night-time, depending on when those places were originally captured on film, you see? So we've had to generate our own daytime cycle. Some folks live in the dark areas and travel to and from each day, but in many of the administrative areas like this one, we have to let people know when it's the end of the day. Mostly because they would never go to sleep otherwise!"

Kitty stood up.

"Now then young lady. I know you've got a lot running around in that head of yours right now, but you try and get some sleep and I'll come back in the morning and take you to breakfast. That sound okay? Things will seem much clearer on a good night's sleep and a full stomach I always say!"

With this she turned on her heel and walked to the door. She found the switch for the room's floor lights and turning with a sharp nod to Gertie switched them off, plunging the room into sudden gloom. Then she opened the door and was gone.

# XXII.

"Everyone you see here, including me, works for a group called The Guiding Light." Kitty was explaining to Gertie the next morning in between bites of her breakfast pastry. "The 'Light' have actually been around for centuries, longer than this place has existed, but our operations took a dramatic leap forward when we discovered what the films would enable us to do."

Kitty and Gertie were sitting in the canteen hall, a vast space filled with benches, tables, chairs and booths of all styles and eras. This room had obviously been put together by moving things from lots of other rooms to create a usable and functioning space. Gertie guessed it must have been like a history of eating food in films; there were military style serving benches, big neon diner counters, and tropical bamboo bars, all sitting next to each other along one side of the hall where she and Kitty had queued up to get their breakfast.

"But what exactly does everyone do?" asked Gertie.

"Oh we've got all manner of people here, who do all kinds of crazy stuff. A lot of it is to do with science, some of it using something called computers, all very much beyond me. We have some of the 20th century's smartest people here, doing things completely unheard of back in the 'World'. Then you've got the people who look after everyone else here in the Æther, the technicians and the medical staff.

I myself am part of a group called Real World Ops, we are the ones who travel to and from the World, running missions and gathering intel and supplies. You met our head yesterday, Director Earhart. Real smart cookie, and one of my personal heroes as it happens, a true aviatrix."

"Wait," interrupted Gertie "You don't mean Amelia Earhart do you? The famous pilot? Was that the grey haired lady?"

"Indeed I do! Yes that was her" replied Kitty

"Wow! But she disappeared mysteriously years ago didn't she? I remember reading about it in a book once"

Kitty put on a show of looking secretive whilst she sipped her morning coffee, learning in and talking in a quieter voice.

"Well, yes and no. She disappeared from the World because she ended up coming here. She was actually one of our top Agents back there until her situation was compromised and she had to move here permanently for her own safety." She sat up again and grinned. "We have lots of people in the World who are secretly 'Agents' of the Light, many have never been here at all, but they are all fully up to speed with what we do here... our gate operators for example."

Gertie chomped on another mouthful of chocolate cereal with a quizzical look on her face. When she swallowed it she said "Okay, so I've been thinking about the film...the one that got me here. Is it all films that create gates? Or only certain ones? Or is it something to do with the projector?"

"Hmmm, tricky." said Kitty, "I know. Let's finish up here and then go on a little tour back to the gate room prep area, or the Glass House as it's called. When we're there I'll tell you the story of how the gates were created and show you how it all works."

# XXII.

Now then. Are you comfortable there dear? Marvellous. Then I shall begin.

This story starts on a Wednesday. The 22nd of April to be exact, in the year 1896. Miss Alice Ida Antoinette Guy, a 23 year old secretary for the L. Gaumont et Cie camera company in Paris, was on her way to the company's photographic laboratory on the Rue du Plateau. Alice was an elegant and striking figure, as sharp as a pin and wickedly funny, her jet black hair scraped into a bun, all cinched of waist with cascades of crinoline under her neatly pressed dress. I like the sound of her myself, and I'm certain you would too. Now she'd become rather inspired after seeing the Lumière brothers show their film at a screening for the Society for the Development of the National Industry and had managed to persuade her manager, Monsieur Léon Gaumont, to let her use one of the company's brand new film cameras to shoot her own picture in her spare time.

She'd given the resulting reel of film to one of the laboratories chemists to be developed earlier that day, and was excited to see the results of her work. She'd called the film La Fée aux Choux or the fairy of the cabbages. It was only a minute long and was a simple retelling of a popular folk story that depicted a newlywed couple visiting a fairy to receive their new baby, born from a field of cabbages.

Although the equipment they were using was still very new, the chemists and photographic technicians at the laboratory, like Alice, had also been experimenting with the cameras for a few weeks. They had been testing the cameras by filming these very rooms we are sitting in as a matter of fact. They believed that they had got the development process down pat, so were happy enough to put Alice's handy work through the same process. On this occasion however there had been a bit of a mix up with the chemicals and an extra compound had been introduced which only the assistant chemist had noticed. Believing it to be fine, the chemist in question, Henri Durand, set up the camera projector ready to view the film as soon as Alice had arrived.

The moment they ran the film it was obvious something wasn't right. The film produced a strange purple glow which neither Alice nor Durand could account for. Durand approached the projection screen and was shocked to discover the feeling of an electrical charge running through his body. When the film ended Alice and Durand could only look at each other in disbelief. An odd compulsion made Durand decide to run the film again and he once more approached the screen, again feeling the electric charge coming off it. He went closer with the intention of touching the purple light, but discovered that when he did his fingers passed straight through the fabric of the screen and seemed to disappear into thin air.

The next day, somewhat frightened of his experience with the film, Durand decided to pay a visit to the President of the company, a certain Gustave Eiffel. You've heard of the Eiffel tower I presume? Good.

Now little did Durand know, but Eiffel was a long serving member of The Guiding Light. He doted on Alice as if she was his own daughter, so he advised the chemist to hide the roll of film after making a single copy for Alice to show her manager, Gaumond, and to keep with the film details of the chemical mix that he'd used to produce it. Eiffel then arranged to have several key members of the Light join himself, Alice and Durand at his secret apartment in the Eiffel tower itself. What followed, I think it is fair to say, has changed the course of history.

Being of the type to have extreme curiosity in scientific experimentation, Eiffel decided that more needed to be known about the nature of this film and organised a special screening in a theatre on the tower's first floor in two days' time. That Sunday a screen was set up and one of the L. Gaumont et Cie's projectors was borrowed. Eiffel, Alice and Durand were joined at the tower by several members of the French Academy of Science, each a secret Light, as well as a young adventurer by the name of Arnaud Marron, who had volunteered to help should Eiffel's suspicions prove correct. He was tall and very handsome apparently. After many viewings of the film where various scientific principles were tested, it was deemed Arnaud Marron's turn to step up to the screen just as Durand had done. Like Durand before him, Marron felt the electric charge as he approached, but was pre-warned of the phenomenon and so pressed onward to touch his fingers to the fabric. As expected his fingers passed through and vanished. He breathed in deeply and plunged his whole arm through the screen, left it there for a few seconds and then withdrew it again. As the film shut off he was left flexing his grip, making sure that his hand and arm still worked as before.

Turning sharply on his heel, Marron went over to an area of the theatre containing his own equipment, and started to climb into a deep sea divers suit; an oversized canvas all-in-one with a heavy brass bib and collar which sat around the neck and shoulders. He donned the large rubber gloves, picked up the large brass helmet with its grilled-over glass viewing holes, and nodded to the others. One of the scientists picked up a tube lying on the ground next to a large box with twin cart wheels attached either side, and walked it over to Marron who had made his way back to the area beside the screen. Together they attached the tube to the helmet, and Marron lifted it over his head, placing it on the brass ring around his neck and twisting until it was in the correct position. Then the scientist ran back to the box and started to turn the handle on one of the cart wheels. The box was an air pump you see, it produced compressed air which fed into the brass helmet allowing Marron to breathe.

Marron then signalled to Durand to start the film. Now I'm sure you know what happened next, as you've done it yourself. Marron made his way to the screen and stepped through. When the film had run its length and shut off however, the rubber tube was immediately severed, the room was plunged into darkness and everyone was left in a state of shock. Marron had gone and they had no clue where or how to get him back.

They ran the film again, and again, but Marron failed to reappear. After scratching their collected heads for some time, it was decided that Durand should go back to the lab, make multiple copies of the film and repeat the process of developing it, with the exact formula he had used the first time. By joining these copies together they hoped to have enough film to keep the gateway open for long enough that someone could enter, assess what was on the other side and then return before getting lost just as Marron had done.

After working the next day on the new copy of the film, Durand joined Eiffel and Alice in the Eiffel tower theatre that evening and once again opened the gateway. Durand clearly felt that this was all somehow his fault for mixing up the chemicals in the first place and so volunteered to go through and try to find Marron. He duly donned a spare diver's suit and helmet, and with Alice and Eiffel manning the pumps, noted the time on the pocket watch he had attached to one of the loops on the brass collar, then started the projector and walked to the screen. He stepped through, with great trepidation, into what lay beyond.

After less than two minutes, Durand reappeared back through the gateway. The front panel of his helmet was open and he was dragging his air hose in his wake with one hand and carrying Marron's helmet with its own severed hose with the other. After Durand had removed the helmet and sat down to rest he chronicled his strange journey to Alice and Eiffel.

When Durand exited through the other side of the gate he had found himself in a dimly lit room which he was surprised to find was identical to the main factory building at L. Gaumond et Cie. Had he just travelled across the city from the tower to the factory? Is that what the gateway did? He thought. Something wasn't quite right in the room however. At first he believed the strange purple light discernible on the wall behind him had somehow affected his vision as everything here was entirely devoid of colour. Lying on the floor of the room was Marron's discarded helmet, but there was no sign of Marron himself. Durand called out but there was no answer.

He concluded that as Marron's body was clearly not lying there next to his discarded helmet that he must have survived his air supply being cut off. Reaching up he undid the bolt on the front flap of his own helmet, cautiously opening it to taste the air in the room. It seemed fine and he could breathe normally.

It was then that he happened to glance down at the pocket watch he was carrying and realised that the hands seemed to have stopped moving. After staring at it for a minute he noticed that in fact the small dial showing the number of seconds passing was moving but almost imperceptibly slowly. So time was clearly moving at a different speed this side of the gate to the side he'd come from.

Realising he had a lot more time than he originally planned to explore this space, he came to the conclusion that Marron had tried to do the same. By taking the time to watch the second hand move on his pocket watch and counting in his head the number of actual seconds passing he worked out that 10 seconds of time on Alice and Eiffel's side of the gate was equal to about 1 minute of time on his side of the gate. This meant he had about 18 minutes before he needed to return to the gate and step back through.

Twisting his helmet to remove it, he placed it on the floor and struck out to see if he could find out what had happened to Marron. Still believing himself to be back at the Gaumond laboratory he was very surprised to find the next room he encountered wasn't the one he was expecting... it was an identical copy of the room he'd just come from, but with lots of different objects in it. There were crates, and pieces of scenery and various items of furniture which he had never seen before but, like the previous room he was in, nothing had any colour at all. He moved through to the third room, which was even more of a surprise. It was a huge glass pavilion, this very room in fact. But Durand didn't recognise it as one of the buildings at Gaumond, because for him it didn't yet exist. It wasn't going to start being built until at least a year later in his time. The bright light in the room hurt Durand's eyes and he started to feel dizzy, his stomach turning. He felt like he was going to faint, so turned around and stumbled back into the previous room. He realised he could go no further in his search for Marron, so decided to come up with another plan.

Looking around the room he found some loose pieces of canvas, some paint and a brush. Taking these into the gate room, he made some quick calculations, scrawled a hasty note to Marron on the canvas and set it down, along with his pocket watch on the floor in front of the gate.

The note read: "Be here when the watch reads 16:00 hours. I'll come for you then, Durand." With this in place, he picked up his helmet and placed it back over his head securing it with a twist. Then he picked up Marron's discarded helmet as evidence and stepped back through the gate.

# XXIII.

*Z49,214*

"Okay." Said Gertie "I have SO many questions. Who is Alice Guy? She sounds amazing, I want to know more about her. And what's going on with her and Mr Eiffel? More importantly, did Durand actually manage to rescue Marron?!"

"Calm yourself down dear, I'll get to all of that. Well… most of that" reply Kitty with a smile. She was sitting in the anteroom between the Glass House and the gate room elegantly folded into an armchair, with her knees together and her feet off to one side. Across from her Gertie was perched on the chaise longue, knees drawn up underneath her oversized woolly jumper.

"Now, because of the time difference here in the Æther, Durand only had to wait 24 minutes on his side in the theatre before opening the gate again. You look confused dear, I know... it's hard to wrap your head around that bit sometimes isn't it?"

"I think I understand, sort of… I've been here for three days, yes? So how much time has passed in the real world?" asked Gertie quizzically

"Less than a day, roughly speaking… but don't think about that right now, it's not relevant to the story. Also I'm a time traveller remember, it all gets even more confusing when you add that little doozy into the mix" replied Kitty, using her sing-song voice to soothe Gertie's addled brain.

111

"Shall I continue?" she asked. Gertie nodded in reply.

"Marvellous. So. After the 24 minutes was up, Durand started the film once more and, this time without the need of the protective suit or its air supply, stepped through the gate. Within seconds he returned with Marron, his arm around the man's waist, helping to support his weight. Clearly Marron was suffering from a lack of water, and was feeling quite weak."

"What had happened to him? He'd gone at least 4 days without a drink or food right?" Gertie said excitedly

"Oooo, you clever girl. You catch on fast. Yes, it had been roughly 108 hours for Marron since he had first stepped through the gate, that's four and half days, but just over a day and a half for Durand, Eiffel and Alice. It was a mistake he wouldn't repeat. Monsieur Eiffel took charge and instructed Durand to secure the film from the projector and pack up the equipment, whilst he and Alice helped Marron out to the lift and up into Eiffel's apartment. He knew that it was important for Marron to rest up and to be given small sips of water over time, not to drink too quickly. Believe it or not you can actually end up being much more ill if you do that."

"That's what the Nursey people did for me when I woke up here. I really wanted some lemon squash, but they kept saying I had to have water." Gertie chipped in.

"Well, there you go. It worked for you and it had only been a few hours. When Marron was feeling up to it he told the others what he'd seen. You had a similar journey I would have imagined. But because at that time this room was still flooded with daylight, Marron had felt the effects of the strange light - or Quintessence as we call it - and instead of turning straight around as Durand had done, tried to push on into the room beyond. By the time he'd got there the effects of the Quintessence had nearly overcome him and he wandered in a daze through the rooms beyond, eventually getting lost and disorientated. Eventually he found his way back to this room and, by wrapping his shirt around his eyes, he made his way back into the gate room to discover Durand's note."

"That was a very clever thing for Durand to do. But what if Marron hadn't made his way back at all? What would they have done then?" asked Gertie.

"Well, I would have imagined that they still would have come here to explore, but it would have taken them a lot longer to understand where we are and what this place could bring to the world." explained Kitty. "But as you say, Durand was a very clever man, as were Eiffel and Alice Guy. Together they were the first people to come here, and establish the first stronghold. But it was Durand's cleverness that led to us having a system of gates and, ultimately, a way to use those gates to move in time. Now, you sit quietly for a few minutes and listen to the rest of the story."

# XXIV.

Let's skip forward two years down the line. Now, all thanks to Alice Guy's success in making motion pictures, the company she worked for, L. Gaumond et Cie if you remember, had switched from making photographic equipment to making movie cameras. Alice was made head of production at the company and continued to make more and more films to demonstrate the use of Gaumont's cameras to its clients. All of this fitted nicely into her newfound secret work with the Light and their continued exploration of the Æther.

During this time Durand had attempted to replicate his original mistake with other rolls of film but it seems that only the original La Fée aux Choux reel would produce a result. He could however copy that reel multiple times and create a number of gate reels to be used in multiple locations if needed. This allowed the Light to send Marron and other agents into the Æther with supplies and provisions enough to spend extended periods of time there. They slowly started to explore and change the spaces they found. By wearing eye protection whilst traversing the Glass House they discovered that they could counteract the effects of the Quintessence and soon erected blinds and screens to block out or defuse the light where needed.

What the discovery of the Æther meant to the Light was that they had a new secret location, completely separate from the world around them, where they could set up a base of operations in their centuries old fight against the machinations of another even more ancient order called the Obscurus.

The origins of the Obscurus can be traced to the early civilisations of Ancient Egypt where a small group of powerful men started to use their influence to control and shape the world around them. Over time this group became bigger and more influential and has been manipulating and altering the world around them ever since. Every secret society you have ever heard of is just one small piece in the Obscurus puzzle, the Illuminati, the CABAL, the Inquisition, the Knights Templar, the KKK, you name it. Every unspeakable act you can think of throughout history has been at the hands of the Obscurus, and they've really been stepping up their pace in the last hundred years. Every assassination, from Lincoln to Archduke Ferdinand to Kennedy and Martin Luther King has been at their request.

It all sounds a little bit like the plot of a cheap movie to be honest with you, but it is real. I've had many a run-in with Obscurus agents in my time with the Light, limited as it has been, they truly are stinkers to the man.

Anyway, let's get back to the story.

In October of 1898 the Gaumont company had arranged to open a new office in London. Durand saw this as an opportunity to experiment further with the Æther gate and sent Marron with a copy of the film over to the London office. A new cinema had recently been set up at the Royal Alhambra Theatre in Leicester Square and Durand wanted

Marron to connect with a local agent of the Light so that they could operate the gate and test travel to and from different places.

Eiffel offered to set up a permanent gate room at his mansion on the Rue Rabelais, as he and Durand had cooked up some grand scheme to use the spread in popularity of cinema to create a network of gates throughout the world. *IF* this test worked out successfully. Durand had tagged the film he'd sent with Marron and wanted to see if he could detect which gate was which when each was opened consecutively. He also wanted to test if someone could enter the Æther from the new permanent Paris gate and exit again through the London one, and vice versa. This would both revolutionise the activities of the Light, as it would create a form of instant travel for Light agents, and make the spread of information between networks much quicker. In the end it would have an even more revolutionary effect than Durand could ever foresee.

Working as they often did on Sundays, Durand opened the Paris gate and stepped through to the Æther. On the other side he quickly looked for the mark he'd added to each frame of the film when he'd copied it in order to track which film was which when viewing, but was shocked to find it wasn't as easy as he'd hoped. Not because it wasn't easy to spot, he saw it almost immediately, but because along with the mark he'd placed he saw hundreds of other marks all with varying degrees of brightness and tone. There were at least forty different marks he could spot, and of these more than a hundred variations of each. What was strange is that the marks resembled those he had planned to make on subsequent films, but hadn't yet done so. These marks were made up of a series of lines and dots, each line denoting 5 and each dot 1, arranged in a square, so four corner dots with a line under two of the dots made the number 9.

The mark for the Paris gate, a single black dot at the top left, was the strongest and sat the most prominent, but the others were still very visible. In fact, when the gate shut off, he could still make out the residual glow of the gate light, and all of the marks he had previously seen. This gave him an idea, but he would need to wait until completing his current experiment to try it.

Perfectly on schedule the new gate from London opened and, just as with the Paris gate, he saw the two black dot marks for it at the forefront of the gate's discernable light. Just then Marron stepped through once more into the Æther. After making his greetings to Durand he invited him to travel back through the gate to London. Shortly afterwards both men arrived at the Alhambra Theatre as predicted. The experiment was a resounding success, and Marron and Durand celebrated in style that night with a hearty meal at Rouget's.

The next day, before it opened for morning performances, Durand went back to the Alhambra and travelled back through the gate back to the Æther. Once there he set about finding some equipment that Monsieur Eiffel had arranged to be shipped from the Academy of Science. Among this equipment was a brass mantle clock. He set this clock to match that of his pocket watch, currently set to Paris time, and placed it on a small table to one side of the main gate room. Next to the clock he used a small paint brush to write the letter "Z" on the wall, he would do the same in the Paris gate room on his return so that both sides of the gate were synchronised. We refer to this now as "Day Zero" and its how Durand would eventually work out the time, date and location of each of the gates. Each day in the world that passed in the Æther he or one of his assistants would mark a tally on the wall next to the Z on both sides. We've come up with a far better way of marking this time now, it's all automated on some form of electric counter, but this was how they did it in Durand's day.

# XXV.

Gertie yawned dramatically, she couldn't help herself.

"I'm sorry darling" said Kitty, "It's all a bit boring and technical isn't it. You probably want some more excitement and derring-do don't you?"

"I don't mind really… It IS interesting, it's just I think I'm still recovering a bit and getting used to being here, and I am quite worried about dad and Walt wondering where I've got to." Gertie explained.

"Yes, I didn't think about that. Well, funny you mention that, because it is relevant to the story. We HAVE been sat here for quite a while. How about we pop back to the canteen, get them to whip us up some sandwiches or something and we can go for a walk, explore the outside streets a little, whilst I continue the story?" Kitty saw the concerned look on Gertie's face, "Don't worry, we'll make sure we are wearing suitable eye protection from the effects of the Quintessence. And don't worry about being away from home… Remember we can travel in time, it doesn't matter how long we spend together here, we can just return you to your gate at the exact time you left. It will be like you were never gone."

\*     \*     \*     \*

Gertie and Kitty were sitting on the deck of The Inferno; the galleon of pirate Captain 'One-Eyed' Willy from Gertie's favourite film The Goonies. They were each wearing a pair of curious looking sunglasses that reminded Gertie of the goggles mad scientists always wore in science fiction horror films. Unlike Gertie's normal sunglasses at home, these were oval in shape and had special extra pieces of leather on the top, bottom and sides which stopped the light getting in anywhere but the lenses. The lenses themselves were tinted purple and when Gertie put them on, the outside world in the Æther looked like a perfectly sunny day and her head didn't hurt at all. It was warm outside and Gertie had taken off her jumper, revealing the burgundy Le Shark polo shirt her mum had brought for her dad the Christmas before her accident. It was her favourite top in the world even though it was far too big for her. The strangest thing about being outside here was that there was no breeze, no wind at all in fact. The temperature was constant and always warm but not too hot, "shirtsleeve weather" as her dad always referred to it. Kitty had managed to produce a large blue gingham picnic blanket from somewhere and they had spread it out on the deck of the ship which sat dead calmly in a high-cliffed alcove in the bay overlooking the town square she had collapsed in when she'd first arrived. Whilst they ate cheese and cucumber sandwiches and slices of a really tasty bacon and onion quiche out of a picnic basket, Gertie asked Kitty questions about the Æther.

"So, everything here is here because it was once in a film?"

"That's correct. No one is still quite sure why, but every object, or building here was captured at some point on cellulose film in the real world. There doesn't seem to be an order or sequence to when or where things were filmed rather that each thing had just naturally slotted into place where it fitted. The only thing that is a focal point here is the gate room, because this was the exact room Henri Durand projected Alice Guy's original film of La Fée aux Choux and opened the first doorway into this place." explained Kitty, pausing between delicate bites of a sandwich.

"But what about all the actors? Why aren't they here? And what about animals or plants? I've not seen any of those at all… even the grass down there isn't real grass."

"Well that's the curious thing. It seems to have only been non-organic, non-living elements that have come through. The boffins here refer to it as "inorganic material". Rock, metal and other minerals, water, air, even the clouds in the sky, all of these are here and make up everything that is here. But people, plants, animals… anything that grows or lives, those things only exist here because we have brought them here. We've tried growing things here, but the Quintessence makes it hard, nothing seems to like it."

Gertie grabbed another slice of quiche and thought all this through whilst taking big bites and munching noisily. She hadn't yet mastered the art of taking small bites, like Kitty did, in order to continue being part of an ongoing conversation.

"So… what happened to Alice and Mr Eiffel?" She asked, changing the subject.

"Not a great end to that story I'm afraid to say. Alice fell helplessly in love with an English chap called Herbert Blaché who worked for the London office of Gaumont. His mother was French by the way, which explains the funny last name. Anyway he was much younger than her and a bit of an imbecile, always making silly mistakes. I think Alice thought she could fix him or some such thing. After a whirlwind love affair travelling around Europe together they got married, and when Herbert was sent to America to start a New York office for Gaumont, Alice resigned from her job and went with him. Secretly she had arranged with Eiffel and Durand to set up the first American gate you see. Trouble is, after a few years there, Herbert fell in with a group of bad eggs. Unfortunately they turned out to be Obscurus, and Herbert was corrupted by them, secretly subjugating and undermining all of Alice's activities at every turn."

"Oh no!" said Gertie, "But she seemed very clever, surely she didn't fall for that?"

"Blinded by love I'm afraid. Sad really, and she had no one out there to rescue her. Monsieur Eiffel found out what was going on and tried to get to America, but he was an old man by that point and never liked travelling via the gate system. Once the war broke out in 1914 it became impossible to travel by conventional means." Kitty picked up another sandwich and took a dainty bite.

"She should have married Mr Durand or Mr Marron, they sound like much nicer people." Suggested Gertie sagely.

"Love moves in mysterious ways, or so I'm told. No idea to be honest, never had much truck with it myself." said

Kitty and winked at Gertie. "Eventually, after the war ended, Monsieur Eiffel did manage to get some Light agents to come to Alice's aid and return her to France. He died a year later I'm afraid. Alice never got over her ordeal and never had anything more to do with the Light or making movies."

Gertie thought for a while over another big bite of quiche. "Isn't that something that you could fix using the gates? You know, go back in time and stop it from happening?"

"Not how it works my dear. We have to be very careful about what we change and how we change it. The way it was explained to me is that time is a bit like a flowing river, you can move around some of the smaller rocks in its path and it will just find another way to keep flowing in the same direction. However, if you try to shift its flow in a different direction entirely, you cause more problems than you solve. We can only make small changes, not big ones. Ripples in the water, not waves."

"Right. Like when Marty McFly gets hit by a car outside his mum's house instead of it being his dad, he ends up having to fix things by getting them together another way or he'll disappear from existence." Gertie said, nodding as if she knew the secrets of the universe.

"And once again, I have no idea what you are talking about my darling. Who's this Marty McFly?"

Gertie sat forward excitedly "He's a character in a film. Back to the Future... it's about time travel! The town square over there is from the film, I recognised it when I first got here."

123

"Ah yes, the town square. It's actually a very important part of film history apparently. One of our technicians who is a bit of a film buff says it's known as Courthouse Square and was a permanent back lot set for Universal Pictures. Used in lots of motion pictures apparently." Kitty explained.

Gertie watched as she shifted her pose by sweeping her long legs out and round to the other side of her body. She still couldn't get over how elegant Kitty always seemed to be, she even looked effortlessly stylish in her silly sunglasses.

"Okay, so... you were explaining earlier about how the gates let you move about in time? Something about Mr Durand and day zero?" asked Gertie excitedly.

"Well for that, I suggest we take ourselves on a little trip to the past. How are you feeling now you've had a little fresh air and some lunch?"

"Ooh much better, yes. Are we really going to travel through time? Using the gate? Are we?" Gertie leapt up, giddy with anticipation.

"Calm down dear. No. You are definitely not ready for that. Only trained agents are allowed to use the gates." Kitty gracefully stood up in one fluid motion and placed a reassuring hand on Gertie's shoulder. "No, what I meant was travel in a more metaphorical sense. We can take a little wander and visit Monsieur Eiffel's house and the original Paris gate room. It's all here in the Æther, only a few streets away actually, all thanks to Henri Durand himself filming it using the Gaumond cameras." Kitty said calmingly.

"Oh." said Gertie somewhat disappointedly. "Silly of me really."

"No, that's okay. I know it's probably a disappointment to you. It IS all very exciting." Kitty sank down on one knee so she was level with Gertie's face and put both her hands on her shoulders. "Maybe you COULD travel through the gates someday, but there is lots and lots of training to do first. You can't just go into the past without a lot of preparation beforehand. You need to know how to blend in for one. One tiny mistake and you could really put a spanner in the works."

Kitty stood up again and placed her hand on the back of Gertie's head, gently tilting it upward.

"Come on, let's go for a little walk and see a mansion house eh? Apparently it no longer exists back in the World so this is a once in a lifetime opportunity kiddo." She joked, beaming at Gertie.

Together they packed up what was left of the picnic, folded up the blanket and placed it on top of the picnic basket. Gertie picked up her jumper and tied it around her waist then grabbed the handle of the basket and started swinging it nonchalantly as they walked down the gangplank of the Inferno.

"Let's head across the square and over to what we call the 'French quarter' off to the left there." Instructed Kitty, looping her arm through Gertie's and hugging it to her side.

After crossing the town square they wandered down street after street lined with tall buildings of all shapes and sizes, shop fronts, glass fronted offices, brownstone townhouses, Kitty explaining that these were a mixture of buildings from New York, San Francisco and other American cities. Eventually they moved into a cobblestone lined street and the buildings changed to an older style, more like ones she'd seen on holiday in France. At the end of the cobblestone street was a huge twin set of steps, dotted with street lamps which seemed to go upwards forever. At the top of the steps Gertie could just make out a white building with a domed roof. Kitty explained that this was the Montmartre neighbourhood and that next to the steps was a cable car for anyone who didn't fancy the climb. To Gertie's relief they didn't go up the steps but turned left into a side road at the end of which, Kitty pointed out, was their destination, the mansion of Gustave Eiffel which once sat on the corner at 1 Rue Rabelais in Paris.

The building was a grand stone building of three stories, the second story of which had six full height windows along each side of the corner building topped with ornate carvings and decorated with wrought iron Juliet balconies. On top of these windows sat a stone parapet with a setback third storey whose windows on one side matched those of the storey below topped with arched roofs. On the other side, along which Kitty and Gertie now walked, the second and fifth of these windows were replaced with large round porthole windows. The whole of the third storey was decorated in fish scale-like iridescent tiles which seemed to change colour in the bright sunlight of the Æther depending on the angle you looked at them from. To the rear of the mansion sat two double-height archways with black iron gates, which led into a courtyard. This actually turned out to be the front of the building as the whole thing flowed round into a horseshoe shape in front of them as they entered. Kitty and Gertie strode into the courtyard and towards the grand entrance way of the mansion, a tall curved metal porch way filled with glass like an ornate conservatory that reminded Gertie a little of the doorway to the Grand Picture House back home.

Kitty pushed open one of the sets of double doors and held them open for Gertie to walk through. Stepping through she was presented with another set of glass doors, each framed with decorative scrollwork around the edges. Beyond this was darkness until Gertie realised that the sunglasses she was wearing were obscuring her vision. The room that was revealed when she took off her glasses was even more impressive than the foyer of the Picture House. A three storey high gallery, panelled with great carvings and tapestries, each studded at regular intervals with ivory busts of Romanesque figures, dominated by a marble staircase rising towards an oak doorway framed with ornately carved columns. Gertie stood with her jaw hanging open in awe.

"I know. She's a real doozy isn't she? We're heading this way though" Kitty said, gently guiding Gertie towards an impressive looking stone archway to the right of the entranceway.

They headed through the arch and straight towards a vast floor-length mirror on the far wall which, when Kitty pushed against it, turned out to be a concealed set of doors leading into a plainly decorated room. She really did absolutely love secret doors. At one end of this room sat a large wooden desk and chair whilst the other end of the room was completely empty, a large flat white wall its main feature, the only other piece of furniture a bureau against one wall with a mantle clock on the top. On the desk sat a collection of large wooden boxes, which seemed to Gertie to be all joined together somehow. It reminded her a little of the projectors in the Picture House, in fact she could now see a lens poking out of one of the boxes. Next to this was a large leather-bound book which Kitty walked over to and opened.

"This is what I brought you here to see my dear." explained Kitty, "This is Durand's log book of every gate event up until the boffins got involved and computerised it."

Gertie stood next to Kitty and looked down at the book. At the top of the page was a symbol made up of dots and lines in a square shape. Next to this was the gate's original designation, this one read "Berlin", and underneath a list of location names, dates, times and operators - "Titania, 20.08.30, 11:00, Hans Müller". Every now and again the location name would change to something different.

"You see how the films occasionally moved around? This happened a lot in the early days before permanent movie theatres were set up in the late '20s and onwards." Kitty pointed out. "Every Light gate operator was responsible for keeping a record of every scheduled gate event and phoning it into a central unit responsible for the logs. The log runs into the hundreds of thousands and it helps us pick the perfect time, date and location of each gate we need for a mission"

"Okay, but how could you possibly know every time a gate has been used? What about the ones in the future?" Gertie asked, slightly confused.

"Remember, time travel darling. We know that, aside from a few collectors and enthusiasts still doing so, that celluloid film stopped being used in the early 21st century. We also have another method of tracking…remember Durand and his initial experiments? When he saw all of the different marks in the gate room?" Explained Kitty.

She gestured to Gertie to follow her over to the other end of the room. On the wall between the bureau and the large white wall Gertie could see ink marks. The very first one was a 'Z' then underneath a line, next to that two lines, then three, then four, then four with a diagonal line through it. Gertie realised these were tally marks, she had seen them scratched into walls by prisoners in movies.

"Okay, I think I understand about the gate log, and I'm sure you're going to explain about Mr Durand and his experiments, right?"

Kitty nodded.

"What I don't really get is what this has to do with it. If this is a count of everyday that passed in the real world and the one in the real gate room on this side corresponds to it, then what has that got to do with the gates and using them to time travel?" asked Gertie, her face scrunched up with confusion.

"It doesn't… well not exactly." explained Kitty, although this just made Gertie's face scrunch up even more. "It's just a way for me to demonstrate to you that time here is different from time in the World. Which is why Durand had time to do everything he needed to in order to make the gate system work for us. This day, today, is marked as day Z49,214. That means almost 135 years have passed in the World since Monsieur Durand first marked day zero in this place." she gestured to the wall "and in the actual gate room back out there."

"Right" said Gertie, sounding doubtful "I don't really get it, and it hurts my head too much to think about it, so I'm just not going to." She beamed a grim at Kitty.

"You know, young lady, the more time I spend with you, the more I like your moxie." replied Kitty, clearly amused.

Gertie looked confused again "Okay… what's moxie? Is it good?"

"Yes my dear, it's good… very good. Now let's get out of here. It's been a long day and I think it's time we went and did something else less taxing on your brain.

"I've arranged for you to come stay the night with me at my apartment, then tomorrow we can go see the techs and find out about getting you home. That sound okay?"

Gertie nodded, so Kitty held out her hand for Gertie to take and, grabbing the picnic basket with the other hand, strode purposefully out of the room with Gertie in tow.

# XXVI.

That night Gertie had a nightmare, her first in 3 years. She was standing on the high street in her old home town watching as her mother came out of the chemists on the other side of the road. It was the day she'd died. Gertie's mum was fiddling around in her purse, routing around trying to find something. She was walking slowly forward towards the curb, not looking at where she was going. Gertie suddenly realised she would walk right into the road if she didn't look up soon. She shouted "MUM!" at the top of her voice. From the other side of the road her mother looked up and saw her across the street. A strange smile spread across her mother's face as if she'd suddenly remembered something she'd forgotten. Slowly and with clear purpose she nodded gently at Gertie, closed her eyes and stepped forward, straight into the path of an oncoming car. Gertie screamed and ran, trying desperately to get to her mum, but from out of nowhere a stream of people walked in front of her obstructing her path. She forced her way through, jostled and pushed by the people in her way and ran into the road where the traffic had now come to a standstill. People were starting to crowd around the figure of her mother lying on the floor a few feet in front of the car that had hit her. Gertie rushed over and pushed between them, bending down to touch her mum's prone figure on the road. But as she got a closer look at the figure's face, it wasn't her mum's at all, but

Kitty's. Her face covered in blood and cuts just as it was the day she'd first arrived through the gate at the Grand Picture House.

She awoke with a start and it took a moment to remember where she was. The strange purple light filtering around the edge of the blackout blinds at the windows threw strange shadows across the bedroom. She lay back down, closed her eyes and tried to go back to sleep.

In the morning she would be going with Kitty to meet the technical team to find out about going home. Not that there was any such thing as morning here, only the time when everyone got up and went to work. Kitty had explained that most people who lived in the Æther worked on the same daytime cycle but a small contingent were running on an alternate cycle to everyone else, the "night shift" as she had referred to it. It was during one of these night shifts that Gertie had originally come through the gate, which is why no one had been manning the gate room. If a technician had been on station they could have either returned her straight away or at least made note of her gate's designation. Unfortunately for Gertie the gate room had been shut down as no active operations were currently taking place, so no one knew she'd even arrived until one of the canteen staff had been crossing the town square on the way to work and discovered her passed out.

She obviously managed to drift back to sleep again as, before she realised any time had passed, she was woken by a gentle knock at the door. It opened slowly and Kitty popped her head around the gap.

"Rise and shine, sleepy head. Let's go grab some breakfast and see about getting you home, shall we?"

*      *      *      *

Gertie and Kitty stood in the doorway of a huge auditorium with a sloped floor and banks of long, curved desks running at intervals across its width. At the lower end of the room was a vast array of screens that filled the whole wall, each one showing something different: graphs and charts full of numbers, tables full of lines and lines of text, photographs of people with statistical details and paragraphs of words underneath. Gertie couldn't make any of it out, but it looked very impressive and utterly overwhelming. Kitty waved at a tall, black skinned woman with super curly brown hair and amazing olive green eyes who was standing talking to one of the people sitting at the desks on the other side of the room. She beamed a wide smile and motioned for them to come over.

As Gertie and Kitty crossed the room, the woman came to meet them half-way. She was wearing a pair of denim dungarees over a pink gingham short sleeve blouse and looked just as glamorous as Kitty always did.

"Gertie, this is my friend Bobbie. She's one of our head supervisors for the gate system." Kitty stood behind Gertie with her hands resting on Gertie's shoulders "Bob, I'd like you to meet my little 'mess' as I believe you called her, Miss Gertrude Granger. We've come to find out how y'all are getting on finding her a way back home"

"Hey Kitty girl, and may I say you are looking fine as a dime as always." Bobbie replied, she winked at Kitty and then took a knee in front of Gertie to hold out her hand for a handshake.

"Very pleased to meet you Miss Granger", said Bobbie, imitating Kitty's posh mid-Atlantic accent and loosely shaking Gertie's hand. Dropping her head so she was looking through her eyebrows, Bobbie's eyes darted back and forth between Gertie and Kitty and she asked in her own New York drawl "She been treatin' you okay?"

"Mmmhmmm" was all Gertie could get out of her mouth as she nodded enthusiastically. She wasn't great at talking to adults a lot of the time, only those she felt comfortable around, but her dad had explained that it was always polite to say something, even if it was just an "Mmmhmmm" every now and again.

"Well, alright then" replied Bobbie, kindly realising that she was not going to get much else out of the girl. She stood back up and motioned them over to the man she was talking with when they had come in.

"This is Virgil, he's one of our top technicians and an expert in the gate system. He's been looking over the computer logs for the gate room on both the day Kitty travelled back from her mission in France, and got sidetracked through to your time, and the night you came through the gate and ended up here." explained Bobbie "Over to you Virgil"

The man sitting at the computer terminal wore a pair of those old-fashioned 'eyebrow' glasses just like the ones

Gertie's Maths teacher had, but his hair was jet black with streaks of bright blue in it and was sticking straight up in spikes. On one side it was really short and had lines cut into it showing the pink skin underneath. To Gertie he looked just like someone from the future, except for the glasses and the bright yellow chunky knit cardigan he was wearing. He only looked to be about 10 years older than Gertie and she immediately felt a little embarrassed around him.

"To say you've thrown us a bit of a curve ball is quite the understatement." Virgil said in his well-educated English accent. "Our system keeps track of every gate event as well as biometrics of everything that comes through. See, here is a recording of Agent Simpson's last return from two days ago."

Gertie had no idea what biometrics were, but Virgil pointed to the flat screened display standing on his desk and Gertie saw a Kitty shaped blob of orange, yellow and green standing in a sea of purple. Arranged around the shape were groups of numbers with titles like 'blood pressure', 'heart rate' and 'temperature'. To the side of the screen Gertie saw Kitty's name next to a small square photograph and other details about her, a bit like Gertie's dad's passport did. Underneath this were details like those in the book Kitty had shown her in the gate room at Eiffel's mansion house. In this case, "London, Gaumont, 01.05.37, 11:23, Francis Baker", and underneath this a picture of a series of symbols made up of lines and dots in a square shaped pattern.

"Now, this is the record of the night you came through."

The screen changed to one showing what Gertie could clearly see was her own shape, picked out again in oranges, yellows and greens, but glowing more fiercely than Kitty's did. The groups of numbers were there, but to the side there was no information, just a blank picture of the head and shoulders of a body in two-tone grey, with the words "unknown" written where Gertie's details should be.

Under this Gertie could just see a series of question marks where the gate details should be, and no funny looking symbols as there had been on Kitty's entry.

"It's clear we wouldn't have any ID details for Miss Granger but, as you can see, there are no entry details for this gate at all in our system either. It's just, either never been logged, or isn't one of Durand's gates at all."

"But how is that possible?" asked Kitty. "I thought when the new system was brought online it scanned for every trace of every gate ever opened? Regardless of the old logs."

"It did." replied Virgil "But it was looking for both a copy mark and a corresponding luminosity and wavelength for quantum degradation. This gate doesn't seem to have a mark at all."

Gertie didn't understand anything that they were saying anymore. It was all starting to become too overwhelming for her and, with a sudden burst of bravery, she managed to get over her shyness enough to speak out.

"Please!" she blurted, "I don't know what you are saying. What does this all mean? I just want to go home."

"Oh Gertie darling, I'm sorry" Kitty said in her low soothing voice, "Here, sit down in this chair and I'll try and get you up to speed."

Kitty grabbed one of the room's spinny office chairs and wheeled it over for Gertie to sit in.

"Now, I've only just realised we never did talk about Monsieur Durand's experiments in the end did we? About how he worked out that the gates could be used for more than just travelling to places, but to go to those places at different points in time too?"

Gertie shook her head slowly.

"Well, I guess now's the perfect time to do that, and we've got a better expert than me in Virgil here, who can explain it to you." Kitty turned to Virgil and tilted her head towards Gertie as if to say "Go on then"

"Okay…" started Virgil, "Did Agent Simpson explain about the copy marks?"

"Mmmmmhmmm" replied Gertie. Then, realising she might have to give more details, went on to say "She told me Mr Durand put marks on all the copies of the gate film he made so he could work out which one was being used."

"Very good, well yes, that's part of the story. But there was another factor." Virgil explained. "Durand found he could spot the gate mark here on the Æther side of the gate, but he also discovered that he could see all the other gate marks as well. And he also found that those marks were still visible even when the gate wasn't active."

"Yes, Kitty explained that bit too. But it all started to make my head hurt so she didn't go any further." said Gertie.

"Okay, well I'll try and simplify it all a bit for you. Durand worked out that by projecting filtered light onto the wall in the gate room he could create a connection with a gate FROM the Æther, rather than rely on having a gate operator open it from back in the World. Once he'd worked this out, he realised by changing the filter to different light lengths he could isolate out different gates. With me so far?"

"Not really, what do you mean by filter and what's light length?" asked Gertie

"Hmm well a filter is literally a piece of glass that changes the light projected through it into something else. For example, adding a blue coloured filter turns the projected light blue. But what's really going on is that the filter is changing the wavelength of the light to something different."

Gertie's brow started to furrow in that way it always did when she was thinking REALLY hard. But as Virgil had only just met her he didn't notice and just carried on regardless.

"You see, light travels from one place to another in waves, just like the sea does. The length of the light wave is the distance between the top of the wave and the bottom. Every perceivable colour is basically light with a different wavelength. So to change blue light into green we just make its wavelength smaller… by about 100 nanometres."

"What's a nanometre?" interjected Gertie.

"It's one billionth of a metre. Immeasurably small to the human eye." explained Virgil.

"Okay, I think I get it. Each gate is basically a slightly different colour and you can find them by changing the colour with a filter?"

"Sort of. Except we are not talking about light that's visible, but light that's outside of the range our eyes can see. Anyway, you seem to get it enough for me to move on. So by filtering the projected light Durand could lock on to each of the different gates, visible by the symbol he had given it coming to the fore. But what If each gate was opened hundreds of times? Just because you could see the gate mark, you still wouldn't know at what point in time that gate had been opened."

Virgil was now getting quite animated, this was clearly his favourite subject and it was exciting him. She saw Kitty and Bobbie look at each other and roll their eyes. Gertie had started to feel relaxed around Virgil for some reason and so got herself more comfortable in the chair by curling one leg under herself and leaning against the desk to the side of her, ready to listen.

"Durand found that if he changed the *luminosity* of the projected light… in other words how bright the light was, he could match the projection to each time a particular gate was opened. Remember he had years to work all of this out before we started actually using it in an effective way. So by having each gate operator keep a record of the dates and times each gate had been opened, he could eventually correspond that to the recorded wavelength and luminosity of the projected light on the Æther side of the gate and create a paired match."

Virgil stopped talking and there was silence for a good half a minute, whilst Gertie just sat staring at him in a far off way.

He smiled kindly and said "Does that make any sense to you?"

"Oh, yes, yes... I get it now. So..." Gertie tailed off

"So?" echoed Kitty.

Gertie suddenly became aware of the rest of the group, she hadn't realised she'd been concentrating so hard on Virgil. She sat up straight again and said, "So... how does this all fit with finding my way home?"

"Right, yes." replied Virgil "The problem is that without a gate mark to lock onto we have to scan every possible combination of wavelength and luminosity in order to find one that corresponds to your gate. I'm not even sure I can do it. It helps that we know it's only been used a small number of times, only two that we know of. But it's still a very small needle in a really big haystack."

"Erm... I might have, kind of, watched the film a few more times than that when I was trying to work out where Kitty had gone." confessed Gertie.

"Oh" said Virgil, trying not to sound disappointed. "How many times?"

"Like twenty, I think"

"Twenty!?! No... no, actually that helps. If we are looking for lots more gate events then it will be easier to find potential matches. That's good, yes, that's good."

With this he turned back to his computer and started to work on a solution, completely absorbed by his thought process and typing furiously. After an awkward pause whilst no one talked for a moment, Bobbie clapped her hands together and said,

"Well okay then. I guess that's the end of our little history lesson."

She came over to where Gertie was sitting and put a reassuring hand on top of her shoulder.

"Listen honey. I think the long and short of this is that until Mr Genius here figures out a way to find your gate, you are gonna be stuck here with us. Sorry about that."

# XXVII.

Gertie collapsed on the sofa in Kitty's living room and closed her eyes. After finding out she wouldn't be able to get home, maybe ever, she and Kitty had spent the day wandering around the San Francisco quarter, near Kitty's apartment, to try and take her mind off it. Gertie loved walking up and down the steep winding roads of Vermont and Lombard Street and the amazing houses around Haight and Ashbury. She never imagined being able to visit San Francisco, and the beautiful thing about the Æther was that these roads were right next to each other instead of miles apart as in the real world.

Despite all this she still felt a little empty inside, she really missed her dad, and even Walter a bit. She knew that Kitty wasn't really a replacement for her Mum, but her nightmare the previous night had scared her. What if she really was stuck here forever…did Kitty even *want* to look after her? She was so glamorous and adventurous, why would she want to be saddled with looking after a 12 year old girl. Maybe she was only doing it out of guilt for not covering her tracks well enough when she'd appeared at the Picture House. Gertie's head was spinning. This was all her fault. She should have just left it and not tried to find out where Kitty had gone, and she definitely should not have tried to follow her when she did. But she'd done it out of selfishness. First the Picture House and then Kitty were the most exciting things to happen to her in her entire life. After her mum's death she'd felt so lonely and she was left with a great sadness and a void in her life that needed to be filled, and the cinema, and then Kitty and the mystery of the film had seemed to fill it. And now she was stuck in a strange place, with lots of strange people she didn't know and she missed home so badly.

Just then Kitty came into the living room armed with a tray containing some tea and a big bar of chocolate. She placed the tray on the coffee table and sat down in the armchair on the opposite side of it to where Gertie was on the sofa.

Kitty's apartment was small and simple. When Gertie had asked her why, of all the amazing buildings represented here in the Æther, she had chosen it over moving into a huge mansion house like Gustave Eiffel's, Kitty had explained that with all the time she spent on missions she just needed somewhere small and manageable but that felt like home. The apartment was actually that of the character Sam Spade in the film The Maltese Falcon, one of Kitty's favourite films as well as one of her favourite books. In fact the film version was apparently based on the real apartment the book's author Dashiell Hammett lived in when he wrote the original story. This was one of the reasons Kitty was drawn to it. Because of the curious nature of the Æther everything in the original apartment was monochrome, but Kitty had made it her home by grabbing pieces of furniture from other places and paint and wallpaper from the stores of various supplies that had been moved over from the real World.

"How are you doing dear?" she asked gently. "Feeling okay? Here this will help, trust me.. Always does."

Kitty broke off a strip of chocolate and handed it across to Gertie as she sat up from where she was lying down. Gertie said nothing but took the chocolate from Kitty and broke a big chunk off with her teeth. It was really good and she could feel its rich melty gooeyness filling her mouth with a warm, comforting sensation.

"See", said Kitty "Told you it would."

Kitty paused for a moment watching Gertie take another bite of chocolate.

"We'll get you back home, I promise. Remember that time is on our side. Quite literally in fact."

She reached forward and picked up her mug of tea from the tray, the steam billowing gently away from the top of the mug as she blew on the hot liquid to cool it.

"Even if we can't locate your gate, we'll search for another one that we can use, as close as we can to the time you left. Until then, we'll see about finding you something to do. And some new clothes to change into. Would you like that?"

Gertie nodded quickly and reached for her own mug. She pressed it to her lips but could already tell the tea was going to be too hot to drink, so put it down again.

"Yes please. And could I… could I have some more chocolate?" she asked, shyly "please?"

"Of course darling, do help yourself. It's the least I can do. After all I got you into this mess didn't I? Why don't we finish this tea and I'll send a message over to the supply stores and see what we might have clothing wise that will fit you."

"It's… it's really not your fault…" said Gertie between bites of chocolate. "I shouldn't have played with the film and I shouldn't have walked through the gate. It was silly of me. It could have been dangerous. Please, don't blame yourself."

"Oh I'm not, don't worry." replied Kitty, winking and smiling brightly at Gertie "I don't blame you either dear. I blame the damn fool who left that film lying around for you to find!"

Gertie couldn't help but to smile back at her. She picked up her mug of tea again and as she did so a sudden thought struck her. This whole situation was because of the film. If she'd never have found the film, never opened the box, Kitty would never have been diverted off course on her return from the First World War and they would never have met. Gertie would never have become obsessed with finding her again and never used the film to travel here. If only there was a way to stop all of that from happening.

That was when the plan started to formulate in her mind. A plan to change everything.

End of Reel Two

# Intermission

The line went dead. She could do nothing now but hope that her message got through.

She hugged the telephone to her chest and pushed herself harder into the gap underneath the old desk, listening as the hurricane-force wind howled outside. The door started to clatter and rattle even harder on its hinges. Above her there was a sudden rending shriek of noise as if the world was being pulled apart by two giant hands. Part of the roof of the building was torn off and blown 20 feet away to smash against the ground, splintering into pieces. The storm raging outside had no regard for property or people, it screamed and smashed everything in its path like an angry god.

She closed her eyes tightly and hoped with all her strength that they could find her before the others discovered her hiding place or she was buried alive.

# Reel Three: The Mission

# XXVIII.

Gertie had been in the Æther now for two weeks. She was still getting used to the strange day-night cycle everything worked around, so the passage of time didn't feel quite as it should have. As promised, Kitty had drummed up a new set of clothes for her, quite a lot of new clothes in fact, and she was enjoying wearing whatever she wanted and not having to put on school uniform for half the time. She did miss school, but mostly because of her friends, and she really missed her room and her own stuff. There were so many new people to meet in the Æther that she didn't think about her brother and dad so much anymore, usually just in the evening when she was alone, trying to get to sleep. She'd started to think about them just being frozen in time, like statues, standing around the Grand Picture House and not even realising she wasn't there. It helped, but it was still quite an odd thing to wrap her head around; the idea that if and when she got back home again it would be as if none of this had happened. That she'd just stepped back through the gate and into the auditorium as if she had never left. Neither her dad nor brother had seen her leave so they wouldn't even know about the gate, wouldn't know about the Æther, wouldn't even know she had gone anywhere, or done any of this. And she wouldn't be able to tell them, even if they would have believed her if she tried. It was such a big secret to be holding in, even though she wasn't even home yet, she felt like she would burst keeping it trapped inside her. Instead she concentrated on the plan. And that was another secret she had to keep hidden.

After Gertie had been in the Æther only a week, Kitty had been pulled back into active duty. She had to start preparations for her next mission, so was no longer able to spend all her time with her. Instead, she had arranged for Gertie to be given a very strange little gadget that, Kitty explained, was like a mini computer but so tiny that it fitted in her pocket. Gertie had just started to use computers at school, but they were big beige-coloured boxes that had to be connected to bulky television-shaped display units, nothing like this. For starters nearly everything on the computers at home were written in words, sometimes there were big blocky pictures alongside the words that you had to click on with the mouse. This device was small, about the size of her mum's makeup compact, and made of dull metal, like a very thin box. The top of the box was made of jet black coloured glass, and when Kitty got Gertie to touch the glass it lit up and projected an image into the air above the device, a bit like a miniature cinema screen, which showed an array of small pictures. Gertie moved the device around but the projection still hovered in the same place about 5 centimetres above the glass screen. Kitty explained that if she touched each of the pictures the screen would switch to something new, such as a map or a list of places.

"Now, click on that little picture of an arrowhead", said Kitty.

She was sitting next to Gertie on her bed and they were both staring at the projection the device held in Gertie's hand was making. When she clicked on the arrowhead the screen full of tiny pictures was replaced by a map of the apartment, a bit like the architect's drawings she'd once seen on her dad's desk at home.

"This is an interactive map of the Æther, it will not only help you navigate your way around whilst I'm off in the World, but it also shows the location of everyone else here so you can find someone if you need to. We all have these devices on us at all times you see, except when travelling through the gates, then we turn them off and leave them behind in the gate prep room."

As they looked at the screen Gertie could see a small blue dot in the centre and right next to it a small orange dot

"That blue dot is you, and the orange one, me. Now place your finger on my orange dot..." Gertie did so and a box popped up with Kitty's name and picture and an orange lozenge shaped bar that read "message".

"You can send me a message whenever you want, and I will get it instantly, and reply if I can. Now just push the box off the screen with your finger and it will disappear."

Next Kitty showed her how to search for a specific person's location and how to get the map to plot a route to that person. She chose Bobbie and could see she was currently in the gate room.

"If I'm not around, you can always message Bobbie or even Virgil, they've both said that would be okay. Now, pop that down on the bed and hold out your wrist so I can put this on."

Kitty held out a thin black metal bracelet which looked like it had been broken into two pieces. Kitty placed the two halves of the bracelet either side of Gertie's wrist. As they were brought closer they snapped together to form a single band. The band was surprisingly warm, and as Gertie turned it over and over she could see no visible join.

"This is a tracker, so even if you put your smart device down and forget to pick it up, we still know where you are. This also helps you find the device again. Squeeze the band between your fingers."

As Gertie did so the device on the bed started to vibrate and make a beeping noise, which stopped when she let go of the band.

"Now try walking out of the room without the device."

Gertie stood up, walked across the bedroom and through the door. As she disappeared from sight, Kitty heard her shout "Whoa!"

The band on Gertie's wrist was now vibrating, but it stopped as she walked back into the room.

"Seems like magic doesn't it?" said Kitty, "Certainly felt that way to me when I first came here. I'm just a small town girl from Connecticut. Never even heard of a computer until I arrived. As for this...it's like something out of a Jules Verne novel. Now… sit back down."

Kitty patted the bed next to her. When Gertie had sat down she reached behind her back and brought out a small package wrapped in brown paper. She handed it to Gertie and said, "I brought you a little something else too."

Gertie opened the package carefully and found a delicate silver watch inside. The watch had a metal bracelet strap and a white face with very fancy looking numbers on it.

"It's set to the same time as your own, back in 1987. Now you'll always know what time it is there. Let's put it on you shall we?"

Kitty gently put the watch onto Gertie's other wrist and checked it fitted properly.

"It's beautiful, thank you", said Gertie watching it shine in the light.

"It is absolutely my pleasure dear. Now. I'll go and make us something to eat shall I?" With that Kitty got up and left the room.

Gertie looked at the watch for a few seconds and then turned to the device sitting on the bed next to her. She stared at the little green dot that represented Bobbie as it moved around the map of the gate room.

"This is it." thought Gertie to herself "This is the key."

# XXIX.

*29th October, 1922*

When Kitty entered the Royal Bar at the Winter Palace Hotel in Luxor she immediately started searching for her mark, the archaeologist Howard Carter. She made her way slowly across the highly polished parquet floor towards the bar in order to grab a drink and blend in. The bar seemed quiet for a Sunday night. She'd been told that the place was usually filled to the rafters with eager Egyptologists and their wealthy patrons, as well as writers, artists, high ranking Army officers and officials of the British colonial service. Perhaps the recent unrest in the area, due to Egypt fighting for its independence from colonial rule, was keeping them away. The threat of riots and bombings still a possibility even though a settlement had recently been put in place. Or perhaps it was just that the next dig "Season" was yet to start and they hadn't yet arrived in the country or travelled, as Kitty had done, down from the capital city of Cairo.

She was dressed elegantly in the newest fashions of the time; a long flowing emerald green silk dress, covered in beading, with a wide, bejewelled headband keeping her delicately waved hair in check. The research team back in the Æther had done a fantastic job of getting the outfit together and she felt she fitted seamlessly in with the smattering of other bright young things she'd seen moving around the hotel. She'd arrived in Cairo a few days before via the Kursaal Theatre gate and, thanks to the local Light operatives, managed to book passage on the recently built paddle steamer P.S. Sudan. She was playing the part of an American heiress and socialite holidaying in Egypt. She'd secretly been longing to travel this way ever since reading Agatha Christie's novel Death on the Nile, so built her cover story from parts of the book's plot just so she could. It wasn't going to be written for another 15 years so what was the harm... at least that's how she'd justified it to Director Earhart.

Often on her missions there was an element of danger, stopping agents of the Obscurus from diverting the course of history to their own aims as she'd done in France for example, but this one was different. It was more of a pre-emptive strike. Planting the seeds of truth that would lead her mark to continue towards their greatest triumph, and keep them on the correct path if any outside agents tried to intercede. There was still a possibility that the Obscurus had people in the area, but Kitty felt she could let her guard down a little and enjoy herself for a while.

Just then the bartender arrived with Kitty's drink - a Sidecar - her favourite cocktail. She slowly sloshed the rich burnt orange drink around the broad bowl of its long stemmed Coupe glass, momentarily lost in the reflections of the room it picked up on its travels. She began to wonder how Gertie was getting on back in the Æther. She hated leaving her, but after all she had a job to do so that was that. Of course, it was the job that had landed her with Gertie to begin with, but she was sure she'd be in good hands with her friends back in the Æther. Gertie seemed to be coping quite well, a little too well perhaps, Kitty felt. Maybe she was still in shock, she thought, it *was* a lot to take in, and with the added worry of not knowing she could get home easily to top it all off. Except that Gertie seemed to be doing fine. She did seem a little preoccupied at times and asked a lot of strange questions, but then Kitty knew she was a clever young woman and perhaps asking a lot of questions and keeping her thoughts to herself was just what Gertie did. She was a little like that herself to be fair.

She turned herself around on her bar stool and surveyed the room, sipping lightly from her drink as she did so. Intel had said that Carter was a bit of a loner so would most likely be by himself. All the people she could see populating the room seemed to be in groups, and she wasn't yet able to pick out Carter in any of them. It was a warm night, so she decided to make her way out to the terrace and get a view of the river, there was a chance perhaps that Carter would also be there.

The terrace was about as busy as the bar had been, consisting of just a few groups of people sitting at the low tables having quiet conversations with each other. She chose to stroll down the length of the terrace to get a better view, and as she neared the end she realised she wasn't the only one who had had the same idea. Leaning against the terrace wall was the man she'd come here to find, Howard Carter.

One week from now Carter was about to uncover one of the most important finds in world history, the undisturbed tomb of Tutankhamen, filled with treasures and antiquities never seen before or since. The problem was that six months previously, at the end of the previous dig season, Carter's partner and patron Lord Carnarvon had informed him that this would be the last season he was willing to finance. The dig had been going on for the last five years or more with no results. Both Carnarvon and Carter were dejected, disheartened and worn out. Kitty now needed to, not only make sure Carter kept going at the dig site, but that when certain opportunities arose after the find had been uncovered that he stayed the path and wasn't corrupted into selling out and succumbing to Obscurus influence.

Carter was a tall, scruffily dressed man in his mid forties with dark brown hair slicked down into a side parting. He had a cold and serious face, and his most striking feature, a large curved nose, was underlined with a bushy grey-streaked moustache. It struck Kitty as fitting that this face belonged to a man who had spent much of his life chipping away at stone walls. She could easily understand why he had a reputation as a loner, it would be hard to find kindness and empathy in such a stern face. But that was what she now had to do; befriend this man and gather him into her confidence so that history would benefit from his efforts. She put all thoughts of Gertie out of her head and moved forward with her opening gambit.

"Breathtaking, isn't it?" She enquired, settling herself against the terrace wall next to Carter and indicating the river Nile, a hundred yards away across the sandy river bank. "As Longfellow once wrote: forever new and old, among the living and the dead, its mighty, mystic stream has rolled."

159

"Hmm" was Carter's clipped response, his voice gruff and weary.

"Really?" Kitty replied with an amused tone, "I would have imagined in your line of work, that the river represented something far greater than just water, no? Is it not the 'gift' of Egypt, giving life to all those civilizations you seek to uncover the possessions of?"

Carter stood up and turned to Kitty as if to confront her, but seeing her for the first time paused as if lost for words. After a few moments he visibly relaxed and leant his arm against the wall.

"Destroys more than it gives life to these days. Water is one of the archaeologist's greatest enemies."

"I was right then? You are an archaeologist? I was warned this place would be swimming with them, but you are the first person I've seen who actually fits the bill" Kitty said, smiling brightly at him.

Carter put out his hand for Kitty to shake and said *"Carter. Howard."*

Kitty gently gripped his outstretched hand and replied, light-heartedly mocking his own introduction "Hartz... Eleanor."

"And what brings you to the banks of the Nile Ms. Hartz?"

"I've wanted to come here since I was a little girl. I've always had a bit of a thing for ancient ruins, you see. I thought I'd travel the world for a while seeing how many of them I could visit. And you Mr. Carter? What are you looking for here in the Valley of the Kings?"

Kitty turned her back on the Nile and perched elegantly against the stone terrace wall, looking sideways at Carter with her head tilted.

"Well if my luck runs out before the end of this season I'll be 'looking' for something else to do it seems." he replied somewhat grumpily.

"I don't believe that there is any such thing as luck. If something is going to happen it will. The important thing is to keep trying and never give up. My mother always taught me that, to give up, even if it seems like the easier choice to take, will almost always turn out not to be the case in the end. If you are looking for something and you know it should be there, then it is. You just have to keep looking. Leave no stone unturned, yes?" Kitty told him, in her most soothing singsong voice.

"Yes. Quite. You are correct, of course. I know he's there... I can feel him. All the evidence suggests this to be the case. Carnarvon's had me on some fool's errand up on the ridge, but my gut tells me to go back to the centre of the site, near the North East corner where we found old Ramses."

"Well then that is what you should do Mr. Carter. If your heart, your head and your gut are in agreement, then who are we to argue with them?" She let out a gentle laugh "Are you a meticulous man Mr. Carter?"

"Oh yes, extremely so. I pride myself on it"

"Then continue to be so and I'm sure what you are looking for will present itself sooner than you think." Kitty finished the last of her drink and stood "It was a pleasure to meet you Mr. Carter, but the air is cooling and I fear the time has come for me to retire for the evening. So I shall wish you all the best in your search and hope that we might bump into each other again in the future."

"As do I Ms. Hartz and thank you. You've helped me more than words can express." Carter gave a small bow to Kitty in acknowledgment.

"Good night Mr. Carter."

"To you too, Ms. Hartz."

# XXX.

Kitty had been away now for a little over a week and Gertie had kept herself busy studiously enacting the various parts of her plan. She'd started by path finding; working out various routes to and from the apartment and each of the landmarks she needed to get to. She'd obviously begun with the quickest routes, but then found several alternatives which would skirt around the more populated areas of the Æther in case she would need them.

She hated having to wear the strange sunglasses needed to travel in the streets outside, so was very pleased to discover that many parts of the city were connected by an underground rail system. This, as far as she could tell by the signage and style, was made up of various parts of the New York subway, Paris Metro and London underground. These transit systems seemed to be automatic, as Gertie never saw a train driver, guard or conductor of any kind present at the stations or on the platform or train, as she rode around, occasionally glancing at her smart map to see where she was and who else was near. Just as it was back in the World, these trains had rush hours, where more people used them at given times to get to their various jobs within the Æther, but she could hardly call it rammed. Certainly not in the way she'd witnessed on her trips to London with her mum. As far as she could tell the Æther wasn't very heavily populated anyway. Still, she tended to travel outside of these peak times as she had nowhere to be anyway.

Another really good reason to use the tube system was that occasionally the Æther suffered particularly violent storms which seemed to drift in out of nowhere, make a lot of noise, throw down water like waterfalls and disappear as quickly as they came. Kitty certainly had *not* warned her about that. The first one happened on the second night she was alone in the apartment and it frightened her so badly that, without realising it, she'd climbed under Kitty's bed and curled up into a ball. Even though there was no one in the apartment to witness, Gertie had still felt very embarrassed after the storm seemingly disappeared without trace after 30 minutes. She'd braved looking out of the tinted windows of the room to see steam rising from the ground in great clouds, as the Quintessence evaporated the rain in shimmers of rainbow colours.

She'd asked Bobbie about this the next day and she'd explained that "Just like with all the objects captured on film, every thunderstorm and sudden downpour from every movie is here in the Æther as well. Over time these storms have merged and now travel around the place like super storms. Don't ever get caught in one or you'll be soaked to the skin in seconds. Oddly though, the rain is warm so it's like standing fully clothed in the shower."

This had given Gertie yet another idea to add to the plan, so she'd quizzed Virgil about whether anyone had studied the storms and was an expert in predicting them, just so she could be prepared for next time. Virgil had pointed her in the direction of one of the gate techs named George, who had taken an interest in the meteorology of the Æther. George had told her that, even though there was some randomness to them, the storms came roughly every thirty days, so he predicted the next one would happen near the end of the day on Z49,262. This gave Gertie her window… she just hoped that Kitty wasn't back from her mission by then.

# XXXI.

Kitty had spent the last week shamelessly enjoying herself as a typical rich American tourist would have in the nineteen twenties. She'd visited all that Luxor had to offer, the sun court of Amenhotep III, the grand colonnade, the avenue of Sphinxes, and the temple to Ramses II with its giant statues. She'd wandered the vast ancient city of Thebes with its temple to Amun-Re, its Great Hypostyle Hall and its necropolis guarded by the giant Colossi of Memnon. She'd travelled by camel to the temples of the Gods Horus at Edfu and Sobek at Kom Ombo. Now she was sitting enjoying a spot of breakfast on the terrace of her hotel. Her intelligence report had said that her mark, Howard Carter, would be visiting the hotel that day to check for any telegraph messages before heading back to his dig site in the Valley of the Kings. He had spent the last two days uncovering the steps to what he believed to be the entrance of Tutanhamen's tomb and had sent an urgent message the previous night to his patron, Lord Carnavon, about his discovery. He was now awaiting an answer before continuing the dig. All she needed to do was sit, wait and hope he spotted her as he made his way back out of the hotel.

Kitty was just starting to worry that Carter hadn't yet shown up when he came striding out of the hotel door with a look of thunder on his face. He looked tired and dishevelled, his already dirty clothing wrinkled and unkempt. Kitty beamed a smile at him and Carter glanced in her direction but continued walking angrily away. Before he reached the top of the steps Kitty called out.

"I say? Everything alright Mr. Carter?"

Carter stopped dead in his tracks and looked at her in confusion.

"What?! Oh, sorry. Forgive my manners, Ms. Hartz isn't it?" said Carter, the confusion leaving his face. He still wore a frown of anger, but his body language relaxed slightly as he stood looking over at Kitty's table.

"You look positively fuming Mr. Carter, whatever can be the matter? Dig not going well?" asked Kitty kindly

Carter shook his head as if brushing away the anger like flies and strode towards Kitty.

"Err, no. I mean, sorry. Yes, the dig is going very well, very well indeed as it happens. I'm just angry that there's been no word yet from Carnarvon."

"Sit, Mr. Carter, you must tell me all about it." Kitty indicated the empty chair opposite and leant forward, her elbows on the table and her head nestled in her palms indicating that she was giving him her full attention.

Carter sat, looked up at the sky for a moment and then back to Kitty.

"It's the most extraordinary thing Ms. Hartz. I think I've finally found him."

"Found whom Mr. Carter?"

"Tut-ankh-Amen. We uncovered some hidden steps and when we dug further down it turned out to be an entrance way. I found a royal seal there indicating a tomb.

It's odd. It seems that the whole site was just forgotten and covered over with the detritus caused by the digging of Ramses tomb. There are workmen's huts right next to it, but they clearly never knew that something was beneath them." Carter told Kitty, getting more and more animated as he did so.

"But that's wonderful Mr. Carter. Perhaps you were right all along! But why did you look so angry just now?"

"Oh, I wired the old fool in England to tell him. He should be here when we crack open the seals, you see. I hoped I might have heard back from him by now. I don't want to just plough on in case others discover what we've got here. There hasn't been a new discovery for over ten years! It's going to be big news."

With this Carter finally relaxed into his chair. A wave of exhaustion seemed to wash over him.

"Well Mr. Carter, you must do what's best for the find. That's your priority now. If you will accept the advice of a mere woman, of course?"

"Naturally Ms. Hartz. After all, I believe it was you who steeled my resolve the other night to move where we were looking in the first place."

"Then let me add this Mr. Carter. In the privileged position I am in, I'm no stranger to publicity and believe me, it can be a wild and unruly beast. If you can get a hold on it and keep it on your side, the best you can, then you might stand a chance of coming off unscathed."

Carter looked puzzled, but smiled kindly and nodded.

"Thank you Ms. Hartz. I will do just that."

He stood up swiftly and gave a slight bow to Kitty

"Now I must get going. You've given me an idea in fact. I think my course of action now is to prepare everything properly and secure the site ready for when the old man can get here. I'm going to make sure everything is done correctly. Once again, Ms. Hartz, it's been a pleasure."

"Thank you Mr. Carter. Remember, always trust your instincts and continue to be meticulous and you'll be okay. This is yours. You are in control, don't ever let anyone take that from you. Now I shall wait with bated breath to find out what it is you've uncovered."

Carter bowed his head once again and turned on his heels, striding purposefully away wearing a much more quizzical look on his face than his previous one of anger.

Kitty poured herself another cup of tea, happy in the feeling that her work was once again done for the day.

# XXXII.

Gertie had spent the last three weeks gathering everything she needed together. First she'd gone to the main stores and grabbed a notepad, some large sheets of paper and a pack of coloured felt tip pens. These were now spread out on the table in front of her. She'd been using them to plan out everything she needed to do, when it needed to be done and where she needed to be at each given point. At the same time she'd also grabbed some writing paper and a fountain pen. She'd used these to write Kitty a note explaining everything and letting her know how much Gertie had appreciated everything she had done for her. She had no idea if Kitty would ever see the letter, she wasn't really sure how this was all going to work out and what the effect would be on Kitty and this place, but it seemed like the right thing to do, so she did it. Finally she'd grabbed a large canvas backpack, not too big to carry but big enough to hold everything she was going to need, including the original clothes she'd arrived in.

She'd then spent a little time each day, travelling each of her intended routes, keeping note of everyone she encountered on her interactive map, even if they were in buildings away from her on the edge of the map. She'd noted which areas were quietest and at what times. She timed how long it took to get from point to point, mapped out the exact steps she'd need to take, the exact routes she had to follow and the alternatives should she come across something unexpected.

She'd made frequent visits to the gate room, the prep room and the control room and charted the flow of people in and out of them, noticing patterns and cycles in each person's daily life. She'd asked endless, boring questions of both Virgil and Bobbie, making sure she understood, without being obvious, how the gate system worked, how it was operated, who monitored it and when.

Finally she had everything perfectly planned out. She was ready. She poured over every detail of the plan one last time, then neatly folded everything up and stashed it in the side pocket of the backpack. Now she just had to wait for the time to be right. Timing would be everything.

# XXXIII.

Her current work in Luxor complete, Kitty travelled back to Cairo by rail and stationed herself at The Mena House, a newly expanded hotel with a direct view of the Great Pyramids of Giza that was the current hot spot for travellers and colonials alike. The hotel itself was a collection of large square villa style buildings, with many balconies and terraces for views of the pyramids and surrounded by groves of palm trees. It was on one of these terraces that Kitty sat enjoying coffee and waiting for an appearance of her next mark, Arthur Merton, a journalist for the Times. She was here to persuade the news reporter to travel to Luxor and seek out Howard Carter, in order to get the inside scoop on his find in the Valley of the Kings. She was hoping that this would lead to an eventual deal being struck between the Egyptologist and Merton's employer giving them full access to the dig thus ensuring the world was fully informed of the breath and value of the artefacts yet to be discovered. The Guiding Light network had picked up talk of a potential cover up and takeover being orchestrated by the Obscurus and fed this information through to the Æther. They must be getting desperate after their Great War plan failed to get them anywhere and Kitty was here to do everything in her power to stop this from happening. She'd already laid the groundwork at Carter's end and she was here in Cairo to meet with Merton and his wife to push him in the right direction.

Kitty was dressed for the day in a light green pleated sports dress, lace up shoes and a straw cloche hat with a matching scarf wrapped around it which fell down her back to offer extra protection from the sun. She'd prefer to wear her usual casual trousers, but as these were yet to be fashionable for women, she was slowly getting used to the loose fitting dresses of the '20s. They still afforded her free movement if she needed it, although she would have to be careful in any combat situations as they weren't exactly made of resilient or sturdy fabrics.

She reached forward and poured herself another cup of coffee from the tall brass coffee pot on the table in front of her. As she did so she scanned the terrace for signs of the Mertons. She knew they would be at dinner at the hotel later that day, but hoped to bump into them on the terrace this afternoon, so that she was already introduced and could join them without too much preamble that evening. As she looked to her right toward the pyramids she was shocked by the sight of a man walking down the stone steps through the palm trees towards the terrace. She recognised his face immediately, even though it now sported an eye patch over his right eye. It was the same Obscurus agent she had tackled at the field hospital in the Somme in 1916! She tilted her head forward so that her cloche hat cast shadows on her face and turned so that its asymmetric brim obscured her features. She couldn't afford to be seen. The man walked swiftly through the scattered collection of tables and wicker chairs on the terrace scanning their occupants as he did so. He was wearing a scruffy beige linen safari suit which had seen better days and a dust covered pith helmet. "Honestly" thought Kitty to herself, "Could he look more like the stereotype of an evil henchman?!"

She decided to abandon her post on the terrace and follow the man at a discrete distance. She watched as he exited the terrace onto the road towards the great pyramid and, grabbing her parasol, leaped up to follow him. Within one hundred yards she managed to slot herself behind a group of people making their way up the road and could see the man stride up the hill ahead of her. He reached the top of the road and veered off onto the left hand track away from the Pyramid of Khufu and into the eastern cemetery complex. As her group were continuing on to the pyramid ahead, Kitty had to strike out on her own in order to keep up with the enemy agent. The cemetery complex was full of twists and turns around the many tomb entrances and smaller Queen's pyramids, which thankfully would have afforded Kitty many chances to conceal herself from the man ahead if she'd needed to. However the man just kept walking purposefully ahead, straight around the outside of the complex and towards the great statue of the Sphinx.

"What is he up to?" Kitty asked herself.

The agent hadn't paid any attention to any of the scenery around him, or looked back once since leaving the terrace so Kitty decided to be bolder and catch up with him as best she could in plain sight. She had her hat and her parasol to conceal her, and had no reason to suspect the man had even seen her on the terrace at all, or suspect who she was. A change of outfit, a new haircut and a dusting of makeup did a surprising amount towards transforming her into someone else. After all, the enemy agent had last seen her six years ago and only for the briefest of moments, coupled with the fact that at the time she was dressed as a nurse, makeup less and with a headscarf on.

As the man rounded the sandbank at the edge of the cemetery Kitty could see ahead of him the giant Sphinx and the impressively straight sandstone causeway running behind it to the Pyramid of Khafre on the hill to its right. Under the impression that he might be meeting a potential contact at the Sphinx she hung back slightly, skirting close to the sandbank to conceal her presence. She watched as the Obscurus agent approached the giant feet of the Sphinx. As he got to a point between them, directly in the shadow of the statue's head, he swiftly looked around him left and right as if searching for something. Clearly not finding what he was looking for he struck out once more and disappeared through the great stone archway into the Valley Temple of Khafre at the bottom of the causeway. Kitty broke into a sprint and crossed the space from her concealed spot, passed the Sphinx and through the archway in less than a minute. As she cleared the entrance she was pleased to catch a glimpse of the man as he disappeared left into the temple's vestibule. She trotted swiftly on light feet towards the vestibule entrance, collapsing her parasol as she did. Pressing herself against the stone pillar she poked her head around the entrance to see if she could see the enemy agent. To her surprise he stood 20 feet inside the room with his pistol pointed directly at her. She pulled her head back around just in time before the loud *"crack"* of gun fire sounded and the limestone pillar exploded from the bullet's impact at the point where her head had been.

"Ah, Hell!" she said under her breath and, grabbing the parasol with one hand by its ribs and the other its handle, she swiftly unsheathed the hidden blade concealed within its bamboo shaft.

Keeping low, with the sword pointed towards the floor, she sprinted across to the entranceways opposite pillar, glancing into the vestibule beyond as she did so. She saw no sign of the man and, as no more shots were forthcoming, she ducked low and plunged through the doorway into the room. The agent was nowhere to be seen. The room was vast and empty, three times her height and open to the sky, so afforded no hiding spots. She sprinted quickly along the granite wall on her right to the edge of the opening leading into the temple's pillared hall. After a few deep breaths she poked her head through the opening. The room beyond was expansive and like the previous room open to the sky. Dotted along its length were two rows of perfectly preserved granite columns, topped with lintels to form a colonnade. Between this and the opening stood two standalone columns no longer connected to the rest. After a moment she spotted the agent at the far end of the hallway half concealed behind a pillar. He fired another shot, but it went vastly wild, impacting on the granite wall at least two feet away from her. Clearly his depth perception was affected by only having the one eye, she could use that to her advantage, she thought. Once again keeping low, she sprinted through the opening and across the gap to the first standalone pillar on the left hand side of the hall, on the opposite side to the agent. She was now obscured from him by several feet of granite. She swiftly pushed the advantage and moved to the next pillar along, and then the next. She was fairly certain that this was the last pillar giving her cover, so she poked her head around it to her right and was once again rewarded with a near miss and a shower of granite dust from the enemy agent's pistol shot.

Rapidly rolling her body around the pillar back the way she had come, she rounded its width and sprinted across the hall to the opposite row of columns on the same side as the enemy. She raised her sword in front of her and ran directly at the wall opposite her, bounced off it and back towards the next pillar along, flattening her back to the cold granite surface. She was surprised the agent hadn't been ready with another shot from his pistol, perhaps he wasn't anticipating her moves as much as she might think. She took a few deep breaths and prepared herself to do the same move again to try and take the man out, assuming he was still hiding in the same position of course. She sprang out, glancing to her left as she headed for the opposite wall, but there was no sign of the enemy. She headed for the last pillar, coming to rest on the right side of it. Slowing her breathing in an attempt to listen for the man's position she could hear nothing but the cool desert wind reverberating around the hall. He had to be just around the other side of the pillar. She ducked and turned the corner ready to strike with her blade only to find the man was no longer there.

Kitty stood, not knowing what to do next. The hall was completely silent, no sounds of movement, no sign of any other life except her own. Suddenly she felt something cold press against her lower back and the man grabbed her around the neck from behind with his rough and powerful hand. He had somehow managed to outflank her!

"We meet again Mademoiselle. Much has changed since the last time we saw one another, more for me than it is for you it seems." said the enemy agent, his English thick and awkward and ladened with a heavy French accent.

"I don't know how it is that you have tracked me here, but I have you now and there is nothing you can do to… URK!"

Kitty struck quickly before the man could finish his victory speech. She stabbed backwards with the main part of her parasol, its pointed tip catching the man in his stomach, winding him. She spun around quickly, bringing her blade up as she did so and drew a thin red line across his throat. He fell backwards against the granite pillar, and slumped forward, dead. His pith helmet fell from his head and hit the ground, the sound echoing loudly around the empty hall. Kitty stood looking at him, breathing heavily into the silence that followed.

"Why do you bad guys always have to gloat!" Kitty said to the lifeless body in front of her, "Leaves you completely distracted from the task in hand."

She collapsed to the ground, the blade and parasol still clutched in her now trembling hands. A sob shuddered through her body and she began to cry, the tears drawing lines down her dust strewn face. She'd had to kill people before, mostly during her time working in France as an SOE agent, but this was the first time since she'd joined the Light. After a minute or so she pulled herself together, slid her blade back into its parasol handle and wiped the tears from her cheeks with the hem of her dress. This was her job, she was expected to do whatever it took to stop the enemy, the mission was bigger and more important than the life of one man. She stood up and looked down at the body of the enemy agent.

"Now I'm going to have to do something with you so you're not found, you stupid man. People will start to ask questions, and we can't have that."

# XXXIV.

Gertie was sitting on the edge of her bed in Kitty's apartment, the canvas backpack lying next to her, stuffed and zipped ready to go. On the dining table in the living room sat the letter to Kitty. Now she just had to wait and hope everything fell into place. She'd occupied herself with tidying and sorting the apartment, running over the plan again and again to make sure everything was committed to memory. George had said that the storm was due to happen near the end of the day on Z49,262 but couldn't say when that would be exactly. All she could do now was hope that the storm didn't arrive before the bell sounded that announced the end of the working day. It wouldn't be terrible if it did, it would just mean she'd have to find a hidehole somewhere en-route and hope that she wasn't discovered in the meantime.

Everything was so quiet in the apartment, and all she could hear was her own breathing, load and fast.

"Keep it together, old girl." said the voice of her dad echoing through her head. She took deep breaths to calm herself down. "Won't be long now."

Just when she thought she would burst, the 'Bing bong' noise came through the speaker in the hall. The day cycle had ended at last, thankfully before the storm appeared. All she had to do now was hope that the storm would break soon. Thankfully she didn't have to wait long. Almost as if it was holding out for the day cycle to end and everyone to return to their homes and retire for the day, the telltale signs of the storm began to appear. As she looked out of the window of her bedroom, Gertie saw the clouds begin to gather and the light levels begin to drop.

She lifted her wrist to look at the thin black tracking bracelet Kitty had given her previously. She'd asked Bobbie if it was possible to take it off, coming up with the excuse that it sometimes felt funny to keep it on when she needed to wash. Bobbie wasn't particularly happy about it, but eventually explained how, making Gertie promise to put it straight back on again after she'd finished washing. She tapped on the bracelet three times at the spot where Bobbie had told her to and it dropped in two separate halves into her lap. She picked the pieces up and let them come back together again to form a single loop, then quickly stood and walked over to her bedside table and laid it down next to the mobile device that was already there.

This was it, it was now or never. She turned on her heels and, scooping up the backpack off the bed, she walked quickly out of her bedroom, through the hallway and out the door of the apartment. Outside the storm was just getting going so she took the stairs two at a time, reaching the front door to the street in seconds. She could now hear the first drops of rain strike the pavement outside through the door. Looping her arm through the strap of the backpack she settled it properly on her back and tugged at the straps to make it firm. Then she pulled open the entry door and sprinted out into the rain. She needed to make it the three streets to the subway entrance without getting caught in the coming deluge. At least she was certain that everyone else in the Æther would be sheltering and hidden away so wouldn't run into anyone. As the rain began to hit her she was surprised by its warmth, Bobbie was right, it was exactly the same temperature as the shower. She was an accomplished runner at her school sports days, so could sprint very quickly but was still out of breath, and already quite wet, by the time she made it to the steps down into the subway entrance, just as the clouds opened and the heavens began to fall.

Gertie hit the bottom of the stairway flying and slipped on the water already accumulated there from the rain, almost losing her balance. She jumped up onto the ticket barrier and slid herself across it, swinging her legs over the rotating bar so she didn't trigger any of the sensors that tracked entry and exit into the transit system. She'd made it this far without incident so stopped and took a breath. If there had been anyone around to see her it would have looked to them like the steam from the warm rain coming off her body and clothes formed a hazy cloud around her. She slowed her breathing, and after a few beats started slowly across the hall towards the stairs down to the platform. At the top of the stairs she stopped and bent down to see if she could see anyone below. Finally, convinced she would be alone, she walked gently down the stairs, making as little noise as possible and entered the platform. She looked around and then, turning right, walked quickly to the rear of the room and hid behind one of the upright, tile clad pillars that dotted its length.

After a few minutes she felt the strange sucking of air and deadening of noise that pre-empted the arrival of the train, and sure enough, 30 seconds later it appeared out of the tunnel next to her. The train slowed quickly and smoothly to a stop and its doors opened. As Gertie had hoped, no one exited the train. Everyone but the designated night staff, none of whom would be using this station anyway, was already home and going to bed, if not already there. Still she waited in her pillared hiding spot until finally the "beep, beep, beep" of the door alarms warning passengers of their closing in 20 seconds, echoed along the platform. Gertie broke cover and headed for the doors of the end carriage of the train, just making it through into the train's interior as the doors closed, narrowly missing her backpack. With a quick glance along the length of the train, she crouched down behind the first set of benched seating facing the doorway.

From this position she could see underneath the seats for the entire length of the train, and noted that the lack of visible legs meant she was alone in the carriage, just as she had planned. She relaxed and closed her eyes for a moment as the train moved away from the station. In her head, she started the countdown of the six stops she would need to travel before having to switch trains to another line. She opened her eyes again and watched as the graffiti that covered the walls of the train caught the blurred lights outside the windows travelling in arcs as they passed.

# XXXV.

Kitty collapsed on the bed in her room at Mena House, exhausted. It had taken her nearly two hours to first find a suitable hiding place for the body of the Obscurus agent, then manoeuvre him into it and cover the whole thing up. She was amazed that she hadn't been discovered doing it, but it was now done. Hopefully the body wouldn't be found for many years after she had eventually returned to the Æther. She had no idea what ending the life of the enemy agent would do to the time stream, she hoped this still counted as a ripple, too late to do anything now she supposed.

In an hour's time she would need to be ready to continue her mission and introduce herself to the Mertons at dinner, but for now she could rest after her ordeal. As she lay on the bed she thought once more of Gertie. She hoped that Virgil had managed to make some progress into locking on to Gertie's mystery gate. She would be very sorry to see her go, she'd gotten very used to having her around, but Gertie was very young and needed to be with her family. Kitty decided to make it her next mission to get Gertie back where she belonged, even if that meant travelling to an adjacent gate and making their way from there. If they could get to the Grand Picture House before the time Gertie had opened the gate, then she could sneak back in moments after she had originally left and no one would be the wiser. It would, of course, be preferable to use the original gate, especially as once it had been identified it could be locked out and prevent Gertie from just coming straight back to the Æther again. And of stopping more potential accidents such as the original one that misdirected Kitty in the first place from happening, naturally. It hurt to think of never seeing Gertie again, but it was in the girl's best interests. It wasn't the place for a young girl to be mixed up in the life of a special agent, there was always the chance that one day something could go wrong and Kitty wouldn't return from a mission. Gertie had already lost her mother, Kitty didn't want her to lose anyone else.

When it was time, Kitty got herself up off the bed with only a small amount of wincing and groaning and made her way across to the wash basin to clean herself up ready for her evening's work. After washing she redid her makeup, reset her hair and put on a lace front silk dress with draped side panels and a floral embroidered belt, heeled shoes and silk stockings. Satisfied with her look, she left the room and made her way downstairs to the large dining hall, hoping to spot Mr. and Mrs. Merton.

∗    ∗    ∗    ∗

The dining hall consisted of two high ceilinged rooms, elaborately decorated in the Moorish style with several vast horseshoe arches in two-tone brickwork allowing passage between the rooms. The larger of these rooms held three long tables which stretched its entire length, each surrounded by seating enough for all the hotel's guests. The smaller room, which Kitty headed towards, was focused on more intimate dining around circular tables reserved for parties of the hotel's wealthier clientele. This is where she believed the Mertons would be dining, and after a quick scan of the room spotted them at a table next to the room's impressive looking fireplace.

Kitty made a particular show of coyly looking around the room as if to find someone she might know, standing on tiptoe to look over the seated diners' heads. After a few scans she slumped visibly with a look of disappointment on her face. As she hoped Mrs. Merton had spotted her plight and waved at her, beckoning her to their table. Kitty made a point of mouthing "Who, me?" at the lady, laying a palm at her breast and, when Mrs. Merton nodded, walked quickly over to their table.

"Is everything okay my dear?" asked Mrs. Merton in her over pronunciated upper-class British accent. "You look a trifle lost."

Mrs. Merton was a short, kind looking woman in her mid-forties. As with all women her age she was dressed in a very stiff and formal manner of those who had grown up through, first the Victorian era, then the reign of Edward VII. Her fine cotton dress ran from collar to ankles and all the way down the length of her arms, so that only her head and hands were to be seen. Sat next to her was a more serious looking man, with a heavy moustache and bald pate, dressed in out-of-fashion black formal evening dress of stiff upright collar and white tie. Her mark, Mr. Arthur Merton.

Quite apart from their dated dress-sense, the couple also sported the unfashionable tanned skin of those whose vocation is to spend long periods in hot countries.

"I am rather, yes." said Kitty, emphasising her well-to-do mid-Atlantic accent. "I'm travelling alone you see, and hoped I might spot someone whom I knew so I could dine with them."

"Well, you are more than welcome to join us, if you'd like? And we won't mind a jot if you do eventually spot someone and wish to leave us. We've spent enough time dining here to worry much about standing on ceremony. Isn't that right Arthur?" Mrs. Merton turned to her husband, who looked up at Kitty for the first time.

"What? Oh, yes, erm...absolutely. No problem at all. Please, join us." Merton gestured to a seat across the table from him. Kitty nodded and sat down, placing her beaded purse on the table in front of her.

"American, eh?" He continued, "What brings you across the pond to this Godforsaken place?"

Kitty laughed politely and answered, "I was fortunate enough to come into some money and thought I'd see a bit of the world, before it all gets destroyed by silly wars and the like."

"Yes, quite. Awful business. I hope you didn't lose anyone? I know so many boys didn't make it back" replied Mrs. Merton kindly.

"Only an older cousin. My brothers were too young to be called up, fortunately. You?"

"No. We have never been blessed with children, which in a way spared us the pain and anguish of seeing them have to go to war. It was bad enough that Arthur had to be there for work."

"Oh, and what is it you do then Mr...?" asked Kitty.

"Merton." replied Arthur, "I work for The Times. Overseas correspondent. Not as exciting as it sounds, to be brutally honest."

"Gosh, I think that sounds very interesting. Here I am going on about seeing the world and you've probably already done so." Kitty leant forward, her elbows on the table and her face cupped into her hands.

"Not really, just lots of mud and trenches in France, followed by sand and trenches in the Suez. That's how I ended up here. Bit of an affinity with the natives."

"Yes, I imagine you've been quite busy with all the troubles going on here. Still, hopefully that might come to an end now that an agreement has been reached?" asked Kitty, sitting back in her chair again.

"Not bloody likely" Merton replied grumpily.

Thankfully Kitty was saved from having to come up with a way out of the subject by a waiter appearing at the table enquiring about drinks. She ordered her customary Sidecar whilst the Mertons' ordered wine for the table. Seeing her husband's mood descend Mrs. Merton changed the subject swiftly and asked Kitty:

"Have you seen much of Egypt yet, dear?"

"Oh, yes. I took a trip along the Nile on a paddle boat and spent some time around Luxor, visiting all the astonishing temples and tombs they've uncovered. I was lucky enough to meet a chap there who thinks he might have uncovered something rather interesting in the Valley of the Kings."

"Really? I thought that place was tapped out?" replied Merton, his interest piqued.

"Apparently not. According to this chap Carter he thinks he might have uncovered some forgotten Pharaoh or some such. Says the find had been completely overlooked."

Just then the drinks arrived and Kitty sat sipping at her Sidecar as she watched Arthur Merton deep in thought.

"Not *Howard* Carter surely? Used to work for The Antiquities Service as Inspector of Monuments? Last I'd heard he was digging for trinkets on Lord Carnarvon's concession?" said Merton suddenly with an astonished look on his face.

"Yes, that's the chap. Seemed very excited. Said he might have found a completely untouched tomb buried under a pile of rubble from a nearby dig." replied Kitty brightly.

"But, that's astonishing." said Merton, clearly flummoxed.

"Quite", replied Kitty, knowingly "Perhaps it might be worth popping over there and seeing what all the fuss is about, considering your profession Mr. Merton?

"Yes...yes indeed. I might just do that." said Merton distractedly. Kitty could almost imagine the cogs whirring in his brain, as he thought it all though. "If he really has found something extraordinary it could be an exciting thing to write about."

"It certainly would Mr. Merton and, if it turns out to be newsworthy, you'd end up being the 'man on the ground' so to speak." replied Kitty subtly.

With the seed of the idea firmly planted in Arthur Merton's brain Kitty now felt she could make her exit. Finishing her drink she turned to look across into the larger room, and feigned recognition of someone standing the other side of its archway. She beamed a smile and waved at no one in particular.

"I've just seen a friend come in, would you mind awfully if I go and see them?"

Without waiting for a reply, Kitty stood up.

"It's been a delight meeting you both, and thank you so much for letting me sit with you. I don't know what I would have done if you hadn't rescued me. Good luck with Mr. Carter, I look forward to reading all about it in The Times Mr. Merton."

With that Kitty was gone and walking off through the archway leaving the Mertons with a look of surprise and confusion on their faces.

# XXXVI.

*Z49,262*

Gertie had to change lines three times before reaching her final stop on the transit system. Each time she took pains to wait until the last second before exiting the carriage, heading for the nearest cover as she did. Then pushing deep into each station platform and waiting until the warning noise before plunging into the next carriage. As she'd planned she came across no other person on the trains, not even the sounds of other human beings anywhere she travelled.

The last train she boarded was a little different to all the others. It consisted of a series of single, bullet shaped cars on rails, with sliding glass-domed roofs and only two passenger seats in each. She'd asked Virgil about it when she'd first come across them as she vaguely remembered seeing it in a science fiction film on TV once. He'd gotten very excited and said it was from the film Logan's Run, in 1976, an "Absolute classic!" as he'd described it and then gone a bit glassy eyed for some reason. She'd entered this last section through a brightly lit corridor onto the platform which was unlike all the others she'd been on. It was a completely white room with strange cut-out curved walls. Both the floor and ceiling were painted the same shiny white as the walls which were interspersed with glowing panels with lights inside. In the centre of the ceiling was a huge crystal shaped light fixture and dotted around the platform

191

were plastic potted plants. It was one of the strangest rooms Gertie had been into in the Æther, almost as strange as the bedroom she'd woken up in when she'd arrived. It was rather more like a hotel foyer than a train platform.

Having made sure there was no one on the train, she quickly headed to the last carriage. As she sat in the seat the glass roof slid forward to enclose her and the train started moving. It headed into a semi-circular tunnel which was clad in shiny silver, interspersed with the same light panels as the platform. As the train moved rapidly through it the silver walls acted like a mirror reflecting the carriage and Gertie within it multiple times. It was hurting her head so she closed her eyes and settled into the comfortable black leather seat for the short ride which would take her to the main administration buildings.

After what seemed like only a minute or two the train started to slow and came to a standstill next to a rather more rundown version of the previous platform. This time everything was dull and dirty, the walls were square not curved, and there were no plants to be seen. On one wall was a sign made up of single letters, some of which had fallen off at some point leaving only the ghost of its shape, spelling out the words "Cathedral Plaza" in block capitals. At the rear of the platform stood a large door perforated with huge holes. Gertie got out of the train car and as she walked towards the door it slid open, revealing a dimly lit corridor beyond. She moved off cautiously down the corridor, listening for signs of any other people moving around, but could hear no one.

After a hundred yards or so the corridor ended in a left turn. As she reached the turn she saw that she would have to pass through a strange brightly lit section, which was like a square with curved edges. The section was covered in mirrors and had a series of strips of white neon lights running all the way up each wall, over the ceiling and down the other side, leaving a gap through which to walk on the floor. As she walked through the mirrored passage she entered a double-height room painted black with a shiny black floor. Along each of the walls were panels of lights, occasionally turning on and off, giving the impression of fields of stars twinkling in the night sky. Above these at a sloped angle were four panels made up of squares of lights in blue, yellow, green and red. Each had a circle in the centre and made Gertie think of huge eyes looking down at her. The shiny floor made her shoes squeak as she walked so she walked as quickly as she could to the other side.

Through the set of double doors at the end of the room she found herself in a white corridor lined with doors to other rooms, like those of a hotel. Along the length of the corridor ran a brown carpet with orange interlocking hexagons with smaller red hexagons inside each larger one. The exit she needed was at the very end of this corridor where it widened and turned on itself. At the turn was a set of double doors, with an emergency "Exit" sign above them. Gertie already knew that these doors led into the warehouse-like room she'd come across when she'd first arrived, with all the stairs and platforms and tall white pillars. She was getting closer to her goal.

Carefully negotiating the platforms she found the set of stairs leading upwards to the room with the stadium seating and warship coming out of the wall. Beyond this room lay the gate prep room in the Glass House and beyond the gate room itself. She ducked behind the end of the block of seating and listened. When she was satisfied that no one was around she slid around the end of the seats and walked sideways along the length of the seating. From the end of the row she could see the open doors leading into the Glass House. It was now time to be bold, she needed to walk into the gate area looking like she was going there for a reason just in case someone happened to be present. If someone was there she'd come up with the excuse that she wanted to check when Kitty was coming back, as she was getting lonely without her. If the area was empty, as she had planned it to be, then the plan was still on.

She stopped, took a few deep breaths, stood up straight and broke cover, heading directly for the doors at a normal pace. She walked into the Glass House and called out:

"Hello? Anyone there?"

Without waiting for an answer she continued towards the gate room without breaking her stride. So far there was no answer, but perhaps the gate room was still staffed and they hadn't heard her. As she reached the gate room door, she stopped and called out again:

"Hello?"

Again no reply came. She quickly turned around, walked back through the anteroom and scanned the Glass

House prep room for anyone hidden away, ducking and weaving between the rows of clothes rails. She was fairly sure no one was home, but you can never be too careful. Satisfied, she walked back into the anteroom, swung the backpack off her shoulders, unzipped it and pulled out the set of clothes she'd originally arrived in before dropping it onto the floor. She quickly stripped off the clothes she was wearing and changed into her original set. She paused to feel the texture of the polo shirt on her cheek as she put it on, remembering its touch and the sentimentality wrapped in it. Once she was done, she neatly folded up the other set of clothes and left it on the chaise longue. She grabbed the notepad from the backpack, zipped it up and put it back on before heading swiftly back to the gate room and sliding the door closed behind her.

Once the door was secured she shifted into overdrive. She headed over to the centre of the gate room, approaching the large projector that dominated the space there and placed her finger on the touch screen that controlled it. The projector powered to life and the room was suddenly filled with a soft, purple-tinged light. Quickly consulting her notepad, she followed the sequence she'd pieced together and noted down, from each of her visits. Each nugget of instruction gleaned from the various technicians she'd quizzed and then jotted down from memory as soon as she was out of sight. She quickly found the index of gates and clicked on the magnifying glass icon to bring up the search function. Typing in the words Uckfield and the number 84, she was pleased to see only 4 gate events showed up.

Selecting the one marked: "Picture House, 12.08.84, 19:00, Alice Smallwood", she was overjoyed by the sounds of the projectors computer controlled filter mechanisms whirring into action. Her heart was beating so hard now it felt like it was going to burst up out of her mouth. A large pulsating button appeared on the screen labelled "Engage". This was it, no going back now.

She swung the bag off her shoulder and tucked the notebook back in through the zip before putting it back on again. She walked back to the projector, tightened the straps on her backpack so it was secure, took a deep breath and clicked the button. She waited whilst the light on the screen intensified and changed hue almost imperceptibly. She could just about make out reversed out moving images on the screen at the end of the room. Finally after what seemed like a lifetime, as she waited with her breath held, the touch screen changed to show a large green "active" marker. She exhaled dramatically, and with a purposeful stride walked swiftly towards the screen and was gone.

# XXXVII.

*1st December, 1922*

Kitty was sitting on the terrace at the Mena House reading the day's copy of The Egyptian Gazette, the go-to English language newspaper for world news. After flipping through page after page, she finally came across the article she'd hoped to find. Entitled "Sensational Discovery at Thebes", the story described how "In a message from 'The Times' of London's Cairo correspondent we hear of a remarkable archaeological discovery in the Valley of the Kings". It went on to quote Mr. Merton's original article as follows: "On Wednesday afternoon Lord Carnarvon and Mr. Howard Carter revealed to a large company what promises to be the most sensational Egyptological discovery of the century."

She folded the newspaper up, placed it down on the table in front of her and allowed a satisfied smirk to cross her lips. Clearly Mr. Merton had managed to befriend Mr. Carter just as she had hoped. Now she had to trust they would be resolute in that relationship going forward and let nothing coerce or break their bond. There was nothing more she could do now, she'd done her job in getting the world's spotlight on the discovery. There was no chance the Obscurus could cover it up and take over. She was certain they would still try but had faith in Mr. Carter that he would hold on tightly to this career defining moment, with the help of Mr. Merton and the press of course. She'd managed to take care of that pesky Obscurus agent as well, so her cover was still intact. She could only hope that his disappearance didn't have any adverse effects.

She reached for her cup to finish the last drop of her coffee and then stood up. It was time to go home.

*     *     *     *

She exited the gate in the Æther to pandemonium, and for a second thought she'd seriously screwed things up by taking out the Obscurus agent. Then Bobbie came striding over to her.

"Your little tweety pie's really gone and done it this time!" she told Kitty, grabbing her luggage from her.

"Do you mean Gertie?! What happened?"

"She gone flown the coop, girl", explained Bobbie.

"What?! How?"

"Oh she's a clever one alright, played us all like a deck o' cards. Come along now, the bosses want a word."

Bobbie motioned towards a group standing in the centre of the room and Kitty saw Director Earhart, Section Officer Foster and several other members of Real World Operations looking puzzled as Virgil tried to explain something to them. She and Bobbie made their way over.

"Ah, Valentine. Good of you to finally join us", intoned Office Foster. She'd never gotten out of the habit of calling Kitty by her old SEO codename. "Seems your little protégé has given us something of a problem."

"Could be catastrophic in proportion", added Director Earhart.

Kitty looked between the Director, Foster and Bobbie with a confused look on her face.

"Sorry, I don't understand. What's Gertie done?"

"If I may?" asked Bobbie looking at the others for permission to continue. Director Earhart nodded. "It seems that whilst you've been back in the World on 'mission', your girl has taken it upon herself to come up with a little mission of her own."

This did nothing to remove the look of confusion on Kitty's face.

"Seems she's been playing super spy and learned all our tricks and trades without us even realisin'. Slipped her tracker off then used a big ol' storm to cover her tracks as she made her way here during the night shift. Then figured out how to get this contraption on and working. Disappeared through it back to the World", explained Bobbie.

"Can't we just follow her? Get her back before she does anything stupid?"

"Don't you think we've already thought of that, Simpson!?" said Director Earhart, angrily.

"We found out where she's travelled too, but for some reason or other, that Mr. Genius here can't fathom, we don't seem to be able to get a lock on it. Like the gate's offline for some reason. We also had your scheduled return to deal with, which has slowed us down."

"Seems our little anomaly is now AWOL, Valentine" added Officer Foster, "We need to get her back or neutralise her before she causes any permanent damage."

"Not sure it need come to all that Adelaide, dear." Director Earhart put in, rather more kindly than before. "But we do need to find her, Agent Simpson. She's an untrained minor who knows too many of our secrets. She's loose back in the World and out of step with her own timeline. It could be catastrophic."

Kitty stood for a minute, processing everything she'd just heard. Finally she turned to Director Earhart.

"I think I've got an idea of what she might be planning. If you'll indulge me, I'll see if I can fix this."

The Director nodded. "I hope so, Simpson. I hope so"

"Right, the first thing I need to do is change out of these ridiculous clothes." With that she strode towards the Glass House with Bobbie in tow carrying her luggage.

# XXXVIII.

Gertie leapt down from the raised screen and pelted across to the side door as soon as she was through the gate. This was the cinema she grew up watching films at, she knew the layout better than her own house. She knew that the side exit led directly to the street as this is the way everyone left the theatre after each film ended. She'd been through this door so many times, she was able to just run without thinking. With any luck the technician operating the gate wouldn't even know she'd come through. She was moving so fast and was too busy concentrating on the emergency exit sign ahead of her to notice that all the lights had gone out and the gate had shut the moment she'd come through.

In moments she was out on the street, the exit doors flapping shut behind her. She negotiated the steps down to the street, turned sharply right and ran full pelt down the road towards the path that ran past the library building at the top of Luxford Field. It was a warm summer night and only just getting dark and she needed to find a hiding spot as soon as she could and wait it out until dusk. The street lights were flickering into life around her as she ran along the path and into the car park without stopping. She barely made the corner out of the pedestrian entrance to the car park into Belmont Road as she banked sharply to the right, almost colliding with the concrete bollards. She continued sprinting past the doctor's house and across the road then through the entrance into the graveyard at Holy Cross. Only then did she slow her pace. Evensong had just finished and she didn't want to run headlong into anyone who came out of the church. Walking at a slightly faster than normal pace she headed to the back of the church and into the rear graveyard. At the entrance to this graveyard next to the road was a wooden porch which her dad had told her was called a lychgate, and had been there since the Middle-Ages. It was essentially a tiny timber frame house with a tiled pitched roof, but where the walls, windows and doors hadn't yet been finished. It did however have two built-in benches running only each side between its two  doorways and she slumped down onto one of these when she reached it, finally, utterly exhausted. This was a good enough place to hide for now, it had views of both the road both ways and the graveyard behind. If anyone came for her, she'd be able to bolt the other way. She'd often used this area as a cut through on her way to primary school, and there were a mass of alleyways, or "twittens" as they were known, she could duck down and lose people in. All of a sudden all the nervous energy and adrenaline that she had built up all day was released and she started to shake uncontrollably. She pulled her legs up to her chest and curled up small on the bench, closing her eyes.

When she opened them again it was pitch black. She must have fallen asleep. "Oh you idiot Gertie!" she thought to herself. Rubbing her face she uncurled stiffly. The ache of the day's physical strain was acute and painful. She stood up somewhat awkwardly and started back towards the church.

Her plan was to sneak in through the back door and find the blanket box in the vestry that she knew from her brother were kept there for keeping the choir boys warm at winter services. She suddenly had the thought that it might be locked, for some reason she just assumed that churches stayed open all the time. She was sure she had heard her dad say something about churches offering "sanctuary for weary travellers", but on the other hand there was a lot of stuff in there that could be stolen. She had no idea how long she'd been out but, stopping to listen, she could hear no sounds of people around her.

She reached for the rusted ring handle on the back door and tensed her body hoping that it wasn't locked. It turned and she heard the latch come up on the other side. She pushed but the door was heavy oak and she was still weak from her day's work. Putting her shoulder to the door she leant all her weight against it and was rewarded by it swinging open almost too quickly. She dug her heels in to stop it swinging wide but not quick enough before it caught on the uneven stone floor and made a loud high pitched squeak like fingers on a blackboard, and stopped dead in its tracks. She froze, listening for any response to the noise. She waited, rooted to the spot, for over a minute before gently letting go of the door handle and tiptoeing towards the archway into the vestry. She could just see through into the main part of the church from here. The doors through to the entrance porch were open and a sudden moment caught her eye. An old grey haired man was carrying stacks of books and piling them up on the table next to the doors. Must be a caretaker tidying up after Evensong, that would explain why the door was still open she thought. She remembered seeing him here before and was pretty sure he was deaf as a post.

She'd never really liked churches. They always felt cold and smelled damp. They had never filled her with joy or happiness which is what she had been told churches were supposed to do. The last time she had been here was the day of her mother's funeral. They weren't a particularly religious family, but in a small town like this, everything revolves around the church. Christenings, carol services, marriages, funerals, you name it. It all happened here. She'd hated being here that day. She had just sat in silence, staring at the floor, waiting for it to be over. It was funny to think that all that was still to happen here, that in just over a month her younger self would be sitting in one of those pews wishing she was anywhere else in the world.

She shook herself out of her reverie and turned to the large wooden box against the left hand wall of the vestry. Carefully lifting the lid she was pleased to find a neat stack of thick woollen blankets waiting for her. Selecting a dark tartan one from near the top of the stack, she gently closed the lid again. Tucking the blanket under her arm, she peeked through the archway into the church to make sure she hadn't been rumbled, then retraced her steps to the door back outside. Carefully lifting the door upwards so it didn't make the horrible scraping noise, she gently swung it closed behind her as she walked backwards into the night. She let go of the handle after the latch had caught again and breathed a huge sigh of relief. She quickly stuffed the blanket into her backpack and set off down the path out of the church grounds. Even though it was now dark, she needed to be vigilant in case anyone was out looking for her. Between the exit out of the church and the top of the road she was heading for went past the car park she'd walked across before and she felt that was too dangerously close to the cinema for her liking. Summoning all her will, she broke into a run back along the road, past the doctor's house and down the right hand fork into the small road that ran behind the Rocks Park estate.

The road was dark and overgrown and had no street lights. This was definitely not a place she would normally walk along at night. She remembered vividly walking this way back from school when a boy disturbed a wasp's nest in one of the trees and was stung repeatedly all over his body. She shuddered just thinking about it. She got her head down and walked on. At the end of the road there was an old Sussex Oast house that she had always dreamed of living in one day. At this point the road narrowed and turned into more of a path and beyond this was a large plot of allotments and the main road beyond. Due to the fact that she really didn't know anything at all about vegetables and how they grow, Gertie had never understood allotments. To her they always looked abandoned and overgrown. They always seemed to have collapsed weather beaten sheds, or busted up greenhouses, and the plants looked like a wild and untamed mass of vegetation. They were also seriously spooky places to walk past at night time. She made her way along the path at the top of the plots at an urgent trot until she reached the other end.

The other side of the plot of allotments was one of the main roads in and out of town, so she needed to be super cautious. It wasn't good for a girl her age to be out this late, and if she was spotted by a passing driver they might report her at the police station up the road. Thankfully, if she timed it right, she'd just need to get across this road and she could lose herself in the imposing buildings of the industrial estate on the other side. Concealing herself between the fence at the side of the allotment and the tree line, she pulled the blanket out of her backpack and draped it over her head like a headscarf. From here she could see a long way down the road ahead in both directions. She waited for what seemed like a lifetime until she could see no sign of headlights coming either way, and made a break for it. On the other side, she kept her pace up and, passing the Uckfield Club building on her right, headed for the back of the old Playhouse Theatre, now occupied by J. Picard & Co. seed merchants. She was finally almost in sight of her final destination.

Now was the tricky part. She needed to somehow navigate around the side of the building site that sat between herself and the high street beyond to where Bridge Cottage stood. In her day, Bridge Cottage had undergone restoration and turned into a museum open to the public, but at this time in 1984 it was still derelict, only having been saved from demolition the previous year. She'd be safe to hide out there for the next few days, which was all she would need. The trouble was, because it was at the end of the high street she couldn't risk being spotted by passersby. Worse still any of the local bobbies that patrolled the high street at night, looking for vandals or hassling gangs of youths hanging out in the park or by the Barclays up the road. This meant she'd have to somehow get in to it from the back. She walked into the car park behind the seed merchants, and up to the large wooden fence that surrounded the building site. Pushing through the bushes so was right against the fence she stopped to let her eyes adjust to the gloom and then followed it around to the western end which ran down towards the River Uck. The area around the rear of the fence was very overgrown and in the dark even having the blanket over her head didn't protect her from the bramble bushes. Several times she got caught up and at one point received a sharp scrape across her cheek when she managed to free herself. Just before the fence turned a corner and the ground fell away towards the river below, she came across a small clearing, and found that several fence panels had been loosened and pulled to one side. Clearly some enterprising local boys had managed to get along the river bank and up to the fence, jimmying the panels open so they could muck about in the site at the weekends. She took off her backpack, squeezed herself through the gap and pulled it through behind her. She could just make out the shape of the cottage ahead of her, so she scrambled up and over piles of rubble and around the stacks of building materials until she reached the line of bushes at the back of the building.

Bridge Cottage had sat on this plot since it was built in the late middle-ages and was, at the time of its construction, considered a large and luxurious house for a wealthy landowner. By modern standards though it was more like a quaint and poky little hovel. The doors and windows were barely the same height as Gertie and she remembered having to duck to get through the front door. It used to be a family home (in fact at one point two families) up until the late sixties when it was finally abandoned to rot. It currently looked very different to how Gertie remembered it, and could easily be confused for a modern home. In 1987 it looked very much like a Tudor building with wooden windows and black and white zebra stripe beams, but right now it still had glazed leaded windows (albeit broken and dirty) and was covered in wooden weatherboards. The rear portion of the roof where she was now was tiled all the way down to the first floor over the top of an extended lean-to and there was a single wooden door into the back of the property which had a rusted latch with a padlock attached to it. She searched around her to find something to try and smash it with and eventually found a half brick lying a little way off. It took her three or four attempts, but was eventually rewarded with a clatter as the rusted lock hit the floor. She leant her weight against the door and it juddered open by about half a metre then jammed in place. Once again she found herself having to squeeze through a gap, but eventually made it into the house. She had to throw herself against the door to get it shut again and was plunged into darkness as soon as it did.

All she could do was to stand still and wait until her eyes adjusted to the dark. When they did she found herself in a long hallway with several doors leading off it. The floors were bare stone and there were what she hoped were cobwebs everywhere. As she walked cautiously towards the front of the house she discovered a staircase to her left. Assuming this went up to one of the upper bedrooms, she decided that she'd done enough for today and would find somewhere to sleep for the night. Being very careful in case the wooden stairs collapsed she made her way up to the first floor, tensing every time one of the steps creaked under her weight. On the upstairs landing she tried the first door she came across and found herself in what was once a back bedroom, now completely empty with only a threadbare carpet left behind. Mercifully this room's window wasn't broken at all, just very dirty.

Gertie spread the blanket out and using her backpack as a pillow lay down, wrapped herself up and tried her hardest to go to sleep. Full of anguish about the task ahead and frightened of being discovered she imagined that sleep would never come, but exhaustion soon took over and she was asleep in less than a minute.

# XXXIX.

Kitty ducked behind a screen and quickly changed into her standard outfit of loose trousers and a blouse. If she was going to travel to the 1980s she was going to do so properly attired for the job. Thankfully there had been a bit of 1940s revival in the '80s, so the clothes fitted right into her wheelhouse. Whilst she was dressing she shouted out to Bobbie.

"Would you be a dear and grab me some suitable luggage there Bob old thing?"

"Jeez, what did your last servant die of?", Bobbie joked back.

"Talking back!", laughed Kitty.

She spent the next few minutes grabbing various outfits, shoes, boots, a makeup kit, and finally a serious looking two-tone cropped jacket she'd had her eye on for a while. She grabbed a big stack of £1, £5 and £10 notes from the correctly marked drawer in the currency vault, and then headed to the weapons section. Typing in her code into the keypad she unlocked the gun cabinet and selected a small silver 9mm ASP pistol, several clips of ammunition and a leather shoulder rig with holster to carry it all in. She also grabbed an U.S. Army medical kit and small combat knife. When Bobbie saw the gear going into Kitty's travel bag she exclaimed:

210

"Damn Kitty girl! And there was me thinkin' this was a rescue mission", Bobbie laughed. "You expecting some trouble?"

"It always pays to be prepared, darling. You never know what you could be up against", Kitty retorted.

"Just make sure you don't get caught holdin' that heat. This is England we're talkin'. Ain't the same as back in the states. Carryin' a shooter will get you arrested quicker than being black at a student rally!"

"Ah, so that's how you ended up here is it?" joked Kitty

"You know it ain't you crazy ol' coot. Now shift them buns, time's a tickin'"

Kitty dropped everything into her holdall, zipped it up and strode back into the anteroom to where Director Earhart and Officer Foster were waiting.

"The good news is we've found you a workable exit, Agent Simpson. It's going to involve some travel and a very tight timetable but it's as close as we can get you to Gertie's last known point", said Director Earhart. "You'll have to brief our operatives on the other side as soon as you get there, but their standard mandate is to help any agents travelling via the gate system. You should be fine."

"Thank you Director. I just hope I'm able to get there in time."

"What's she planning to do, Valentine?", asked Officer Foster.

"I think she's going to try and divert the time stream. Make it so she never got stuck here in the first place. Change her own future… but she has no idea of what that will do, what it will cost her. I'm not even sure it would work, certainly not the way she thinks it might."

"It's vital that we stop her then. Damn girl. Too clever for her own good", said Foster, shaking her head.

"Quite. Well, your mission is approved Agent Simpson. Best get to it. Virgil has everything prepped for you in the gate room. Godspeed", added Director Earhart.

With that Kitty nodded to the Director and her Section Officer and walked swiftly into the gate room where Virgil was waiting by the projector terminal.

"Apologies Agent Simpson", said Virgil as soon as he saw Kitty. "I can't help but think this is my fault. She just kept asking me questions about stuff, I just had to keep answering. You know how I get when people actually buy into my geek trips."

"Not to worry Virgil. She's a very bright and cunning young lady. Sounds like she played us all a little. Even waited until I was out in the World", replied Kitty kindly. "Anyway, we must move on. What do you have for me?"

"First off, here's as much information as we could gather from the computer records about Gertie's family, including all known addresses." Virgil said, handing a manila envelope to Kitty. He waited whilst she slipped this into the top of her holdall. "As we can't seem to access the same gate that she used, the closest one we could find is about 20 miles away in Burgess Hill. But we can't get you there until a week later."

"That should be fine. It still gives me a few days to gather intel and hopefully get to her before anything happens. If she's trying to do what I think she's trying to do, that is." Kitty looked at the monitor on the projector. The entry on screen was under Burgess Hill and was marked: "Orion, 19.08.84, 20:00, Lucy Preston".

"Right. Let's get this show on the road. Dial up the gate please Virgil", asked Kitty, a determined look spread across her face.

As Virgil navigated the controls she heard the gate filters whir into place.

"Ready when you are, Agent Simpson."

Kitty nodded at Virgil and turned towards the gate as the light in the room changed to a brighter and deeper tone. She breathed deeply and walked towards the gate, just as she had done many times in the past. This one felt a little different however. This one gave her butterflies and made her feel a little sick. This one felt more important than any of the others. Kitty reached the event horizon of the gate and disappeared through it.

# XL.

Gertie woke with a start to the sounds of cars and people outside. She looked around the room bleary eyed, forgetting for a moment where she was. The events of the previous day came flooding back and she closed her eyes again tightly. Her body ached all over from the exertion and adrenaline she'd been putting it through. She opened her eyes and looked at the watch Kitty had given her, the only thing she'd brought with her from her life in the Æther. She hadn't been able to bear the thought of leaving it behind. The time was now 8.10am. As it was a Monday in the school holidays she figured it would be okay to leave her hiding spot in a little while, as long as she avoided anywhere her or her friends would normally be hanging out she should be okay. She'd also planned to use some of the money she'd lifted from the Glass House prep room earlier in the week to buy some food from the Gateway supermarket across the road. But that was all later, right now her stomach started to grumble reminding her that it had been hours since she had last eaten anything.

She stood up, dusted herself off and looked around the room for the first time. It was decorated in the style of the early sixties, with patterned yellowing wallpaper and what Gertie instantly recognised as the same horrible brown carpet her aunt still had in her living room. The paper was peeling off in places and in one corner of the room the wall was crumbling so you could see the wooden lathes underneath the plaster. It was pretty hideous as bedrooms go, but it would do Gertie for now. At least it was at the back of the house and she wouldn't be spotted from the High Street. She picked up her backpack and headed out into the landing. This was in much the same state as the bedroom, but someone had taken up the carpet so the floorboards showed. She slowly made her way down the stairs into the hallway. At one end was a big oak door that led to the garden in front of the house facing the High Street. At the other was the door she'd come in through last night. Like upstairs this floor had two doorways leading off the hall. She guessed that the door closest to the front door led into the living room, or front room...whatever the family used to use it for. So she chose the other door and was pleased to come out into a small passage with an indoor toilet on one side and around to the right a small kitchen. She headed into the kitchen and propped her bag up on the Formica top of the unit next to the sink. She pulled out the supplies she'd managed to sneak out of the stores in the Æther and arranged them on the draining board. Then she hopped up onto the counter and pulled open the bag marked Chocolate Chip Brioche Rolls with the strange French sounding manufacturer. It didn't matter where and when these things came from Gertie thought they were delicious and ate three in quick succession.

Curious, she leant over and tried turning the tap on and was surprised when it spluttered and coughed but then produced running water. The water was a bit dirty at first, but after it ran for a little while it became clear. She tried a little. It was very cold and tasted a little bit metallic, but it was better than nothing. She suddenly had an idea and leapt down from the counter top. She walked into the toilet next door, with its awful sunflower wallpaper. It was one of those old fashioned toilets with the cistern high up on the wall, a large down pipe connecting it to the toilet bowl below. The cistern had a chain pull with a wooden handle. She leant over and gave it an experimental tug. The chain came down quickly and went straight back up when she let go. Nothing happened. Then a few seconds later she heard water trickle into the cistern above her. The trickle turned into a gush and then the sounds quietened and stopped. She gave the chain another pull and this time was rewarded with the sound of the toilet flushing. She couldn't believe the water was still on! The sound of the sloshing water suddenly made her want to wee, so she quickly tested that the wooden toilet seat was still attached before sitting down and going. After Gertie returned to the kitchen she opened up a box of something called Twinkies. They turned out to be so sugary and sweet she had to wash the taste down with the last of the water from her canteen bottle. She refilled it from the tap, then repacked her backpack and got ready to head out.

# XLI.

Kitty stepped off the stage of the Orion Cinema and waited for the gate to shut off behind her before calling out.

"Hello operator? Inbound traveller Number 27061138 requesting assistance."

After a moment the main auditorium lights flickered on and a figure came through the door at the top left of the room. She saw Kitty and jumped.

"Oh! Blimey!" She dropped the clipboard she was holding and stood with a look of panic on her face. "Sorry...erm, did you come through the gate?"

"Operative Lucy Preston I presume?" said Kitty rolling her eyes, "Aren't you supposed to ask me something to check my credentials?"

"Oh crumbs, err...yes sorry. Never had to do one of these before. Blimey, had no idea if this would ever actually happen. Right. Bloody hell, erm what's the phrase. Oh yeah. Sorry. Cum tenebrae cadit...."

"Et Erit Lux. When darkness falls, let there be light", replied Kitty with a small bow "Now the formalities are over, let's get on shall we...I really don't have much time. My name is Kitty Simpson. I'm a Special Agent for the Light."

"Lucy. Preston. That's me... I mean, Lucy Preston. Nice to meet you." She reached down and retrieved her clipboard before walking down to meet Kitty in front of the stage.

Lucy Preston was short and stocky. This didn't stop her from trying to dress in the latest fashions of the day, in her case faded baggy blue jeans with Dr. Marten buckle shoes and pop socks. The jeans were held up with a wide leather belt but she also had a pair of blue clip-on braces which sat over the top of the knitted tank top and white t-shirt she had tucked into them. It wasn't a good look in Kitty's opinion and she had absolutely no idea what to make of the girl's hair. It was backcombed into a big bird's nest mess and had green streaks sprayed into it for some reason.

"Charmed I'm sure", said Kitty with a tilt of her head.

"Whatever you need, I'm your girl", said Lucy, her hand flipping up to her forehead in the three-fingered salute of the Girl Guides.

"What I need to do is get to a place called Uckfield as soon as possible. Also I need a library or wherever it is you keep your public records. And I'd kill for a cup of coffee, gate travel really makes me queasy. I'm open to what order those things happen in, all except the coffee, which most assuredly needs to come first."

"Okay. Erm.. yes! I can do that. Think there's some coffee in the staff kitchen...come this way", said Lucy excitedly. She turned and motioned Kitty to follow her back out the door at the back of the auditorium that she'd come out of.

# XLII.

Gertie had spent the last week wandering around Uckfield trying to find the courage to visit her old house. She knew if she did that she could possibly catch a glimpse of her mother, and she wasn't sure she was ready for that.

She'd spent her first full day back in the World visiting some of the spots that she missed since moving away. Her old school, empty now because of the holidays and the swings up at the rec behind the catholic church at the other end of town. She'd even ventured close to her house so she could see the Elephant Rock again, a limestone mound that looked just like an elephant lying down that she used to play with her friends on at the weekends. That evening she'd waited until about 5.30pm, when she knew that her younger self would be back home having dinner, to go across to the supermarket and buy some food. About an hour earlier she'd brought an oversized black felt beret from a charity shop on the high street and was studiously hiding under it in case anyone in the shop recognised her. She realised this was silly because the last time she'd been in the shop was with her mum, when she was about eight years old. She'd had to spend ages working out in her head when that was at this point in time. She'd come to the conclusion that it was a few years ago now, but you could never be too careful. Anyway, people changed a lot in four years, right? She'd received a few strange looks from the checkout ladies as she stuffed all the food into her backpack, so she walked quickly out of the shop back across the road to the industrial estate without looking back. There she hid in the bushes behind the seed house until she was happy it was safe to make her way back across the building site and into her hiding spot at Bridge Cottage.

Feeling like she'd pushed it a little far on the risk front the previous day she then spent the next few hiding out at the cottage, eating, napping and reading the books she'd brought along with the beret from the charity shop. On Sunday she'd crossed the bridge over to the station and walked to the end of the platform and onto the stretch of disused railway line that went towards Lewes. After walking for about an hour along the increasingly overgrown line, she reached a clearing where the river ran close by. This was the perfect spot for a picnic and she spent a few hours, sitting by the river, dozing in the sun, eating sandwiches and drinking lemonade before wandering back towards Uckfield and eventually to her cottage hideout.

The next day was Monday and she remembered that her mum always visited her friends on the other side of town on a Monday morning. Some kind of mother's coffee morning, she couldn't exactly remember who with. So she summoned all her courage and, backpack and beret firmly in place, made her way across the road from the cottage into the car park and onto a footpath that led out of the back. She made her way through quiet streets and alleyways up past her old school, around the shops at Downsview and down into the Nevill estate on the north east of town before finally coming out onto the main road across from Uplands Drive. This stretch of road wasn't as busy as it used to be since they opened the bypass on the other side of town, so she didn't have to wait too long before a break in the traffic. She shot across the road and up the path that ran up to Cambridge Way. Her old house was at the end of this road at the junction with Claremont Rise. As she walked through the wooden stile at the top of the path she remembered the time she and her friend Nicola were stopped by the police about a year from now. She'd been at Nicola's house for dinner and she'd offered to walk her back as far as the stile as it was getting dark. Even though they could practically see each other's front doors from the stile, the police had taken both their names and addresses down "just in case". As she came onto the road she saw her house again for the first time since they'd moved out two years previously in Gertie's past. She stopped dead and a lump formed in her throat. Until this moment she hadn't realised just how much she'd missed the old house. She could see her old bedroom window at the front over the living room, the painted white stable doors on the garage. The tall, neatly trimmed hedge that surrounded the garden she spent so much time playing in when her brother was a baby. Slowly she crossed the road and walked towards the house. As she got close she tucked herself into the side of the path, obscuring herself behind the neighbour across the road's untrimmed hedge so she was hidden from the front door. She stayed there, hidden from view, watching her house for what seemed like an hour but was actually only minutes. She was so lost in her thoughts that she completely failed to hear the footsteps coming up behind her.

"Gertie?!" said a voice she instantly recognised.

She turned around slowly and there, behind where she had been hiding, stood her mother.

# XLIII.

Kitty's mug of coffee had been truly awful. Whatever Lucy Preston's talents were, making coffee wasn't one of them. Although, to be fair, it had still helped with the gate lag. She'd also managed to slowly coax the information she'd needed out of Lucy before the bottom of the mug. It being Sunday night, nothing was going to happen straight away, but Lucy told her that the library in Uckfield would be open from 9am and they did indeed hold copies of the phone directory. Lucy didn't have a car of her own, but said that her boyfriend Dave would be willing to drive Kitty to Uckfield first thing in the morning as he went through town on his way to work. Lucy had offered to let her sleep on the sofa at her parents' house where she still lived, but in the end Kitty declined. Mainly she couldn't face the prospect of fielding all the inevitable questions that would come along with Lucy suddenly turning up late with an unannounced mystery guest. Let alone when they heard her accent for the first time! She didn't have time for cover stories, she needed all her brain power on working out her next moves in finding Gertie. In the end Lucy set up a camp bed in the projectionist's room and rustled up some cushions and a blanket or two to help keep her warm. She left with the promise of returning with Dave in tow at 8am the next morning.

Kitty spent the next half an hour trying to get comfortable on the camp bed. In the end she gave up and went foraging for snacks at the small kiosk in the Foyer. A bag of popcorn, a strange cola flavoured crushed ice drink called a Slush Puppie and a packet of Galaxy Minstrels in hand she sat in the best seat in the house and watched a rather entertaining film called Romancing the Stone, which was handily already spooled on the second projector. She really liked the female lead but that Jack Coltan guy was a bit of an egotistical blowhard. She found the soundtrack surprisingly good too, nothing like the kind of music she was used to, but she felt like it had a beat you could dance to. Eventually tiredness took hold and she retreated to the projectionist booth and crashed out on the camp bed for the night.

Kitty awoke to Lucy shaking her gently.

"Wakey wakey! Time to get up, sleepy head", teased Lucy nervously

She sat up and wiped the sleep from her eyes. She took a couple of deep breaths, in through the nose, out through the mouth, then stood up.

"Ready when you are Ms. Preston. Lead on."

Together they walked out the front door of the Orion and onto the street in front. Parked by the curb was a strange squat looking car in a truly horrible greeny brown colour, with the word Allegra written in script on the edge of the bonnet. It looked like someone had taken a normal car and squashed it front and back so it was shorter and fatter. Lucy walked to the passenger door and opened it up, motioning for Kitty to climb in. Sat in the driver's seat was a skinny man with spiky black hair, who Kitty assumed must be Lucy's boyfriend Dave. Just to confirm this, the man held out a thin bony hand and said:

"Whatcha. I'm Dave. Please ta meet cha."

Dave was dressed in a jet black shirt done all the way up to the neck and a jet black blazer covered in brightly coloured badges, with various symbols and slogans on them. Kitty took his hand and was rewarded with a surprisingly firm hand shake, so firm it almost hurt. Quite taken aback, all she could manage in reply was:

"Kitty. Simpson."

"Droppin' you at the library in Uckfield, yeah?" asked Dave

"If you would be so kind", replied Kitty. She turned to Lucy who was still standing on the curb holding the door open. "With any luck I'll be back in a few days. Will you be here?"

"Yeah, should be. My days off are Tuesday and Wednesday, but I'm here every other day from 10am. Hope the mission is a success. I'm dead excited!" With that she closed the car door for Kitty and stood on the pavement and waved as Dave pulled off.

"Mind if I put on some toons?" asked Dave. He didn't wait for a reply but pushed a small piece of white plastic into a hole in the dashboard with lights and buttons around it. Suddenly a blast of loud guitars and shouting came from a speaker in the door next to Kitty. Dave looked sheepish.

"Sorry 'bout that." With that he turned the left hand button and the noise became quieter.

The rest of the drive continued in near silence, just the drone of whatever music it was that Dave had put on. Eventually Dave turned off the main road onto a country lane where a white wooden sign indicated the way to Uckfield. They drove for a while as the road got more and more narrow, with sandstone rocks forming walls on either side. Eventually the road widened again and they were driving past housing estates. A few twists and turns later and suddenly they were at a junction on the high street. Dave indicated right, and when the lights changed headed down the hill into town.

"Just down 'ere. You'll 'ave to wait around for a bit, though. Don't open for anava 'alf an 'our", explained Dave.

As they reached a junction to turn down Library Way Kitty noted the two old buildings on either side. The left hand one was marked Court House but the one on their right had the words "The Picture House" painted on the side. This looked very much like a cinema to Kitty so she guessed this must have been Gertie's entry point. Dave drove down the road and stopped as it turned left into a car park.

"That's the library. Entrance is round the front." He indicated which end was the front of the building. "When you need to get back, you'll 'ave to grab a bus. Walk back that way to the High Street. You need to get the Number 31 to 'aywards 'eath then change. Good luck, yeah?"

Kitty thanked him and got out of the car then stood and watched as he drove down through the car park and disappeared out of sight. With nothing left to do until the building opened, she crossed over the road into the playing field and sat down in the early morning sun to wait.

# XLIV.

Gertie stood rooted to the spot, completely unable to move. Her mum...her mum was standing *right there*. Alive...as in, not dead.

"Gertie", her mum repeated "What are you doing here?"

Gertie's mind went into blind panic, what could she say? Not only was she in the wrong place, she was in the wrong time.

"I...ere...well it's the school holidays isn't it" was the first thing to pop into her head.

"That's not what I meant young lady and you know it", scolded her mum "What are you doing here...in THIS time. How did you get here? They said there was a chance this might happen but I never believed it would." Elizabeth continued, shaking her head.

Gertie was utterly confused. Why wasn't her mum freaked out about seeing her? To her mum Gertie was three years older than she should be! Than she had been when her mum had taken her to school that morning. Did her mum know about the gates? About time travel? How?! As far as Gertie was aware, her mum just spent her days doing washing, tidying the house, taking care of Walter when he wasn't at nursery and going for coffee mornings with other mums. How could she know about the Guiding Light? How could she know about any of it?!

"Well?" her mum asked again.

"I...I...", She stammered. "The Picture House. A week ago."

She never could lie to her mum. Damn it. This wasn't how it was supposed to go. How any of this was supposed to happen. Gertie just stood there, defeated and utterly deflated, not knowing what to do next.

"Hmmm, well you are here, so let's deal with that first shall we", Elizabeth stated, her manner softening in response to Gertie's clear uncertainty about what was happening "Let's get you inside in case you are seen. I'm going to need to phone in and report this. Then I'm going to want a proper explanation as to why you are here. Okay?"

Gertie nodded and, as her mum stretched out her hand, took it and was guided towards the house she had grown up in.

Walking into her old house was one of the strangest experiences of Gertie's life...and she'd had a fair few strange experiences in the last few weeks. It was like walking into a museum depicting your old life. Like everything had been frozen in time, perfectly preserved for future generations to gaze at and wonder what life was like for this family. She knew all of these things so well yet they felt somehow unreal, like someone had recreated them as models from photographs. Her mum led her through the front door and motioned her through the glass sliding doors at the end into the kitchen behind. She sat down at the large wooden table she remembered so well. She ran her hand over its surface, feeling every bump and scratch like it was Braille. Behind her her mum half closed the glass door and picked up the receiver of the phone that sat on the bureau under the main staircase in the hall. She strained to listen to her mother's conversation but was unable to make anything out. The only word she managed to catch was "Understood" which was the last one spoken before her mum put down the phone again. Her mum paused for a moment as if to collect her thoughts and then turned sharply and walked into the kitchen, closing the glass door behind her. Without a word to Gertie, she busied herself making a tall glass of orange cordial, which she placed in front of Gertie. Then she arranged some biscuits on a plate which she put into the middle of the table before sitting gracefully down on the other side from Gertie. Gertie remembered the plate so well. It was one of her mum's favourite serving plates, blue and white with a picture of a Chinese temple surrounded by trees and birds.

"Now", said her mum, placing her hands onto the table, one hand crossed on top of the other. "Help yourself to a biscuit, and tell me what you are doing here."

Suddenly she closed her eyes and lifted her hand up, palm out.

"No...wait", she paused to compose herself, putting her hand down again "I shouldn't know. If you are here, you are here to do something. Or at least you think you are. Either way I cannot know what that is. It's not my job. Damn it Gert. You've put us in a real pickle."

She opened her eyes, learnt forward slightly and fixed Gertie with a stare. "This is something to do with Aunt Abigail isn't it? I knew her legacy would come back to haunt us one day. Always had an adventurous streak, that one, a mischievous glint in her eye." She cocked her head at Gertie, "You've always had that same glint too, you know."

Gertie and her mum sat in silence for a minute or two, whilst Gertie munched her way through a bourbon cream followed by a shortcake round. The only other sound in the kitchen was the boiler occasionally turning over. After what seemed like a painfully long silence, Gertie's mum asked: "Does anyone know you are here?"

Gertie shook her head and wiped some of the sugar off her lips. Elizabeth narrowed her eyes.

"Not even the gate operative? How did you get past Alice? Actually I imagine it wasn't that hard...always been away with the fairies that one, to be honest."

"I...I just ran straight for the exit, didn't stop until I was well past the library", Gertie managed to get out between her biscuit munching.

"Smart", said her mum. She lowered her head and sighed. After a breath she looked back up at Gertie.

"Well, finish your squash. Then we need to get you somewhere safe, away from here. I've arranged a handoff with my contact in half an hour, so we best get moving." She stood up and looked down at Gertie.

"Got all your stuff with you? Haven't left anything behind anywhere?" Gertie shook her head. She didn't really know what was going on anymore. Was this the end? Had she failed? She supposed that all the time she was here with her mum, anything was still possible. God, she'd really messed this up.

"Mum?" said Gertie, as she stood up, her voice cracking slightly.

"Yes dear?" her mum replied kindly.

"Sorry."

"Don't be silly dear. It will all work out fine in the end, I'm sure." Her mum reached out and put her hand on Gertie's shoulder. She kept it there as Gertie moved around to the other side of the table, only letting it slide off as Gertie embraced her in a big hug.

# XLV.

With the help of a lovely old lady librarian Kitty had tracked down not only the address of Gertie's family home, but secured a photocopied map of the town which the librarian had drawn directions onto. Map in hand, she'd made her way across the car park and up the road past the church, unbeknownst to her following almost the exact route Gertie had taken the night she'd arrived. As she crossed the road she'd driven along with Dave earlier that morning, she noted the unusual wooden lychgate by the church and headed down the delightfully named Pudding Cake Lane. She followed the footpath as it went downhill and continued across the road, eventually coming out onto a road called The Drive. All she needed to do was follow this to the top and she would reach the house Gertie's family lived at prior to moving away after her mother's death.

Once she'd scouted the location her plan was to run surveillance from the car park of the old people's home across the road, hoping to at some point catch a glimpse of Gertie's mother. She could then track her movements and ascertain where Gertie might be. She felt sure Gertie was here to see her mother again, why else would she travel to this time and location.

As she approached the steps down to the entrance of the old people's home, her senses started to bristle and she heard voices across the road just inside the driveway to the

233

Grangers' house. She sprinted across the road and concealed herself behind the hedges that ran around the property. From her vantage point she watched as two figures emerged from the house and onto the street. She instantly recognised the smaller figure as Gertie, dressed in the same clothes she'd been wearing the day she'd turned up in the Æther. The second figure was tall and slim, but had the same wavy coffee-coloured hair as Gertie. This must be Elizabeth, Gertie's mum. Damn. Gertie had already made contact with her. Kitty cursed herself for being too late to prevent it. Now she'd need to follow them and somehow intervene if it looked like anything catastrophic was going to happen.

She watched as they walked across the road and waited until they were almost out of sight before following them. She tailed them as the road curved around and eventually came to a junction. As they turned the corner to the right Kitty sprinted to catch up. Using a hedge for cover she watched as Gertie and Elizabeth walked hand in hand along the road until it came to another junction with a bigger main road. Following along once more she watched as they crossed left at the junction. They walked a short way towards a pub called The Ringles Cross pub. It was a white-washed country style pub that would have once enjoyed the space of fields but was now hemmed in on all sides by houses. As she crossed the junction to follow them she saw Elizabeth approach two men in expensive looking suits waiting in the pub car park. She'd seen enough Film Noir to spot evil henchmen when she saw them. This did not look good to her at all.

# XLVI.

Gertie was feeling lost and uneasy. Not in the sense that she didn't know where her mother was taking her, she'd walked this route many times to catch the bus to the other side of town, more that she had no idea why they were going at all or who it was they were meeting. After leaving the house her and her mother had walked the whole way in silence which had made her feel even worse. After the determination to get here and the single mindedness it had taken to focus on what she'd been planning to do, to have it all snatched away left her empty. She still couldn't believe her mother already knew about any of the things which she herself had only just discovered. Why hadn't she shared these secrets with her? Why hadn't the whole family been involved? If this was all that important to the world and to the future, how could she have kept it from them? She felt numbed by it all. Now what was going to happen? Was she just going to get handed back to some Secret Light member and then sent packing back to the Æther again? Were future events just going to unfold as if she'd never been there to stop them? How could she face Kitty again? How could she face anything again knowing she'd failed? That she'd made no difference after everything she'd put everyone else through to get here? It was all just too much. She wanted to throw herself down on the ground and scream. But she didn't. Instead, she just walked in silence being led blindly by her mum towards whatever was going to happen to her next.

As they crossed at the junction and headed towards the pub down the road Gertie's feeling of uneasiness began to increase. She became aware of the two men standing waiting for them. Suddenly her nerves got the better of her and she began to shake.

"Everything okay, dear?" asked Elizabeth "You're shaking! Oh you poor thing. Please don't worry. Everything will be just fine, you'll see."

"But this is wrong", shouted Gertie, her emotions exploding in a sudden outburst "This isn't supposed to happen. I came here for a reason!"

"And whatever that reason is you can sort it all out with these gentlemen. They will make sure everything is as it should be, I'm sure."

"No they won't, they can't! They won't let me. It's not what the Light does!"

A strange expression suddenly appeared on Elizabeth's face, a look Gertie had never seen before. Her once beautiful hazel eyes became angry and dark with an edge of cruelty.

"The Light? The Guiding Light!? Oh my darling, no. These men aren't from the Light. Is that what this is all about? This is more of your great aunt's doing again isn't it? She was always going on and on about the Light. Some secret group of scientists fighting against evil and trying to divert the course of events or some such nonsense. Could never understand much of what she was talking about myself. She went mad in the end you know, shut up in some home for loonies. Has someone been filling your head with fanciful drivel about changing history? It's all nonsense dear! Now… you run along with these people and I'm sure we'll see each other again soon enough."

"No! We won't!" shouted Gertie, struggling to free her hand from her mother's sudden grip. "This is wrong! Please stop! Don't make me go with them!"

"Oh darling, there's nothing to be afraid of. These people will help you with whatever it is you need to do. They are the ones who are trying to change the world, not some imaginary group of lunatics. They've been shaping the world for centuries. They will set you on the right path, I'm sure of it."

With that she handed Gertie over to the two men who grabbed her by one arm each, as she struggled to get free.

"No!! No!! Please!" pleaded Gertie.

The men waited for a gap in the traffic and then walked Gertie across the road to where a black car was waiting on the forecourt of the garage opposite. As they reached the other side Gertie looked desperately back at her mother across the road.

"But… but I came here to save YOU!" she shouted desperately.

"Wha…what do you mean?" replied her mother, her expression suddenly confused. "Gertie?! What do you mean you came here to save me?"

With this Elizabeth stepped blindly onto the road to cross over to where her daughter was and was stuck head on by an oncoming car.

End of Reel Three

# Reel Four: The Coming Storm

# XLVII.

Kitty watched as Gertie was manhandled across the road by the two Obscurus agents. She heard her shout back across the road to her mum. When she saw the desperate look in Gertie's eyes she broke cover, running as fast as she could across to the other side of the road and towards where Gertie was struggling in the grip of her kidnappers. Just as she did Gertie's mother Elizabeth stepped into the road directly in the path of an oncoming car. Kitty stopped abruptly in her path at the shock of the accident. Everything seemed to move in slow motion as Gertie screamed in anguish, struggling to free herself from the firm grasp of her captors. Elizabeth lay prone on the road a few feet in front of the car where she'd been thrown, not moving. Kitty stood rooted to the spot, unable to contemplate her next move. Thankfully Gertie's assailants made the decision for her by turning and forcing Gertie towards the open back door of the waiting car. She broke into a run just as Gertie turned towards her, seeing her for the first time.

"HELP!" shouted Gertie, her voice filled with desperation. Her eyes widened with the realisation of what had just happened and what was about to happen.

One of the men had managed to climb into the back seat of the car and was dragging Gertie in after him. The other man pushed at her from the outside. Kitty struck quickly and ploughed headfirst into the agent still outside, the force of the impact bouncing them off the open car door and backwards off their feet. She heard the man inside the car shout "DRIVE!" and the car started to pull off. The agent she was currently on top of grabbed at her, preventing her from getting up. She struggled fiercely, beating the man with her fists and thrashing to free herself. The car pulled around in a tight circle behind the one that had struck Elizabeth and Kitty saw Gertie struggling in the backseat with the other agent. As they pulled away Gertie managed to get her head through the still open car door to look directly back at Kitty.

"1896!" shouted Kitty at her, still desperately trying to free herself. "Call 1896!"

She placed her palm on her other fist and used the combined force to strike the enemy agent in the face with her elbow. Finally free she ran towards the car.

"I'll find you!" was all she managed to shout before Gertie was pulled back into the car and the door slammed shut on her as the car picked up speed. Behind her the agent was getting back up, his nose bloodied and streaming. He turned to make a break for it, but Kitty grabbed him by the ankle and flipped him over. She leapt onto the man, pinning him to the ground.

"Where are they taking her?! Where! Tell me!" She screamed into his face.

The man grinned wickedly and spat blood at her.

"Somewhere you'll never find her", he rasped angrily.

Kitty grabbed his head and smashed it into the ground, knocking him unconscious. She'd deal with him later. For now Gertie was gone, and she had no way of following her. Her next move was to secure the Obscurus agent and get him to talk, then find a way of getting to wherever they had taken Gertie.

She suddenly remembered about the accident that had happened only moments before. She had to check on Gertie's mum. She pushed herself off the enemy agent and walked over to the gathered crowd of onlookers who were now standing around the body lying on the road.

# XLVIII.

Kitty was here! She couldn't believe it. Oh but her mum. Her mum had been hit by a car, just like she had before. Gertie hadn't changed anything. All this had been for nothing. But wait... there was still a chance she wasn't dead this time though, still a chance the car was going slower and the impact hadn't killed her. Her mum might still be alive. Her mum. Her mum had handed her over to these men! Why did she do that? And she'd said they weren't Guiding Light. She'd said they worked for somebody who had been changing the world for centuries...was her mum working with the Obscurus?! Were these men enemy agents?

All these thoughts rushed through Gertie's head in seconds. She was shocked and scared and angry and bitter all at the same time. She turned to the man on the back seat next to her who was still holding her wrist tightly and leapt at him, her arms and legs flailing wildly. All her emotions vented in a torrent of aggression. She screamed at the man, a guttural primal scream as she hit him, over and over again. But the blows seemed to have no effect on the man apart from as an irritation. He reached into his pocket and pulled out a handkerchief, then calmly, ignoring every blow Gertie landed on him, pressed the cloth to her face, covering her nose and mouth. The cloth was wet and smelt like the sweet pungent scent given off by rotting leaves and flowers as the summer turned to autumn. It caught in her throat and she coughed. No longer in control of her limbs they stilled and eventually dropped to the seat as the chloroform took hold and she drifted into unconsciousness.

*    *    *    *

Gertie awoke in a small darkened room. In front of her she could make out a large table surrounded by lots of chairs arranged around the outside of it. She tried to move, but discovered that she had been tied to the chair she was sitting on. She opened her mouth to scream, but when she did it filled with the cloth gag that was tied tightly around her head. There was a pain in her stomach and she felt sick. Exactly like the first time she'd stepped through the gate into the Æther. She still had the sweet taste of the chloroform they'd used on her in her mouth, it tasted a little like pear drops which just made the nausea even worse. Where had they taken her? She had to try and escape, try and get away. She needed to find Kitty. She needed to find out about her mum. She was still really confused about her mum. How could she have been corrupted by the Obscurus? How did Gertie not see the signs? How could she not know? Of course she had no idea who the Obscurus or the Light were until a few weeks ago, but still. She imagined she'd be able to tell if her mum had been brainwashed by some evil society bent on the corruption of the world. Wouldn't she?

What had Kitty said as they were driving away? "Call 1896". How could she call up the year 1896?! It didn't make sense. And why? Who in 1896 would be there to answer. She was pretty sure the telephone had only just been invented, so who would even have a telephone to answer? She closed her eyes and thought it through… perhaps Kitty had meant 1896 was the telephone number she needed to call? She could test that easily by finding a phone and dialling the number. But where could she find a phone? If the room she was in had a large table and chairs it was either a dining room or some sort of meeting room. The type of furniture in the room didn't look very "housey" it looked much more "officey", so then this must be some kind of meeting room. If so then that meeting room must be attached to an office. They must have plenty of phones if it was an office, right? The walls of the room looked more industrial though, like those of a warehouse, so maybe this wasn't an office after all. Either way she'd need to get out of here and find a phone. She tested her restraints but they were firm and wouldn't budge. What was it people always did in films? Cut through the ropes somehow? Maybe a concealed knife? Or a sharp bit of metal sticking out somewhere? She felt around as best she could for something, anything that might be sharp but found nothing. Okay, what about calling for the guard to come in and then overpowering him? No, that would never work… firstly she couldn't even speak, secondly she had no strength and thirdly… well she was a twelve year old girl. How could a twelve year old girl overpower or even outwit a large adult man?

It was no good. She would just have to wait until someone came for her. Perhaps at least then she could find out what they wanted from her. Or where they were. Or even WHEN they were if, as she suspected, they had somehow travelled through a gate. But the Obscurus didn't have gates, did they? Kitty had said the only people who knew about the gate system were the Light.

She wished more than ever she had never taken that first step through the gate back home.

# XLIX.

As Kitty pushed her way past a woman standing over the body of Elizabeth, she saw something unexpected. Instead of a dead body lying on the floor, there was Elizabeth, conscious and blinking. Kitty rushed to her and knelt down. She started to put her arm under Elizabeth in order to help her sit up, but a voice from behind her shouted:

"No! Don't. We don't know what the damage is, it's too risky to move her."

Kitty turned towards the voice. There stood a woman in her late forties, with a flowery pinafore over her skirt and pussybow blouse.

"I...I had to do a first aid course as part of my training for the pub. They said never to move anyone who'd been knocked over in case they'd hurt their backs or somefink", said the woman.

"Quite right", replied Kitty, smiling kindly at the woman. "Has anyone phoned for an ambulance?"

"I used the payphone in the pub", said a man in a grey suit standing near the curb shuffling his feet nervously.

Kitty nodded at the man and turned back to Elizabeth.

"Elizabeth? Can you hear me okay?"

"Yes" whispered Gertie's mum, her voice strained and weak.

"My name is Kitty. I came here for Gertie. Do you understand? I need to find out where those men would have taken her."

"Gertie? Is she okay?", managed Elizabeth, a look of panic in her eyes.

"Let's hope so eh?" said Kitty as kindly as she could. "Those men you were with, they drove off with her. I need to find out where. Where will they have taken her?"

Elizabeth's eyes filled with tears.

"What have I done? My little girl… stupid… stupid…"

Kitty narrowed her eyes at her.

"Misguided perhaps, but not stupid. I'd say you knew exactly what you were doing. Seems that runs in the family. She came here to stop this from happening, you know?"

"Yes. I see that now. I should have known" replied Elizabeth. She tried to move slightly and winced in pain.

"Best not to move I would say. She hasn't failed in her mission just yet, now has she?"

Kitty took Elizabeth's hand in hers.

"Now. Where have they gone and how do I get there?"

Elizabeth swallowed with some effort and closed her eyes. When she opened them again she said:

"Brighton. Cinescene. North Street."

Kitty nodded at her and squeezed her hand.

"Take our car. In the garage. Keys to the house in my handbag" said Elizabeth, lifting her other hand slightly to indicate that she was holding onto her bag with it. Kitty reached across and took it. She found the keys just inside nestled between a lipstick, a packet of tissues and a purse.

Giving Elizabeth's hand one last squeeze Kitty stood up again.

"Now you take care of yourself. I'll go get our girl back."

She turned to look across the road to where she'd left the enemy agent unconscious but, of course, he was nowhere to be seen. "I really must work out how to stop them doing that" she thought to herself, then strode purposefully out of the circle of onlookers and back towards the Grangers' house.

# L.

Gertie drifted in and out of consciousness for what seemed like hours. Her arms ached from not moving for so long and the rope wrapped tightly around her wrists was starting to rub. At least her stomach had stopped churning, although the sick feeling had now been replaced with one of hunger. She looked around at her surroundings. The room had very high ceilings and along one wall there were lots of small windows and a single door with a glass panel, all of which had been papered over with scraps of wallpaper. Over time she became aware of movement somewhere on the other side of the door. A few minutes later it opened and a man and woman came in. Gertie judged both to be in their late-forties, certainly older than her mum and Kitty, although the women did have much better posture which made her seem younger than the man. He was dressed in khakis and a white t-shirt with one of those leather flying jackets middle-aged men always wore when they were trying to look younger. The woman was dressed much more stylishly in a buttoned up white blouse under a houndstooth blazer and navy pencil skirt. The man walked over to her and turned her chair around to face out before stepping back.

"Good evening Miss Granger", said the man in a deep, clipped, well educated accent "I hope you are comfortable?"

"Don't be silly Julian, she can't answer you can she? Not with that awful thing tied around her mouth", said the woman, her sneery upper class voice dripping with sarcasm. "Here, let me remove it for you."

The woman walked behind Gertie and untied the gag around her mouth.

"GET OFF ME! GET AWAY FROM ME!" she shouted as soon as the gag was off, her voice croaky and hoarse from dehydration.

"Alright! Calm down dear!" said the man named Julian "If we'd have wanted to snuff you out we would have done so a long time ago. We certainly wouldn't have wasted time and resources in getting you here."

Gertie shot daggers at him and growled.

"Where am I?! WHEN am I?! What do you want from me?" She struggled against her bonds, wobbling the chair as she did so.

"All in good time dear", said the woman "Interesting...you know you aren't in 1984 anymore. Very clever of you. Your mother warned us you were a bright young thing!"

At the mention of her mother Gertie stopped struggling.

"My mother… is she…"

"Dead?" said the woman finishing Gertie's sentence for her. "No idea, I'm afraid. Not my department."

The woman turned to Julian.

"Get the girl some water would you? There's a good chap."

Julian disappeared behind Gertie for a moment then reappeared holding a plastic bottle with a green cap. He unscrewed the cap and put the bottle to Gertie's lips, tipping slightly. Gertie tasted cold water and gulped greedily at it, some spilling down her chin as she bent forward to get more.

"There...that's better isn't it?" asked the woman. "Now. Gertie isn't it?"

Gertie just levelled her best withering stare at the woman.

"Well. My name is Mrs. Olivia De Vere and this is Mr. Julian Fox. As you may have already worked out for yourself we work for a global organisation called the Obscurus group. We boast many important and influential world leaders and business owners in our number. Now, despite what you may have had indoctrinated into you by your friends in the Light, we are not an ancient and malevolent secret society bent on chaos and subversion. On the contrary we are a philanthropic and benevolent group who use our resources to steer the world towards a more mutually beneficial future. That sounds nice, doesn't it dear?"

"No, it sounds like the kind of rubbish the bad guy in a movie would spout!" sneered Gertie, the effect of her verbal attack somewhat diminished by her stomach choosing that particular moment to grumble loudly in hunger. Mrs. De Vere raised her eyebrows at Gertie and turning slightly towards Julian asked:

"Be a dear and get the poor girl some food would you Julian?"

"I'm not your servant Olivia!" he replied fiercely.

"No you are not. No servant of mine would dare answer back!" Mrs. De Vere shot back at him. "It is merely that you have the money and know the way to the shop, you silly man."

She turned back to Gertie as Julian left the room again.

"Honestly. Men?!" she said, rolling her eyes. "Now, as I'm trying to explain to you dear, we are not the 'bad guys' here. You've been fed the wrong information by your so-called 'friends'. The Obscurus aren't evil, we are just trying to make the world a better place."

"I don't believe you! Anyway, you haven't answered my questions. What do you want from me? Where and when am I?", spat Gertie back at her. Mrs. De Vere pulled out a chair and sat down opposite Gertie. She waited for a while in contemplation giving Gertie time to calm herself down then continued slowly and gently.

"Yes. I suppose telling you would help show that we aren't the bad guys you think we are." She paused again, as if struggling with a decision.

"We've brought you home dear. You are back in Brighton in the year 1987. That's the year you came from originally, correct?"

Gertie was lost for words. She sat stunned not knowing what to think. Why would the bad guys have brought her home? Something the Light hadn't been able or willing to do for some reason? She just didn't know anymore. Had Kitty been lying to her this whole time? Were the Guiding Light really the bad guys? They did have a super secret base of operations hidden from the world. They did travel about in time and change the future. She only had Kitty's word for the fact that the Light were trying to prevent bad things happening... maybe they actually caused bad things to happen? Right now it was this woman's word against Kitty's, so Gertie just couldn't be sure. She'd need to be clever and ask the right questions. See if this woman, whoever she was, slipped up and showed the Obscurus' true colours.

"How exactly DID you get me home?" asked Gertie tentatively.

"Simple. The same way you left. Through a gate", explained Mrs. De Vere.

"Sorry... but I thought only the Light had access to the gate system?"

"Well, that's not entirely true. Although we make sure that this is exactly what they think. We don't want them to find out that their system has been compromised in any way you see." Mrs. De Vere sat forward as she said this, conspiratorially. "We have a gate network of our own, separate from the one the Light uses. It's only small and we use it primarily for moving resources to where they are needed most."

"But how?" asked Gertie with genuine interest.

"A short while ago one of the Light technicians defected to our side and helped us retro-engineer our own gate. From there it was a case of expanding our network without the Light finding out. It's all very secret and clandestine. We think of it as our little underground railroad.

We use it to perform clandestine operations against the actions of the Light. To use a kind of film reference you young people are clearly so fond of these days we are like the Rebel alliance, hiding from the Empire." With this she sat back again. Somewhat smugly Gertie felt. She hated it when adults thought they understood the things young people liked, trying to be 'cool'. It just made Gertie think they seemed sad and old and a little bit desperate.

She thought for a moment. "So the Obscurus had a gate system as well, did they?" Perhaps she could use that to her advantage and get away from these people, find out what was really going on and check up on what happened to her mother. Just then Julian Fox reappeared carrying a brown paper bag. She recognised it instantly as the ones they used at the Wimpy down the road and her stomach started to growl hungrily again. Julian placed the bag on the table next to Gertie and stepped back.

"Now, if we untie you so you can eat something, do you promise not to cause us any trouble?" asked Mrs. De Vere. Gertie nodded and Mrs. De Vere indicated to Julian that he should untie her. Moments later Gertie's hands were free and she rubbed her wrists to stop the tingling sensation as blood suddenly rushed to and from her hands. She flexed her fingers a few times to get them working and then grabbed the chair her legs were still tied to in order to manoeuvre it around to face the table. Once in place she tipped the contents of the brown paper bag out and proceeded to attack the pile of food like a hungry animal attacks its prey. It was heaven. The best thing she'd tasted in what felt like a lifetime. She couldn't remember the last time she'd had a Wimpy. Actually she could but she was trying not to think about it. It was on the first proper day her, Walter and her dad had spent at the Grand Picture House. Her dad had treated them to a takeaway for lunch and they'd sat on the stage at the front of the Auditorium silently eating every glorious mouthful. She found herself wondering what her dad was doing right now. He must have been frantic with worry after she'd disappeared. She wondered how he was going to react if she just showed up out of the blue, who knows how long since she'd left. That was a very good point in fact. Mrs. De Vere had said that she was in 1987, but when? Before she'd left? After? If so, how long after?

"Excuse me? Mrs. De Vere?" she asked between mouthfuls of chips. Mrs. De Vere was standing off by the door talking in whispers with Julian Fox. She turned at Gertie's inquiry, holding up her hand in front of Julian indicating for him to stop talking.

"Yes, my dear? Everything okay with the food?" she replied.

"Oh. Yes, absolutely. Thank you. I was just wondering. What day is it?" She wiped her mouth with the back of her hand, then looked embarrassed at the grease stain she produced and decided to wipe it on her skirt.

"October I believe. The fifteenth. The fifteenth?" She turned to Julian for confirmation and he nodded. "Yes, the fifteenth of October. Why do you ask?"

"Well... only I left here in June, so it's been four months. Couldn't you get me here earlier?" She felt this was a very cheeky thing to say, but hoped it would have the desired effect on her audience. Their reaction could be very useful. It could give her a clue as to the extent of the gate network they had or trigger them into getting angry and show their true colours. She felt Kitty would be proud of her spy craft. She suddenly missed Kitty very much, and hoped she would see her again, even if it was just to get to the bottom of this whole good guy/ bad guy thing.

Mrs. De Vere flushed, but quickly composed herself and replied.

"As I said, our network is very small. We only had a limited number of options and we did the best we could. I thought, perhaps just getting you home by any means necessary, would be the best thing for you."

"Oh absolutely", said Gertie, brightly "Thank you. Could I ask one more question?"

Mrs. De Vere smiled in what she obviously thought was a sweet way, but came off a little sinister.

"Of course dear, fire away."

"I'd really like to know what happened to my mother. You know, so I can prepare myself for what I'm going back to. Can you use your gates to somehow find out for me?"

Mrs. De Vere's smile disappeared swiftly and she stared at Gertie for a moment, trying to read from her face what this was all about.

"Funny you should ask that actually. Seems our gate here isn't working right now. It stopped the moment we came through with you as it happens. Don't suppose you have any idea why that is, do you?"

This was news to Gertie. She couldn't think why she would make any kind of a difference. The gate had worked absolutely fine for her when she'd come through in Uckfield, hadn't it? She'd not stuck around for long enough to notice come to think of it. But still, the one in the gate room in the Æther was working perfectly, she'd used it, and she knew that Kitty had used it to go on her mission.

"I really don't know what you mean", she told Mrs De Vere. "I don't even remember coming here. That horrible man covered my mouth with something in the car, then I woke up here, tied to this chair!"

"Yes, that's very true. I hadn't thought of that." said Mrs. De Vere. "Why don't you finish your meal whilst Mr. Fox and I finish our business outside and then perhaps we could have a little chat about everything you've been through in the last few weeks. You can start by telling me exactly how you ended up in 1984 and what you did to get there."

She turned and walked towards Julian who opened the door for her, then followed her out of the room. Once the door had shut Gertie finished the last of her burger then reached down and started testing the ropes attached to her legs to see if she could work them loose.

"Fat chance I'm telling you anything!" thought Gertie. Just then she spotted a movement at the far end of the room. Something that looked like a roller blind had started to move around as if being blown by a current of air. There must have been a window to the outside behind it. She noticed for the first time the deep rumble coming from the other side of the room. It sounded as if she were high up and the wind was hitting the building like waves. As she listened to it the wind surged and then dwindled as it picked up then died down again. Except in this case each time the sound died down a little less and then came back stronger. It sounded like a storm was coming.

# LI.

Kitty sat in the driver's seat of the Granger family's Royal Blue Ford Cortina and looked across the road at the metal shuttered frontage of the old Cinescene theatre on North Street in Brighton, wondering how she was ever going to get in. The traffic was light for a Monday lunchtime, clearly no one fancied sitting in a hot car like Kitty was in the blistering sun and 28 degree heat. The weather had driven many indoors so there wasn't the usual throng of people walking around, those that were brave enough to be out had probably grabbed their lunch and taken it to the beach to eat. She'd seen a sign for car parking a couple of roads back so, after waiting for a bus to pass, she pulled the car around and headed back to drop it off, grinding the gears as she did so. Despite having driven all the way here from Uckfield she was still struggling with the modern gearbox. She'd trained in driving British Army transports during her time in the W.A.A.F. back in the 1940s, but these new synchromesh gear shifts continued to fox her.

Having secured the car safely, she made her way back down Windsor Street. The huge glass fronted modernist building that housed Boots Chemists which dominated the end of the street would give her an excellent vantage point of the Cinescene across the road. No sooner had she reached the edge of the building when she was rewarded by the sight of the small door section of the shutters begin to rattle and

261

lift. When the shutter was almost fully opened a man wearing overalls and a white hard hat ducked out from the doorway, and proceeded to light a cigarette. She waited a few moments then crossed the road quickly and walked up the pavement towards the smoking man. Despite his appearance he didn't strike Kitty as the sort of man you'd usually find on a building site, his shoes were too clean and smart for a start, that and his well-fed belly filling the confines of his overalls.

"Excuse me? Sir?" said Kitty in her best American tourist twang "Could you tell me where I can get myself a pack of those?"

"Oh", replied the man, his manner that of someone who'd been caught doing something they shouldn't "Err… yeah there's a newsagent's up the road there I think. Tell you what, you can 'ave one of mine."

He started to undo his overalls to get to his pack of cigarettes and Kitty spotted his blue pinstripe shirt, and the leather strap of a shoulder holster. She sprang into action, pushing the man backwards through the doorway and back into the building. Grabbing his wrist with one hand whilst reaching into his overalls with the other to locate his gun. The man was taken by surprise and lost his footing, stumbling backwards over the metal runner at the bottom of the door. In seconds Kitty had his gun out and pressed against his neck.

"Where did they take her?!" She hissed menacingly into the man's face.

"I dunno what you're…." the man started to say before Kitty thrust him backwards against the wall and knocked the wind out of him and the hard hat off his head.

"DON'T! Just.. don't. I know they brought her here. Where did they take her?" She moved the gun up to press against the man's temple.

"Please! Don't kill me! I'm just a gate operator!" the man pleaded.

"Then why have you got a gun?!" hissed Kitty.

"It's… jus… just for protection. I don't even know how to use it!" Sweat started to form on his forehead. He was clearly suffering in the heat, but Kitty began to realise this was something else. He was nervous and frightened. Perhaps she'd let her emotions get the better of her, her concern for Gertie was overpowering, and she was prepared to do anything it took to get her back, but this man didn't seem like much of a threat.

"I don't believe you!" Kitty warned. Whilst still training the gun on the man she quickly shut the door shutter again and then grabbed him by the shirt front and guided him further into what was once the foyer of the cinema, now tattered and neglected. She pushed him down onto a cushioned bench which sat against one wall. Dust flew up as his body struck the seat cushion. She stood back and looked around at the dimly lit foyer.

"Wait a minute. Did you say 'Gate operator?'" she asked, turning back to him.

"Yeah", he replied nervously. "I just 'ave to come in and…an' run the gate sometimes, when they need it. Most of the time I just make popcorn and watch films… or play on the arcade machine over there." he jerked his head over to the end of the room where an arcade machine cabinet stood, its screen shooting coloured light against the chrome of the concession stand.

"Are you saying this place has a working gate?" asked Kitty

"Well yeah. Actually no… I mean it did, but the projector blew a fuse as soon as they went through with the girl… Oh…" He realised suddenly that he'd slipped up, but it was too late. Kitty stepped forward and leant over to the man, pushing the barrel of the gun to his sweat-covered forehead.

"Where did they take her?!" Kitty asked once more.

"I don't know! I promise! I did hear the posh bloke with the leather jacket say something about taking her home? That's all I heard though, I swear."

Kitty thought for a moment. So the Obscurus had gained access to gates had they? That was not good news. And what did they mean by home? She'd just come from Kitty's 'home' in this time, so they must have meant something else. She suspected she knew exactly what they meant by it, but she didn't like it one bit. Why would they take her home? What did they hope to gain? She quickly formulated a plan, but she'd need to know more about these Obscurus gates to make sure it worked.

"Okay Mr. Gate Operator, you are going to tell me everything you know about this gate and all about any others you might know about. I'm sure they've told you ALL about it. Bad guys love to show off. You are going to tell me all that now or I'm going to have to make you. For however long it takes until I'm satisfied. As I'm sure you already know, I have all the time in the world." She said calmly. Kitty reached forward and grabbed the man by his shirt front, pulling him to his feet. Together they marched towards the doors at the back of the room that lead into the building's auditorium.

# LII.

For the second time in just over a week Gertie found herself waiting for a storm to break so it could cover her tracks. She had managed to loosen the knots on the ropes holding her legs, but kept them in place by pressing her calves backwards against the chair legs. When the time was right she could release the pressure and the ropes would just fall down allowing her to get free. In the meantime she would take the opportunity to find out more about her capturers and their plans… if they ever came back in the room that is.

The wind was really picking up now, and the roller blind at the end of the meeting room wasn't flapping anymore but permanently blown away from the window, occasionally clapping back when a gust subsided. The noise was now constant, and sounded like someone in the next room had a hair dryer that they'd forgotten to turn off. Mrs. De Vere came in carrying Gertie's backpack and dumped it on the table.

"Thought you might be getting a little cold in here and I noticed you had a blanket in your bag, so I thought I'd bring it in for you." she said, pulling the blanket Gertie had taken from the church in Uckfield out of her backpack. She brought it around to Gertie and draped it across her shoulders, patting her on the back gently when she'd done so. She then resumed her seat across from Gertie.

"Was the food okay? Had enough to eat?" she asked kindly.

"Yes, thanks" replied Gertie. "Although if this office has a vending machine I wouldn't mind a hot chocolate? I remember my dad saying his office had a machine that you could get hot chocolate from."

"Of course!" Mrs. De Vere intoned joyfully "It would be my pleasure."

She got up and left the room again, returning a few minutes later with two polystyrene cups with steam coming out of them. She put one in front of Gertie and kept one for herself, cupping it in her hands as she sat back down to benefit from the warmth.

"These are very hot, so I would leave it for a while before getting stuck in, if I were you. Gosh it's awfully windy outside isn't it, dear? Didn't mention this on the weather report." she opened her eyes wide at Gertie in mock surprise.

"Mmmhmmm", said Gertie, invoking her dad's rule about always trying to say something in reply in order to keep conversation flowing.

"Let's hope it clears up quickly though eh? I'm afraid either way, we're going to have to bed down here for the night. Tomorrow I thought we could go to my house in the country for the day. Then at the weekend we can take you back to your family again. Does that sound nice?" Without waiting for a reply she continued, "When we're at my house we can talk some more about all the things that have happened to you since you left home all that time ago? Well... figuratively speaking of course."

Mrs. De Vere gave a short, smug laugh, but Gertie didn't think it was particularly funny. There was definitely something not quite right about Mrs. De Vere, something false. She certainly didn't feel the genuine warmth she'd got from Kitty when they'd first started to get to know each other. Kitty treated her like an equal, like she was clever and sensible and already knew how everything worked. She made her feel wanted and excited. This woman treated her more like a pet, something that couldn't fend for itself, that needed help, that didn't understand and needed to be educated and taught civility. Like a puppy that needed to be "brought to heel". She leant forward and picked up her hot chocolate, blowing on the top to disturb the steam still rising from the top. She put her lips to the cup and took a tentative sip. It had cooled enough to drink in small measures but still a little too hot to guzzle down. But it was refreshing and warming. The taste took her back to the day she'd spent with Kitty exploring the Æther, when she'd found out about not being able to go back and Kitty had brought out a big bar of chocolate to commiserate. She HAD been brought back though hadn't she? By *these* people. She was back in 1987 now. Okay it was months after she had left, and her dad and brother had been through the agony of her disappearance. She could let these people take her home and they could all move on with their lives together again. Or she could try and get away, try and phone Kitty, see her one more time and find out the truth. If she really was the hero in all this surely she could find a way to get Gertie back to the time she left, so that she could spare her dad and brother all that pain?

Anyway, if these people were the good guys why did they still have her tied to a chair? They had brought her here in order to return home, if she had escaped and run away from them that's where she would be going anyway! They must want something else from her. They wanted to find out something before they let her go, she was sure of it and that's why this woman was being so nice to her.

She made up her mind. When the time was right, she would get away from here. She would find a telephone somewhere and call Kitty to come and find her, then she would wait until she was rescued.

# LIII.

The rest of the day had been a whirlwind of activity for Kitty. Even on missions she'd never had to work this hard. After she'd grilled the Obscurus gate operator about everything he knew to do with the enemy gate network, she'd locked him in the Cinescene's projection booth with some supplies to keep him going and made her way out and back to the car. She'd somehow managed to find her way back to the Orion in Burgess Hill and sweet talked her way into the projectionist booth to retrieve her gear. Then she'd filled Lucy Preston in on everything that had happened and what her next plan of action was going to be.

At 22:30 hours that evening Lucy opened the gate to the Æther and Kitty stepped through. She left Lucy with the task of making sure the Granger's Ford Cortina made it back to them in Uckfield with Kitty's thanks, a suitable cover story memorised in case of any difficulties. On her return to the Æther she briefed the senior directors on the information she'd discovered from the Brighton gate operator. Not knowing the full extent of the Obscurus' corruption of the gate system, the directors decided to keep the information "need-to-know" and enlisted Virgil and Bobbie into helping weed out any potential moles or leaks in the gate staff. One of the most important bits of information Kitty had gleaned from the enemy gate operator was that the network consisted mostly of abandoned gates that had been locked out of the main gate system. So together Kitty and Virgil worked through a list of abandoned gates in Brighton to try and match something that could have been used by Gertie's captors to bring her home to 1987. After hours of looking nothing came up. Instead they set about using the date and location of Gertie's departure from 1984 as a reference point and eventually discovered a small number of anomalies in the database; locked out gate identifiers suddenly appearing at different locations previously marked as abandoned. It was a mess but Virgil set about writing a program to sift through the data and identify other potential matches. Meanwhile, in the hope that Gertie had interpreted her message correctly Kitty tasked Bobbie with searching through the telephone listening station recordings for any sign of a message from Gertie. It was a fraught evening of waiting to see what came up through either search. They worked into the night, long after the end of day shift had been called. Kitty had almost given up hope when they finally got a possible match.

Now that Kitty had Gertie's most likely location, she asked Bobbie to set up the most suitable point of entry to use whilst she'd prepared her gear again to return through the gate and rescue Gertie. She just hoped she could get there in time.

# LIV.

The noise of the wind was incredible, Gertie had never heard anything so loud in all her life. Not long after Mrs. De Vere had left the room to arrange somewhere for Gertie to sleep, she felt the whole building start to sway slightly. Buildings surely shouldn't move this much should they? She was worried the roof was going to be torn off, or the whole building would fly into the air like in the Wizard of Oz. She could just imagine Mrs. De Vere flying on a broomstick outside the window like the Wicked Witch of the West. She decided it was time for her to make her break for it and hoped the sound of the storm outside would cover her movements. She unhooked her legs from the chair and let the ropes drop to her ankles, just as she hoped they would. She looped the ropes off over her shoes and pushed the chair back to stand up. As she did so she wobbled and had to steady herself on the tabletop for a minute. She realised she hadn't actually used her legs properly since that morning and they ached like she'd just run the 100 metres on sports day. She had to step from one foot to the other for a moment to get them working properly again and, satisfied she wasn't going to fall over, pushed away from the table. She grabbed her backpack, stuffed the half finished bottle of water and the blanket into it and strapped it to her back. She heard something crashing outside the window and realised it was the sound of something being thrown against the side of the building by the wind.

Walking as quickly as she could to the door, she stopped and listened to see if she could hear anyone on the other side. Satisfied that the coast was clear, she gently pushed the handle down and opened the door. On the other side, there was a large open room filled with desks set up into grouped cubicles using coloured boards, six desks to a group. There were spinny office chairs and big beige computer terminals everywhere. It reminded her a little of the control room in the Æther but way more boring and down-to-earth. It all looked very new, and distinctly different to the rest of the room which looked old, and rundown with paint peeling off the brickwork walls. She quickly mapped out a path around the various cubicles to the double doors on the other side like she was navigating a maze. Who knew all that time avoiding ghosts in Pac Man would be good practice for this? "Still about avoiding bad guys", she thought and allowed herself the briefest of smiles.

Closing the door gently behind her she ducked low so she could hide behind the coloured boards and struck out along the first line to her left, running parallel to the meeting room she'd just come from. When she touched the boards she was surprised that they were fuzzy, like the felt mosaics she used to play with as a child. Keeping low she made her way along the line of cubicles to the opposite corner. Every now and again a piece of paper was pinned to the boards with coloured drawing pins. Boring pages of small text she wasn't interested in reading. She reached the corner and peaked around to see if the route to the exit was unobstructed. Aside from a few potted plants and a water cooler there was nothing between her and the large double doors leading out of this room. She took a deep breath and turned the corner, walking quickly towards her goal. She'd not reached half way when the doors started to open. Quick as a flash she sprinted forward and into the first opening to a cubicle and squeezed herself under a desk. Her heart started pounding in her chest and it filled her hearing, almost blotting out the howl of the wind outside. She had no idea what she was going to do if anyone had spotted her. All she could do was wait and hope they hadn't.

After one of the longest minutes of her life, Gertie caught sight of the heads of a man and woman over the top of the coloured desk partitions, as they walked past her hiding spot and towards the water cooler. She'd been quick enough for them not to see her running for cover. She slowly unfurled herself from under the desk and edged towards the gap between the partitions. From here she could just about see in both directions. The man and woman had stopped about six metres away at the water cooler and the man was getting water for them both. The woman was dressed in bright colours of neon pink and yellow and the man jeans and a salmon coloured t-shirt. She could see a leather strap running around his shoulders that she knew from watching Knight Rider was a type of gun holster. He was saying something to the woman and she was laughing in that annoying way the older girls always did around boys. They were clearly distracted enough with each other for Gertie to slip quietly out of the cubicle and walk sideways towards the exit. As she got to the cubicle nearest the door she ducked in once more and waited. The man and woman were still standing around laughing, their eyes only on each other. A gust of wind suddenly pushed one of the double doors open slightly and Gertie spotted what looked like a white-washed hallway beyond. Before it could close fully again, Gertie broke cover and was across the last few metres and through the gap in the door in less than 5 seconds.

She found herself on a brightly lit landing above a stairwell. The walls and ceiling were painted white but covered in scuff marks and handprints from previous constant use, a threadbare carpet ran up the centre of the stairs. The stairwell was extremely echoey and the sound of the wind roared down it like the inside of a seashell. Above her she heard a sudden clanging of metal which echoed down the stairs and hurt her ears. A few seconds later it became a constant rhythmic banging, like the cymbals the marching bands used in the bonfire night carnivals. She grabbed hold of the black plastic covered handrail and started walking down, trying to make as little noise with her feet as possible. She made it down one flight, then another. Suddenly there was a lull in the wind and the building rocked violently southwards, almost knocking off her feet. She hadn't realised how much this seemingly solid building must have been moving in the wind until it was released and lurched back to its original position. Almost as quickly it was caught again and pushed backwards as the wind picked up again. She gripped the metal handrail tightly until the movement stabilised. As soon as she felt safe to move again she walked gingerly downward once more. When she reached the fourth floor she heard above her the voices of people approaching and froze. She looked up and tried to conceal herself behind the metal balusters of the railings, hoping that they couldn't see her if they were to look down. A door above her opened onto the stairwell and she heard the voice of Mrs. De Vere talking with Julian Fox. She couldn't make out what they were saying over the noise of the wind and the constant clang of whatever metal object was clinging for dear life to the roof. She watched them turn and start to make their way up the stairs to the floor she was once on. If they headed straight to the meeting room they would find her gone and she would be out of time. She had to move, now.

She broke for the final flight of stairs leading to the bottom of the building and burst through the double doors she found there. The room she ended up in was clearly a lobby where people could take a lift up to the upper floors. Straight ahead were more double doors, so she ran straight for them and through into the ground floor of the building. Clearly this was once the main floor of some kind of shop, along one side were counters that looked like they once had tiles on them, and the room was separated up with tall pillars. The once well carpeted floor was now dirty and patches of it were missing. The room was empty apart from a large pile of wooden pallets stacked against one wall and some metal cages on wheels that looked like they had been filled with plastic sheeting. At the other end of the room was a set of revolving doors, a little like the ones at the Grand Picture House, but much more functional and business-like. She ran straight for these, hoping they were unlocked. As she tried to push against one of the glass doors to turn the doors outward she found that it was, indeed, locked. Looking around in panic, she noticed a small red button on the wall next to another smaller glass door, running to this she pushed and was rewarded by the door suddenly swinging inwards, forced by the wind to open. She ran for the gap and was out the door into the dark lamp lit street.

The noise of the wind was deafening. She couldn't stay out here for long, she'd need to find somewhere else to hide and shelter from the storm. When she walked out of the sheltered porch of the building she'd just escaped from, the wind hit her full force knocking her off her feet. On the other side of the street, metal bins were skidding down the road, followed by the rubbish they once contained. She pushed herself up and braced into the gale. She started to recognise the streets around her and worked out she was somewhere just south of the train station. She could either head south towards the sea against the oncoming wind and hope to find shelter in one of the shops that littered the backstreets of Brighton, or let the wind carry her north and find another building to hide in. Thinking that shops might be the best place to find a telephone, she pressed into the wind and tried walking south, only managing a few steps before she was knocked off her feet once more. She decided this was wasting too much time, and let herself be picked up by the wind and almost carried by it, headed north. As she rounded the end of the next building along, a path led down to her right towards the street running parallel below. Thinking this would shelter her from the wind long enough to get more of a head start she angled herself towards it. As she did she heard shouts behind her and turned to see Mrs. De Vere, Julian Fox and the man and woman she'd seen earlier exiting the warehouse building onto the street and being caught unaware by the storm force winds just as she had. Suddenly free of the squall she ran headlong along the side of the end building and onto the next street. As soon as she left the shelter of the building she was instantly picked up again by the wind and forced to walk at top speed to keep her feet from leaving the ground permanently. A new two-storey office block sat on the other side of the next street down the hill. She guided herself towards it as best she could. She had to stop halfway across to avoid a large panel of wood that had blown out of the corrugated roofed depot at the other end of the road and was skidding towards the empty plot of land to the north. She forced herself over to the end of the building and around the corner, hoping the others hadn't made it to the end of the road above and seen where she was headed. As she rounded the end of the building she was once again sheltered from the wind. The office block sloped down the hill at a 45 degree angle to the east and the wind had managed to get behind one of the protective coverings on the windows and had torn it off. It was now flapping violently in the wind, barely hanging on by a few screws. Her heart sank as she noticed that the now visible window was still protected by upright metal bars, but was relieved to find that the glass behind it had been smashed by flying debris. Confident she could fit through Gertie grabbed hold of the bars and pushed her backpack through the broken window into whatever room was behind. Then squeezed herself through the narrow gap, hoping no broken glass cut at her as she did so. Once she was in and sheltered from the wind she almost collapsed. The noise inside this tiny exposed room was almost too much to cope with. It was like standing right next to a loudspeaker playing static off the radio at top volume. She quickly took stock of her surroundings and spotted an open door over to her right. She made for it, avoiding all the broken glass and bits of rubbish that had blown through the window and accumulated on the floor. The next room was a much newer looking office to the one in the warehouse she'd been held in. It had wood panelled walls and a large oak desk sat at one end. A leather office chair sat in front of it and against one wall stood a grey filing cabinet, its drawers closed and locked and its cellophane covering still half attached.

On the desk Gertie saw a brand new beige telephone, the kind with a flat angled receiver and push buttons. She made a grab for it and dragged it with her, pushed herself into the gap underneath the large wooden desk, wishing with all her strength that she would hear a dial tone when she put it to her ear. Nothing. The line was dead. She pressed her finger on the clear plastic hook switch, once, twice, three times. Suddenly a dull "burrrrrrrrr" noise erupted from the receiver. Quickly she dialled 1, 8, 9, 6 and waited. The line on the other end rang four times and then she heard a "Click".

Suddenly the emotions of the last few days poured out of her.

"Hello? Can anyone hear me? My name is Gertrude Granger, calling any Light agents listening. I've done a very bad thing. An idiotic, selfish thing and now I'm in deep trouble. Help me, ple…"

The line suddenly went dead. She hoped that her message had got through and that Kitty heard it somehow. She hugged the phone to her chest and pushed herself further under the large oak desk. Outside the hurricane howled like an angry god, smashing and tearing its way across the town. The door she came in through suddenly slammed shut and then proceeded to clatter and rattle on its hinges. Above her she heard the sudden shriek of metal being torn apart then the sound of something smashing against the ground beyond the building. She would find out later that one of the plastic skylights on the roof of the building had been torn off and blown across the road. She closed her eyes tightly and hoped with all her strength that Kitty made it to her before the others discovered her hiding place or she was buried alive by the building collapsing around her.

# LV.

Kitty once more exited the gate and stepped down from the stage at the Orion, but this time Lucy Preston was ready and waiting for her.

Lucy had changed dramatically in the three years since Kitty had last walked through the gate. Gone were the ill fitting clothes and the backcombed hair. She stood taller and her hair was now bobbed and straight with a wide fringe and she wore a nautical striped t-shirt and a smart grey blazer over tapered khaki trousers. Definitely an improvement, thought Kitty. This was a very strange sensation for her. Normally she would never return to the same gate or to the same operator at different periods in time. She'd last seen Lucy a matter of hours ago, not the three years it had been for Lucy.

"Ms. Preston. Good to see you again. You are looking well, good to see. Everything mission ready?" replied Kitty.

"All set for our departure, Agent Simpson. I've arranged some accommodation for us in Brighton and have contacted our operative at the Cannon to prep for gate travel if the mission is a success."

"It will be Ms. Preston, it has to be. Oh and Ms. Preston? Call me Kitty", Kitty fired back. "Top work all round."

"Thank you Agent Simp… I mean Kitty." said Lucy, letting out a nervous laugh.

"And how did your previous Mission go? A success I hope?" asked Kitty.

"Package retrieved and transported to the Æther as requested." replied Lucy, beaming a wide smile.

"Exemplary work Ms. Preston. Hmmm, I suppose I best get used to calling you Lucy as well if that's okay with you? Well then, Lucy... shall we?"

"Ready when you are boss!" said Lucy and peeled off a mock salute.

Together they exited the Orion onto the street. The sun was just beginning to set and the street lamps flickered on as they walked towards a shiny white two door sports car parked on the curb.

"Very nice!" exclaimed Kitty as she climbed into the passenger seat "You've clearly done well for yourself whilst I've been away."

"Thanks. It's a VW Scirocco. My dream car. Came into a bit of money so I thought I'd treat meself."

"Well it's certainly nicer than the last car I had the pleasure of travelling to Brighton in. Let's pull her chocks and see what she can do then eh?" said Kitty, tapping the dashboard. With this, Lucy started the engine with a satisfying roar and pulled away, heading towards the town centre and onwards to Brighton.

*    *    *    *

Kitty knew from the message's timestamp that Gertie's phone call was placed later that evening at 9.42pm

Having checked themselves into the Royal Albion Hotel on the seafront, Kitty and Lucy now needed to find the most probable location of Gertie's phone call. That meant tracking down where the Obscurus had taken her upon their arrival in 1987. The timestamp on the recording had enabled Virgil to trace an anomalous locked out gate identifier tracked to the Continentale abandoned the year before, so that was their first port of call. Lucy pulled up on Sudeley Place across from the Continentale, a strange church-like building, daubed in beige and cream with a bright red canopy. Between billboards advertising an "Adult only film club" sat a set of yellow double doors, the handles chained together and windows boarded. Clearly the enemy wasn't using this door as it was locked from the outside.

They got out of Lucy's car and walked along Sudeley Street down the side of the building. The wind was already quite strong and they had to lean into it to keep their footing. Near the rear of the building was a single door marked "fire exit", this seemed the most likely way in. Kitty hid herself behind the wall as it recessed towards the house attached to the end of the building. From here she was obscured from the door. She indicated to Lucy to knock. After a short wait with no answer she knocked again, harder this time. Leaning her face against the door Lucy shouted to reach over the howl of the wind:

"Help! Is anyone there?! I need Help! Please?! Can anyone hear me?!"

After a moment there was a scraping noise and the distinct sound of a key turning in the lock. The door opened a crack and a man's voice said:

"Whadayawant?"

"Oh, please… I think someone is following me. I keep seeing them, but this wind! It's deafening. I don't feel safe, I can't hear anything. They could be anywhere. Could I come in for five minutes, just to make sure they've gone?" said Lucy, putting on her best 'damsel in distress' voice.

The man opened the door wider and stepped out to look around. As he did, Kitty made her move, she swung her whole weight into her elbow, driving into the man's nose. He staggered back through the doorway, and Kitty followed him through. She ran at him, head down and struck him in the stomach, making him bend in half and tumble to the ground. Lucy followed behind, closing the door behind her, re-locking it as she did. Kitty walked over to the man and knelt on his chest, shouting in his face:

"Where have they taken her?!"

The man looked from Kitty to Lucy in shock, his eyes wide.

"What you on about?! You're mental you are! Gettoffme!"

"The girl." hissed Kitty "The girl that came through the gate earlier tonight. Where have they taken her?"

"What girl? I don't know what you're on about!" said the man. Kitty looked directly into his eyes as he said this, they looked shifty, darting to the right as if looking for something.

"You're lying", said Kitty. "Lucy… go and check if there's anyone else home. Take my gun."

Kitty reached behind her and pulled out the silver 9mm she'd brought with her from the Æther, handing it to Lucy who disappeared through the doorway into the next room. Kitty noticed the man start to look scared when she'd pulled her gun. He was clearly just a bully and didn't like it when people stood up to him, she could use that. She stood up, and grabbed his collars.

"Get up!" She dragged him to his feet and shoved him towards the doorway that Lucy had gone through. They came out into the lower end of the building's auditorium into the gap between the bottom of the banked seating and the small screen to their right. The room had seen better days, the seats and carpet grubby and threadbare. Perched on the edge of one of the seats in the bottom row was the enemy gate operator from 1984, even more badly dressed than the last time Kitty had seen him. Lucy stood a few feet in front, her gun trained on him. As soon as the man saw Kitty his eyes widened.

"Oh God, not you!" he said, on the verge of tears. He looked pleadingly at the man Kitty had in her custody and continued "I warned you this would happen! You're supposed to be here to protect me!"

"Clearly, you should have found yourself a new job." said Kitty with a wry smile on her face. "Now. I'm sure I don't need to tell you how this goes. We've been here once before, you and I. Tell us everything we need to know and we'll leave you be. No one will ever know you big strong men got bested by two women."

Kitty marched the man's bodyguard over to him and shoved him down in the next seat along.

"So…", said Kitty, folding her arms as she moved back to stand alongside Lucy.

"Massive old warehouse!" blurted out the gate operator.

"Shuttup you idiot!" shouted the bodyguard. Unperturbed, the man went on:

"Down from the station. Next to a new place. Corrugated roof…Arg!" The gate operator just managed to get the last words out before his bodyguard fell on him grabbing him around the neck.

"I'll kill you!!" shouted the bodyguard as he proceeded to try to strangle the man he was being paid to protect. Kitty looked at Lucy and rolled her eyes. She held out her hand and Lucy passed her the gun. Holding it by the barrel, she cracked the bodyguard across the back of the head with the gun's handle. He dropped to the floor like a sack, knocked unconscious.

"You're welcome" Kitty said to the gate operator who was gasping for breath loudly, having been released from the bodyguard's grip. The two women turned to head back out the door they came in.

"Oh, and seriously, go find yourself another job. This one is clearly disastrous for your health." Kitty fired back at the man as they left.

*　　*　　*　　*

Lucy drove the Scirocco down Trafalgar Street, and had to yank hard on the steering wheel to stop from crashing into the sidewall as they exited the tunnel down from Brighton train station when the wind suddenly hit them full force. The car had been rocked from side to side by the wind all the way there and Lucy had been forced to drive slower than normal. On the seafront road the wind had whipped up the sea so much the waves crashed over the seawall and hit the road, sending sheets of water cascading over the surface. She'd had to keep her foot hard on the brakes as she drove up West Street as the wind was so hard on their backs the car felt like it was flying. They drove slowly down the road looking left and right down every street they passed looking for anything that resembled a warehouse. As they approached the end of the station goods yard across from the Lord Nelson Inn, Kitty cried out. Just beyond the old builders merchants, now an antiques shop, sat a newly built red brick building with a corrugated tin roof. Behind it loomed a huge old warehouse building with the words "Comet Discount Warehouse" painted in large letters on the side. Kitty instructed Lucy to pull up on the other side of the road as she dived out the passenger side to go look. The wind nearly lifted her off her feet as she crossed to the other side of the road heading towards the red brick building. As she did she saw four figures come out of the towering warehouse building beyond and stumble around as the wind hit them. One of the figures, a tall man, clearly had a gun in his hand. A flicker of movement at the end of the street caught her eye and she immediately appraised the situation. Gertie was clearly on the run and these, her presumed captors, were pursuing her. Kitty ducked into the doorway of May's Antiques, concealing herself from the figures as they recovered from the sudden wind and started conversing. The older, more smartly dressed woman seemed to take charge and clearly indicated that the other woman, dressed garishly in pink and yellow, should go with the man in the khaki trousers down the road towards where Kitty was hiding. That left the gun toting man to go with her, presumably in the opposite direction. Kitty slipped back around the corner as the two figures started out towards her, struggling into the path of the wind.

Kitty caught Lucy's eye across the road and indicated that she should keep an eye on them from the safety of the car. Meanwhile Kitty went down the road in order to loop back along to where she'd seen the flicker of movement earlier. As soon as she reached the end of the parade of shops between the two roads the wind caught her again and almost knocked her over. She grabbed hold of a black bollard that sat on the corner to stop herself then, once sure of her footing, moved off towards the back of the warehouse. As she did, a large metal cage on rollers crashed to the floor from behind the rear of the shop next to her. It spun into the road ahead, the stacks of cardboard collected in it flying off into the wind like a flock of birds. She could see the large warehouse block rising behind the red brick building with the tin roof and a vacant plot behind that surrounded by wooden hoardings. On the other side of the road, dwarfed by the imposing high-rise of Theobald House sat a newly built two storey office building with its protective window covers still on. If the figure she saw at the end of the road earlier was indeed Gertie, her instincts told her that she would have made for this building to find shelter. It seemed the most logical place for Gertie to have made her phone call from. She started towards it just as the smartly dressed women and the gunman she'd seen earlier emerged from the back alley of the office block. They stopped as best they could and started looking both ways down the street. She pretended to chase after the metal cage as they looked in her direction. The man laughed at her predicament, but the woman started to pull at his arm, she'd obviously been screaming instructions at him that he was unable to hear over the wind. They turned and started walking away from her.

"I hope something really unfortunate happens to you, you nasty piece of work" said Kitty into the wind, knowing that there was no way she could be heard by the figures at this distance. To her dismay the figures started towards the building she believed Gertie to be hiding in, the man tried to look through the window coverings to the rooms beyond, but evidently saw nothing of interest. The figures moved across to the metal railings surrounding the old train works yards to try and spot a way in. As they did, a gut wrenching shriek sounded from the building they'd just walked away from. The wind had managed to get underneath one of the newly installed plastic skylights and torn it away. Kitty watched in horror as the mass of plastic and metal flew up and then dropped into the street ahead before being picked up again by the wind and sent hurtling towards the two figures standing by the wire fence. The skylight hit them square on, taking the man, the woman and a section of fence along with it as it hurtled north into the works yard.

With a renewed sense of urgency Kitty headed for Gertie's hiding spot, determined to get to her before the building disintegrated around her.

# LVI.

Gertie heard the sound of smashing glass from the room beyond, the Obscurus agents must have realised where she was and were trying to get in. She pushed herself out from under the desk, ready to run at the bad guys as they came through the door, holding her backpack in front of her like a battering ram. Suddenly the door burst open and there stood Kitty. Windswept and dusty but still the most glorious thing Gertie had ever seen. Gertie rushed towards her, dropping her bag and nearly knocking Kitty over as she threw her arms around her.

"Steady on old thing", Kitty said calmly. "I told you I'd find you."

Tears made clean streaks down Gertie's dust covered face as she cried tears of happiness at seeing Kitty again.

"You doing okay?" Kitty asked kindly. Gertie nodded and Kitty wiped away the tears from her cheeks.

"Let's get you out of here shall we?"

"But what about the Obscurus? They were following me!" said Gertie, suddenly finding her voice.

"I'm afraid the storm's already taken care of them for us. They are gone." replied Kitty. She pushed away from Gertie, holding her at arm's length and looking softly at her. 'Come on. I've brought along a friend I'd like you to meet. I think you'll get along splendidly."

With this, Kitty took her by the hand and walked out of the room towards the outside world. As they made their way back through the smashed window and onto the street beyond she looked across the road. The metal fence she'd seen earlier, next to the Harvest Forestry building with its funny fake plastic Brighton Pavilion style Cupola on top, was now gone. She wondered if that had something to do with the horrible noise she'd heard earlier. She shouldered her backpack once more and, hand in hand with Kitty, struck out into the wind. The storm was raging hard, and they really had to lean into the wind to make any headway at all. Kitty turned to say something to Gertie, but her words were lost to the noise of the wind. Instead she indicated that they should cross to the other side of the road and use the shelter of the buildings to move easier. As they crossed the road, she heard the sound of a car crashing into another in the car park that sat underneath Theobald House.

It took them nearly ten minutes to make it the length of the road to the corner with Trafalgar Street. As they got near Kitty gently folded Gertie in step behind her, using her own body to shelter Gertie from the wind. Kitty scouted around her thoroughly before leaning out of the shelter of the shop front on the corner to look up the road. When she was happy the coast was clear she raised her hand and waved up the road. Gertie watched as a low white coloured sports car pulled up next to them and Kitty reached across and opened the passenger door. She flipped the seat forward and guided Gertie into the backseat, before clicking it back into place and climbing in herself. As soon as she shut the door the roar of the storm decreased slightly. Not enough to allow Kitty to not have to raise her voice, however, as she turned around to Gertie.

"Ms. Gertrude Granger, meet Lucy Preston." she said, indicating the driver of the car, a young woman with bobbed brown hair and amazing bangs.

"Hi!" shouted Lucy over the wind, smiling broadly.

"Let's get our girl out of this storm and home shall we Lucy?"

"On it boss!" Lucy replied and started to pull off, heading towards the next road down and onwards towards the seafront.

They made it most of the way down the next road, before the oncoming wind became too much for the car and Lucy had to rev the engine as hard as possible to maintain any kind of forward motion.

"I don't think we are going to make it all the way back to our exit point, Kitty!" shouted Lucy over the combined roar of the wind and the scream of the engine.

"Damn. No idea how long this storm is going to last, either. I suppose we'll have to find somewhere to bed down for the night until its over." replied Kitty.

Just then Gertie had a revelation. She was fairly certain she had a clear picture of where they were, and they could make it on foot.

"The Grand Picture House!" she shouted to Kitty.

"What?!" Kitty shouted back.

"We can go to the Picture House! It's only a couple of roads away and we should be able to get there on foot."

"Once again Ms. Granger, you astound me. You're such a clever minny." replied Kitty, a proud look on her face. "Happy to abandon your pride and joy here Lucy?"

"Sure. I'll just park her up over there and find my way back tomorrow." said Lucy.

Once Lucy had parked the car to her satisfaction they all got out to brave the strong winds once more.

"Lead on McDuff!" shouted Kitty over the wind, indicating to Gertie that she should lead the way.

# LVII.

Exactly 230 days after Gertie had done the same, Kitty stood looking up at the impressive facade of the Grand Picture House. Even in the dark it was strikingly beautiful. They'd navigated to the front of the wall of wooden boards surrounding the plot of land that was home to the old building without incident. Unlike the last time Gertie was here, Kitty was in charge of getting through the gate, not Gertie's dad Edward. So, using the lock picking skills she'd picked up in France during her time there in 1943, she was done and they were through in seconds. Despite the howling winds around them the dark void between the hoarding and the front of the Picture House beyond afforded good shelter and they no longer needed to shout to hear each other.

"Well, Ms. Granger, even in the dark she sure is an impressive thing isn't she? I can see why you'd want to get back to her."

Gertie didn't reply. Kitty noticed she looked oddly apprehensive to be here. The girl sure had been through a lifetime of adventures since she'd last been here. Kitty was guessing that she'd also hoped not to be here again so soon. That Gertie had hoped her trip to the past to save her mother had been a success, and that this place would have become theirs, together. Instead, her mission had failed and she'd come back here again, alone. Her mother still lost to her. Kitty walked over to the girl and gently placed her hands on Gertie's shoulders, reassuringly.

"Sorry. That was insensitive of me. I know you wanted to be here again under different circumstances."

She pulled Gertie into a hug and squeezed softly. She was going to miss this girl once they'd eventually managed to get her home.

"Come on. Let's get ourselves inside and see what the future has in store for us, shall we?"

She let go of Gertie and took her hand, leading her towards the courtyard to the right of the building. Once again she worked her magic on the door's lock and they soon stepped through the side entrance into the Grand Picture House's foyer. The room was in darkness, but she seemed to remember from the last time she'd been here that there was a set of double doors at the back of the room. She gestured to Lucy to pass her the bag she'd brought from the car and rummaged inside for a flashlight. It wouldn't turn on at first, but she gave it a slap on the handle and suddenly a bright beam of light shot across the room. The light bounced off the brass handrails leading to the main entrance, still bright and shiny from their last polish. As she swept the beam around the room, she saw that it was clean and tidy but there were the telltale dust particles floating in the light. A sure sign that no one had been here in a few weeks at least. Which meant no unpleasant surprises or encounters that would need awkward explanations. She picked up her bag purposefully and pointed the flashlight at the double doors leading to the auditorium.

"This way isn't it?" she asked Gertie. Without waiting for a reply she set off towards them. As they entered the Auditorium together she turned back to Gertie and said:

"Would you be a dear?" and indicated with the beam of the torch the area next to the door where the light switches were. Gertie walked over and flicked the brass switch. Suddenly the room was flooded with light.

"Wow!" exclaimed Lucy as she saw the auditorium for the first time. "What an amazing place Gertie."

Gertie stayed uncustomarily quiet as they made their way to the front of the room, to the front row of seats, where Gertie had once stood and watched Kitty washing the blood and dirt off her face from the explosion in Amiens. This time Kitty sat Gertie down and knelt in front of her.

"I have an idea. If you'll indulge me?" she said in her gentle singsong voice. "I think we should use your gate, here, to get back to the Æther. I actually have a little surprise waiting for you there. But first I need to see if we can't do something a little extra to help get you back to your family again once we're done over there."

Gertie looked up at her then, looking directly into her eyes for the first time since she'd rescued her from the office building.

"Okay", replied Gertie, meekly.

"Lucy my dear? Can I ask you to put everything to rights once again when we are gone? I'm sure Gertie here won't mind if you spend the night here in order to wait out the storm. Would that be okay?"

Gertie nodded and Kitty stroked her hair lightly. For a time Kitty twisted her fingers distractedly in the curls in Gertie's hair. After a while she cupped Gertie's head between her hands and looked into her eyes.

"You stay here and get ready to step through the gate. I'll be back shortly to join you." She stood up and, motioning to Lucy to follow her, set off back up the aisle towards the projectionist's room.

# LVIII.

Gertie waited patiently for Kitty to come back. She felt utterly exhausted and utterly useless. Her idea to use the gate system to go back in time and stop her mum from getting hit by a car had failed. Worst still, she was about to step back through into the Æther and face all the people who'd been so friendly to her, and whom ultimately she'd used and betrayed to her own ends. She'd been so stupid and Kitty had had to come and find her and to rescue her. And even though she'd failed to save her mum she could still have caused any number of issues with the time stream. She'd tried to be careful, but then she'd been captured and it was no longer in her control to keep things as they should. She didn't know what she was going to do if she'd actually made things worse. She just wanted to get in her bed back in Kitty's apartment on Post Street and hopefully never wake up again. She buried her face into her hands. Seconds later the projector flickered into life and she looked up to see the black title card with the words "La Fée aux Choux" appear on the screen in front of her. She jumped as Kitty placed her hand on Gertie's shoulder.

"Come up. Let's get this over with. It will all be okay, I promise." she heard Kitty say, her voice almost a whisper.

Without looking at her Gertie got up and allowed herself to be steered towards the stage by Kitty. Together they stepped up onto the stage and walked through the gate once more.

When they emerged on the other side a welcome party was there to meet them. Director Earhart was standing next to the projector with Virgil and Bobbie. All three looked at her with smiles on their faces as she walked slowly forward, guided gently by Kitty. When she'd covered about half the distance between them, the trio parted and Gertie could see another figure emerge and start to walk towards her. It was her mum, alive and well! She stopped dead in her tracks and felt like she was going to faint. Elizabeth covered the distance between them quickly and scooped Gertie up into her arms. They stood hugging tightly for what seemed like forever. Gertie felt the warmth spread around her body and let her mother's distinct perfume fill her nostrils. In that moment she felt the happiest she'd ever felt. When she could tear herself away from her mother's embrace she turned her face to look over at Kitty.

"I...I don't understand?" She looked between Kitty and her mother. "How?"

Elizabeth indicated that Kitty had all the explanations.

"Well. You went to so much effort and seemed so determined. I couldn't let you fail, now could I" said Kitty, gingerly shrugging her shoulders.

Gertie couldn't stand it any longer. She let go of her mother and ran to Kitty, hugging her just as tightly as earlier that evening when she'd appeared in the doorway of the office building.

"Steady on, old girl." said Kitty gently with a laugh.

"I...I still don't understand what this means?" she asked, looking again between the faces of Kitty and her mother.

"Well, obviously we couldn't change the course of history. Things back in the World needed to stay as they were. So back there your mother still died when she was hit by a car. But as you can see, she really came here." explained Kitty.

"But how did you do it? I *SAW* her get hit by that car!"

"Well, in a way you did actually end up saving your mum. Because the circumstances of the accident changed, the car that hit her wasn't going as fast so she didn't die instantly. When I left her back in 1984 she was still alive and awaiting an ambulance to take her to the hospital."

"Okay... then how did she end up here?"

"Well you have Ms. Preston to thank for that." replied Elizabeth, taking up the story. "After Kitty left 1984 to come and rescue you, she tasked Lucy with coming to find me at the hospital. She explained everything and together we faked my ultimate demise, then arranged for my 'body' to be delivered to a specific funeral home. One that the Light uses to remove people from the World and transport them here."

Kitty walked her over to her mum again and together they moved out of the gate room into the comfort of the glass house. Elizabeth sat on the chaise longue and patted the space next to her, indicating for Gertie to sit, whilst Kitty took the seat opposite them. Once she'd sat down Gertie felt her mum move closer to her and felt the touch of her arm against her own. The tingle she felt from her mother's touch after so many years was exhilarating.

"There are, of course, rules to your mother being here. Which you must agree to if you are to continue to see her." said Kitty.

"Okay. Yes… whatever I need to do. No, wait. What are the rules?" asked Gertie.

"Well, I obviously can't come back to the World. But we might be able to arrange visits, and I'll write to you all the time courtesy of Ms. Preston." explained Elizabeth.

"I don't understand. We're both here, why would we need to arrange visits?"

"Actually, that's the other surprise I have for you." continued Kitty. "Remember when I said I had an idea back in the Picture House?"

Gertie nodded but looked confused. Kitty went on regardless.

"Before Lucy threaded up the film to open the gate I had her mark it." A look of understanding suddenly spread across Gertie's face. "Now young Virgil has something to look for, and once he has a match he can have the computer trace any other instances of the gate. Including the one you used to come here."

Gertie just sat, stunned.

"That means you can go home again darling", said her mum gently.

"Yes… but… you are HERE, not THERE. And you've said you can't go back there. I mean I miss dad and even miss Walter, kind of. But I've just got you back again how can I go back there, knowing you are here?" blurted Gertie, her face twisted with mixed emotions.

"Well…" started Elizabeth.

$$* \quad * \quad * \quad *$$

The rules were simple as it turned out. All Gertie had to do was go back to the time and place she'd left from and pretend that nothing had happened. "Easier said than done", thought Gertie. Then she'd have to sit out the next 230 odd days until it was a few days after the storm. After that she could contact Lucy Preston and have her get word to Kitty that everything was fine. At Gertie's word Kitty would travel to the World and visit her at the Grand Picture House once more. She would sit down with Gertie's father Edward and explain to him all about the Guiding Light, their mission and about the gates and, eventually, the Æther. She would gauge his reaction, and if he was open and accepting she would eventually broach the subject of Elizabeth's rescue.

Naturally, as soon as they'd managed to get Gertie home, Virgil would make sure her gate was locked out of the system. They couldn't have Gertie just turn around again and use the gate to return to the Æther. And she had been banned from using any other gates as well. Of course her knowledge of the Æther and the gates and everything to do with the Light meant she was a part of everything now whether they liked it or not, but her escapades in time travel to rescue her mother meant that Director Earhart had put her on probation. It was a condition of her being able to continue seeing Kitty and having visits from her mother that she followed the rules, any deviation from that path would lead to those privileges being removed. It wasn't all doom and gloom, however. The director had mentioned that, if everything went well, and Gertie was able to keep both the Light and the Grand Picture House a secret from the World, that they might conceivably install a proper gate, and allow Gertie to train as an Operator in a few years time. Once she was old enough was how they put it. "Always the same with adults", thought Gertie, "Judging everything by a person's age and not their experience." But it was better than nothing, and in the end she'd had the most incredible adventures already. Just to be a part of that world still was enough for her. If she reflected on that first day, when she'd stood in front of the wooden hoarding around the Grand Picture House, not knowing what lay beyond, not knowing how her life would change, would she still step through that door? Even once she'd met Kitty and she'd felt the energy coming off the screen when she'd discovered the gate to the Æther, would she still step though? The answer was simple.

# LIX.

Gertie stepped through the gate back into the auditorium of the Grand Picture House, seconds after she'd previously left. On the seat in front of her sat her copy of The Lion, The Witch and the Wardrobe, just where she'd left it two months ago, its gilded edged pages glowing purple in the ethereal glow of the gate. Suddenly the gate shut off behind her and she was left standing in the low soft light of the auditorium.

"Dad?" she called out into the silence. Her heart started to pound in her chest. What if something had gone wrong? What if she'd somehow changed the time stream after all and her dad and Walter were no longer here, that they'd changed or ceased to exist. Like that bit in Back to the Future with the photograph, where the figures just fade away. The panic started to rise and she began to feel sick. Forgetting, of course, the effect the gate had on people's stomachs. After an agonising few seconds she heard her dad's voice from the projectionist's box.

"Yes, love? You don't want me to run the damn thing again do you."

"Oh, dad!" she shouted and ran as fast as she could to the back of the auditorium. She made her way up the stairs in the hallway, taking them two at a time and burst into the box. As soon as she saw her dad standing by the projector she threw her arms around him, squeezing him tightly.

"Crumbs, old girl. What's gotten into you?!" said Edward kindly. As Gertie loosened her grip he put his hands on her upper arms and gently pushed her away. "Everything alright?"

Gertie thought for a moment, running through everything that had happened to her in the last two months in her head.

"Yes dad, I'm fine. Sorry. Everything is okay. Really." she replied.

"You had me worried there for a moment, old thing." he ruffled the top of her hair like he was petting a dog. Gertie didn't mind one bit. "That's a nice watch you've got on. Don't think I've ever seen it before."

Gertie suddenly remembered she was still wearing the watch Kitty had given her. The only thing she'd brought back with her that hadn't been on her when she'd left.

"Oh, a friend gave it to me. Early birthday present as she won't be here for it." Gertie replied, thinking on her feet once again.

"Abroad are they? For the summer holidays?" said her dad "Wouldn't it be nice eh? Maybe we could sell this place off and go ourselves?"

"NO!" cried Gertie, a little too loudly. "I mean. It's okay. I don't mind not going on holiday. I'd rather have this It's better than a holiday. We can visit anywhere we wan from here."

"You mean, by watching films?" asked her dad. Gertie panicked. Had her dad been watching her in the auditorium

306

Had he seen her disappear through the gate and then reappear seconds later?

"In the sense that we can visit places, by seeing other people go there in films, yes." she replied cautiously.

"Exactly. Maybe we could make a list of places we might like to visit and see what films we can get that show them. If there's some place that looks incredible, maybe we COULD go there someday. If we start saving."

Just then Walter came into the room. He was noisily drinking through a straw from one of the large drinks cups they'd found stacked in the storeroom behind the front kiosks.

"Alright, snotface." said Gertie, smiling at her brother. He promptly swallowed a big gulp of drink and blew a raspberry at her.

"Oh, you little…" started Gertie and chased after her brother as he turned and fled from the room.

The End

# Epilogue.

Gertie walked into the projection room at the Grand Picture House to find the secondary projector running by itself. On the table next to it sat a large brown leather bag with a wide opening at the top, like the ones that doctors use. She immediately recognised it as her mother's. In front of the bag sat a large collection of notebooks and folders. The topmost book was large and black and had a symbol on its cover that Gertie had never seen before, embossed and picked out in gold paint. As she stepped closer she saw something familiar obscured behind the bag. It was the metal box that contained the gate film. Its lid, open and the combination lock lying discarded on the table next to it.

Before she'd left the Æther Kitty had told her a secret about the film that box contained. She said that she suspected it might be Alice Guy-Blaché's original film. The first copy Durand had processed in his lab, the one that had caused the gate to open into the Æther. She said it may have been given by Durand to his friend Arnaud Marron and that Arnaud might be an ancestor of her Great Aunt Abigail.

She rushed over to the projector and quickly looked out through the inspection hole into the auditorium beyond. The room was filled with purple light. The screen lit up with monochromatic figures holding babies.

She watched as her brother Walter walked up to the screen, touching it with his fingers just as she had done once.

Before she could cry out, Walter stepped through the gate, moments before the film shut off and the power in the building suddenly went out, plunging her into darkness...

# Historical Notes

Many of the Characters and situations depicted in this book are real and happened exactly as described, others are sympathetic or purely fictional additions by the author.

**Mary Borden Turner** (15th May 1886 – 2nd Dec 1968) used her considerable fortune to set up and run the first field hospital, L'Hôpital d'Évacuation, on the Western Front at Bray-sur-somme in France during World War One. It was there she met Edward Louis Spears, just as described here, whom she later married. Already a published author, Spears encouraged her to publish her war experiences in 1929, and they remain some of the most honest and harrowing accounts of the conflict. In recognition of her services to the conflict, she became the first American woman to receive both the *Croix de Guerre* and *the Legion d'honneur.*

**Amiens** was an Advance Base for the British Expeditionary Force during the First World War and faced regular bombings by the Luftstreitkräfte. There are no records of the exact date these bombings started but we know bombing raids by the newly in-service AEG G.IV bombers commenced in the area around this time and as Amien was an important supply line to the Somme campaign it seems like a reasonable date the first of these raids may have happened.

A German V1 'doodlebug' bomb dropped on **Highbury Corner** in Islington at 12:46 on the 27th June, 1944, killing 28 people and injuring a further 150.

**Alice Ida Antoinette Guy** (1st July 1873 – 24th March 1968) became the world's first female film director in April 1986 with the production of La Fée aux Choux which she wrote and directed for L. Gaumont. The film was shown as part of the company's sales show reel and then subsequently lost. No surviving copies of the original film exist.

**Alexandre Gustave Eiffel** (15th Dec 1832 – 27th Dec 1923), whose engineering company built the Eiffel Tower, was president of the L. Gaumont company and would indeed have known Alice Guy. He also had both a private apartment at the top of the Eiffel Tower and a Mansion house on the Rue Rabelais.

**Lady Grace Drummond-Hay** (12th Sept 1895 – 12th Feb 1946) was a notable English journalist who wrote a series of articles for the Chicago Herald and Examiner, chronicling her journeys on the LZ 127 Graf Zeppelin, the world's first passenger airship and the first to circumnavigate the world by air. She also travelled on the maiden voyage of the LZ 129 Hindenburg but whether or not she would have been at the site of its untimely demise is pure speculation.

**Howard Carter** (9th May 1874 – 2nd March 1939), an English Egyptologist did indeed become famous for his discovery of the tomb of Tutankhamen on 6th November 1922.

**Arthur Merton** (Unknown 1883 - 28th May 1942) was a Middle East Special Correspondent for The Times who brokered a deal with Howard Carter for exclusive rights to media coverage of the find.

**The Great Storm of 1987** was a hurricane-force extratropical cyclone that hit southern England, France, and the Channel Islands on the evening of the 15th October 1987, causing heavy damage and at least 22 recorded deaths.

The **Théâtre de la Rue des Trois-Cailloux** in Amiens, **Gaumont Cinema** in Holloway Road, **Royal Alhambra Theatre** in Leicester Square, **Titania** in Berlin, the **Kursaal Theatre** in Cairo, **Picture House** in Uckfield, **Orion** in Burgess Hill, **Cinescene** on North Street and the **Continentale** on Sudeley Place in Brighton all were once working cinemas and some still are!

Printed in Great Britain
by Amazon

16792990R00180